$\mathcal{F}$ALLING *for* FREDERICK

FALLING *for* FREDERICK

CHERYL BOLEN

Montlake
Romance

Text copyright © 2013 Cheryl Bolen
Originally published as a Kindle Serial, September 2012.

Published by Montlake Romance

PO Box 400818
Las Vegas, NV 89140

ISBN-13: 9781611099683
ISBN-10: 1611099684

For John, for everything

EPISODE 1

CHAPTER 1

Siddley Hall, Middlesex

Antonia Townley felt like doing the Highland fling. Simon owed her high tea at the Ritz! He had been so certain there were no Catholic sympathizers in the sixteenth-century Duke de Quincy's household, he had cockily made the bet with her. A smile curving her hot-pink lips, she glanced at the five-hundred-year-old correspondence in her gloved hands. It irrefutably proved she—and not that arrogant Simon—was right.

Even better than getting that trip to the Ritz was the satisfaction of besting that Oxford scholar who deluded himself that he was heavily influencing her dissertation. This California girl had just executed a slam dunk over Simon's balding, bespectacled head.

But before she could gloat over her discovery to Simon, she was anxious to share this letter with Mr. Ellerton. Unlike Simon, he treated her as a valued colleague. He respected her theories. And he had disclosed to her his own discovery, which she had to admit was far more significant than her measly hypothesis. Her theories—which she knew as facts more than theories—were valuable only to historians. Mr. Ellerton's discovery could be worth an enormous amount of money.

Still, she was pretty psyched over her accomplishment. On just her second day combing through the basement archives at what was her favorite of England's stately homes, she had discovered what Siddley's librarian had failed to discover in his nine years' tenure there. In fairness to Mr. Ellerton—who wasn't nearly so authoritarian as surly Simon—she had to admit that nine years would not be enough time to even catalog the contents of Siddley's more than two thousand boxes of historical documents, many of those with ash-delicate paper and faded, barely readable ink.

She'd been bent over box 247 for better than two hours, and she really needed a break. It was getting close to lunchtime, anyway. Mr. Ellerton had said he would share all the details of his discovery with her at lunch. She couldn't wait. She looked at her watch. It was five minutes to twelve. A little early for lunch, but she knew Mr. Ellerton would love to learn of her discovery.

Perhaps the two of them could grab something from Siddley's lunch counter and go sit on a bench in the rose garden or knot garden to eat. As much as she adored combing through these basement archives, she needed to glimpse a bit of sky now and then.

She did hope things had dried. When she'd arrived at Siddley three hours earlier, the sun had just pushed away misty clouds. Eating outside might not be a good idea. The ground was bound to still be soggy from the previous night's rain, and the garden benches were likely soaked.

She placed the Duchess de Quincy's letter back into a clear, acid-free envelope, removed her gloves, and started for Mr. Ellerton's office. She found herself sashaying and chanting "Another one bites the dust-ah" as she strolled beneath fluorescent lights that lit the cold, stone-floored corridor.

The door to the librarian's office was closed. She paused and knocked. She could have sworn she heard a muffled "Help." With no exclamation point. And it sounded as if it came from inside Mr. Ellerton's office.

She tried the knob, and the door opened. Her gaze fanned over the room, especially to the room's other door, which she thought had closed just as hers opened. The middle-aged librarian sat behind his desk, the back of his chair facing her. "Mr. Ellerton?"

This was answered by a groan.

Her first thought was that he'd suffered a heart attack. She fairly flew around the desk—only to be greeted by the most gruesome sight she had ever seen. Blood spilled across Mr. Ellerton's white shirt and beige sweater vest, and there in the center of his chest, a shiny gold dagger protruded.

Antonia froze in her stride and screamed. It was pretty much the kind of scream reserved for ax murders. Or axed murderees.

She hoped like hell it would summon help.

Clearly, Mr. Ellerton was dying. His pudgy hands clasped around the dagger as if he were trying to remove it, but his waning strength was not up to such a demand. She must help!

Tears stung her eyes. "Oh, Mr. Ellerton! What happened?" She would rather gawk at the bloody knife than his contorted face. Which was what she did as she grabbed the knife and yanked it from his chest.

"Shit," he muttered.

Honestly, she could not in her wildest dreams imagine the mild-mannered librarian issuing such foul language, but she supposed this situation did merit such a curse word.

As distasteful as it was to her, she moved closer to him, softening her voice. "Who did this to you?"

Though he appeared to be looking right into her eyes, she knew he was not, because his gaze could not follow movement. "Shit," he ground out once more, then he slumped.

Oh my God, he's dead! She had never been entirely proficient at taking her own pulse, so she knew she likely wouldn't succeed with one she judged to be really dead, but she was curious to know if he was beyond help. Or not.

And why hadn't someone come to help her? Where was that inept assistant? Alistair? She would scream again for good measure. Given the state of her frazzled nerves, such a scream came effortlessly.

Just as she was eyeing the telephone on Mr. Ellerton's desk, Alistair came flying into the room. "What's happened?" His gaze ricocheted from her to his boss, and his eyes rounded. "What have you done to him?"

That was the most assertive thing she'd heard the lisping wuss say in the two days she'd been around him. Why the fellow had been hired in the first place was a perfect mystery to her. Granted, he looked like he belonged in a library. He was no taller than her five-seven height, perfectly pale and thin, and he wore glasses. Not exactly Antonio Banderas. He was even younger than her twenty-three years.

Once again, she could barely contain her impatience with the bumbler. "I'm trying to see if we can save him! Can you check his pulse? Or, better yet, can you call an ambulance?"

Staring at her with horror, he did not move for a few seconds.

"I swear, I'm not the one who stabbed him! I found him like this—only with the dagger in his chest." She peered at her now-bloody hand, the dagger still clasped in it. It was only with the greatest restraint she refrained from threatening Alistair with the murder weapon.

His gaze flicked to the wall above her head. Mounted behind Ellerton's desk was an assortment of antique swords and daggers.

And one of them was missing.

The young assistant snapped into action and came to feel for a pulse. A moment later, he looked up, his face solemn, and shook his head. "I suppose I'd better ring the police."

This was one of those infrequent days when one could drive in England with the top down. Which is exactly what Frederick Percy, the thirteenth Earl of Rockford, was doing. He was in uncommonly good humor, no doubt owing to the mild temperatures and clear blue skies. The sun was especially welcome after the previous night's relentless drizzle.

Another reason for his good humor might also be attributed to the fact that he and Bagsy had decisively trounced Landsdowne and McVey in two straight rounds. All in all, it had been a most satisfactory trip.

Now he needed to get to business. First up on his agenda was an afternoon meeting with Ellerton. Hiring that man to oversee the family archives was not only the first decision Frederick had made when he took over stewardship of the Percy Family Trust nine years previously, it was the best decision he'd made.

The librarian-cum-curator-cum-historian had hardly been able to contain his glee yesterday when he'd told Frederick he was planning to make a stunning announcement.

What was stunning to a fifty-year-old archivist might be yawn-worthy to Frederick, but he would do his best to show polite interest. Ellerton deserved his fullest respect. He was an exemplary employee who was completely dedicated to his job.

Frederick turned off the thoroughfare onto the lane that led up to Siddley. As he often did, he wondered what it would have been like to have seen the estate a couple of centuries earlier when it was surrounded by miles of Percy lands. During the twentieth century, one parcel after another had been sold off, and now just three hundred acres remained.

Three hundred acres this close to the City of London would be worth more than enough to buy a small country. But thanks to the foresight of Frederick's wise grandfather, the lands would stay in the Percy family—or the Percy Family Trust—in perpetuity.

Huge oak trees shaded the lane his sports car sped along. On either side of the lane, sheep clumped beneath the sprawling trees, completely surrounded by green. It was almost incomprehensible that less than two miles away the roaring M4 transported thousands of vehicles each day.

As he came nearer the huge, rambling gray stone house, pride surged within him. Perhaps because his childhood had been spent in one of the smaller Percy properties up in Yorkshire, Siddley Hall still had the power to fill him with awe.

Though a house had stood on this property since the first Percys had come over with the Conqueror, the present massive, turreted "home" consisting of 316 rooms had been built when the Tudors ruled. In fact it was Henry VIII who had conferred the Rockford earldom on this branch of the Percy family.

Just as the house's full roofline—and seventeen chimneys—came into full view, so did another sight. A rather startling one, actually.

What the hell? Why was there a swarm of police vehicles with flashing lights in front of his house?

The Gainsborough! It must have been stolen.

He downshifted, and the Aston Martin raced to Siddley's portico, skidding to a gravel-spraying halt just inches from the first step. As he hurried from his car, he tried to be more rational. Really, the Van Dyke was worth more than the Gainsborough. He would hate like hell to lose it, but a fat insurance settlement would be some compensation. No amount of money could ever replace the portrait Gainsborough had painted of his great-great-great-great-great-grandmother.

"What's happened?" he asked the first person he saw—Mrs. MacIntosh, one of the guides who conducted tours of Siddley's public rooms.

The stooped, gray-haired, cardigan-clad woman had tears in her eyes when she responded. "Oh, my lord, it's so terrible! Mr. Ellerton's been murdered."

He winced. Why couldn't it have been the Van Dyke? Shock and a sudden wave of grief momentarily paralyzed him. It took him a moment to recover his wits. The impact of what she'd said sank in. "Murdered?"

Murders simply did not happen to bookish librarians whose only passions were for centuries-old documents.

"That's what I heard. I suppose you'd better go see for yourself."

"I suggest you and the others close up shop and take the rest of the day off. I know this has been most frightfully upsetting for all of you."

"Thank you, my lord."

Already on his way to the south end of the house and the stairway that went down to Ellerton's office area, he nodded. He went past the great hall as well as the library—both rooms reaching up to soaring wood-beamed ceilings—and sped past the armory, then the great dining chamber with its massive chimney, before he came to the wide stone steps that descended to the basement archives.

He had never been down there when it was so noisy. There must have been a dozen uniformed policemen and another half dozen in street clothes roaming the cool stone corridor, all of them performing some kind of function that he presumed to be important. Most of the activity, though, seemed to be centered around Ellerton's office.

What if Ellerton's dead body was there? He most decidedly hoped he'd be spared such a sight.

Frederick stood in the doorway, his gaze sweeping over the room. Thank God, no dead bodies. Two forensics-looking investigative types hovered around poor Ellerton's desk, and in the corner a dark-skinned, well-spoken detective-looking fellow was apparently grilling a crying woman.

Beside her was that namby-pamby Alistair. The wimp was probably wishing for a closet to hide in. "I know it looks bad for her," Alistair lisped to the detective, "just because she was holding the knife when I walked in..." He trailed off, unable to offer something helpful to the young lady's defense.

Despite the reddened eyes, the young lady was quite a stunner. A little on the order of Kate Middleton, at least as far as the long brown hair and tallish, lean figure were concerned. Her face was entirely different from the duchess's, though. Quite lovely. Large, brown eyes and olive complexion. High cheekbones and perfectly formed nose above a mouth that was not too full, but just about perfect—like her extraordinarily white teeth. Actually, everything about her seemed…perfect.

Frederick cleared his throat. "May I ask what in the bloody hell's going on here?"

All eyes shifted to him.

The man he presumed to be the detective chief inspector eyed him. "And you are?"

"Lord Rockford. This is my house." Frederick normally disliked using his title, but there were times when it was most useful. He suspected this was one of those times.

"I'm sorry, my lord, to inform you that your librarian has been murdered."

Frederick's dark eyes narrowed as he peered at the wall behind Ellerton's desk and saw that one of the weapons had been removed. "I take it that dagger which hung there," he nodded toward the wall of weaponry, "was the murder weapon?"

"It would seem so, but we'll need to wait for official confirmation from the medical examiner," said the inspector.

Frederick's gaze moved to the obviously distraught female. Anyone could see she was incapable of committing such a crime. "Is there a suspect?"

"It's too early to say, my lord." The DCI glared at the defenseless lady, whose composure was in tatters.

"And you are?" Frederick gave the detective a lordly glare.

"Detective Chief Inspector Patel of the Metropolitan Police."

Frederick fully entered the office and shook hands with the DCI. "I'm glad you're here." Frederick's glance flicked to Alistair, then back to Patel. "Will you be needing this lad anymore?"

"No." The detective chief inspector dismissed Alistair.

Then Frederick faced the beauty. "And you are?"

She sniffed and blotted her eyes, wiping away smudges of black mascara. "Antonia Townley." She spoke with an American accent. "Mr. Ellerton and I often shared information, but yesterday was the first time I'd actually met him in person. He allowed me to come here to conduct some of my doctoral research." Her hands were shaking. She must have discovered the body.

"I say, Patel, why don't the three of us continue this discussion away from this room?" Frederick's gaze swung to the pool of blood on the carpet behind Ellerton's desk. No wonder the poor woman was trembling. "I assume the, ahem, murder was committed here?"

"Oh, yes, my lord."

"Follow me." Frederick assumed his most commanding demeanor. They went out the opposite door, which opened to a narrow brick stairwell that rose to the driveway beside the knot garden. It was—or had been—Ellerton's own private entrance to and from the house. The poor old fellow often took his lunch in the knot garden on sunny days like today.

Frederick went to one of the big teak benches and bent to feel if it had dried after last night's rain. "Still too wet to sit on." He remained standing; his gaze went to Patel. When did they start letting such young men be detective chief inspectors? The guy couldn't be a day over thirty. Frederick's gaze whisked over his well-cut, conservative clothing and well-polished shoes. He hadn't realized detective chief inspectors were so well compensated, either. "What can you tell me about what happened?"

Thankfully, Miss Townley had stopped crying.

"According to Miss Townley," Patel began, "she discovered Ellerton's body around noon."

Four hours ago.

Patel continued, "Her subsequent scream summoned Alistair Penworth, who called the police."

She looked up at Frederick. "There was blood everywhere—and that awful knife was sticking out of his chest. He was trying to remove it. I...I helped."

Not a particularly bright thing for a doctoral candidate to do, but understandable under the circumstances. His gaze went to her hands. They were still bloody, only now the blood was the color of rust. That damned DCI hadn't let her wash up.

She glared at Patel. "I know you think I did it, but I swear, I didn't."

"Miss Townley, I am paid to suspect everyone, then to eliminate the innocent."

She nodded solemnly.

"Do you know if the victim was still alive when you found him?" Patel asked.

She nodded, then her hand flew to her mouth. "Oh, my God! That must have been the murderer leaving!"

Patel spoke sternly. "Calm down, Miss Townley, and explain yourself. What are you talking about?"

"When I opened the door to Mr. Ellerton's office—after I heard a moan—I had the impression the other door closed—the door we just exited from. I hadn't noticed that door before." Her tears gathered again.

Patel solemnly nodded. "So the victim was still alive when you found him?"

She nodded.

"Did he say anything?"

She nodded again but did not offer to repeat the man's dying words.

Patel's dark brows drew together. "And were his words intelligible?"

Another nod.

"Miss Townley, will you please tell me what the victim said?"

"He said, *shit*."

If this weren't so grave a matter, Frederick would have laughed.

"That was all?" Patel asked.

"Basically, yes."

"Please clarify what you mean by *basically*," Patel snapped.

Frederick had to give the guy credit. He was immune to her considerable beauty. Nine hundred ninety-nine men out of a thousand would have become completely subservient to her. This detective, though, was so stiff he gave the impression he thought she was guilty of murder. The man must be an imbecile.

"When I asked him who tried to kill him, he said *shit* once more."

Frederick did not for a moment believe this lovely creature capable of murder, but he had difficulty believing Ellerton capable of using his last breath on such a profanity. In the nine years he had known the erudite historian, he had never heard him use slang of any kind. The fellow was very formal, and he was every inch a gentleman.

Patel frowned. "And that's all?"

"Yes."

Frederick turned at the sound of gravel crunching beneath footsteps. One of the uniformed policemen, a paper in his hand, crossed the gravel drive, entered the knot garden, and approached Patel. "Sir, I think you ought to see this."

Patel read the page, then eyed the policeman. "Where did you get this?"

The policeman averted his gaze from Miss Townley. "It was on Miss Townley's laptop."

Patel thanked the policeman, then dismissed him. He handed the standard-size piece of paper to her. "Did you write this?"

She read over it, then looked up at the chief inspector. "Yes, it's an e-mail I sent to my sister."

"This could be motive for murder." Patel stared at Miss Townley.

Her dark eyes rounded. "Because I said I envied Mr. Ellerton's job?"

"You say right here that you'd *kill* for his job."

"It's an expression!" she defended. She began to choke up. "I liked Mr. Ellerton. A lot."

"You also wrote that you thought Siddley Hall the loveliest, most historically significant home in England."

A most intelligent woman, to be sure, Frederick thought.

"That could be a motive," Patel continued. "And we can't discount that a witness saw you beside the body with the murder weapon in your hand."

CHAPTER 2

"Now, come on, Patel!" Lord Rockford admonished. "Anyone can see the poor girl's distraught at finding the body, and you can't honestly believe a slim female like her could overpower Ellerton. Did you notice what a large fellow he was?"

Antonia was grateful to have a champion. If it weren't for all the crappy stuff like finding a bloody dead body and being accused of murder, she'd be practically orgasmic to have the titled, *handsome* Lord Rockford as her champion.

"I will give you that," Hard Ass answered, "but it is possible that because he wasn't expecting an attack from such a quarter, she could easily have caught him unawares."

"I would give you that," his lordship answered, "*if* he'd been stabbed in the back."

So he's handsome and smart!

"Let me ask both of you, then," Patel said, folding his arms across his chest, "if you know of anyone who wanted Mr. Ellerton dead."

She shook her head, then eyed the earl.

"I can't imagine anyone wanting to harm him," Lord Rockford said. "He was incredibly easygoing and well liked."

She sniffed. "I liked him very much."

The detective chief inspector addressed the lord of the manor. "You know of no reason someone would want to harm him?"

"None at all."

It was difficult for her not to stare at Lord Rockford. He was such a complete departure from the other lords of the manor she had encountered since coming to study in England. Where were the sallow complexion, sunken chest, and congenital bad teeth she'd come to expect from Englishmen?

This guy was stare-worthy. Butterscotch coloring. Golden hair and smoky-brown eyes. He was taller than average—she'd guess six two—and though he was lean, his broad shoulders indicated he was probably not a stranger to a gym. He even had an eye for tasteful clothing. Were they in the States, she'd refer to his style as *preppie*.

"Actually," she said, "I may know of something."

They both whirled toward her.

"Mr. Ellerton told me he thought he could prove the existence of the Percy Monstrance."

Lord Rockford's eyes rounded. "I thought it was melted for the gold and jewels during the Dissolution!"

Patel's eyes narrowed. "What's a monstrance?"

Oh, how she enjoyed adopting an authoritarian air with Detective Chief Inspector Hard Ass! "It's a golden receptacle to hold the Catholic communion Host after it's been consecrated. Because they're believed to hold the body of Christ, the monstrances produced in the Middle Ages and Renaissance periods are very elaborate."

"We have a painting of ours," Lord Rockford said. "Come, let me show you."

As they left the garden and walked along the gravel drive to the front entrance of Siddley Hall, the earl walked beside her. "That must be what Ellerton was going to tell me today!"

She nodded. "Yes, I believe he was. He first mentioned it to me several weeks ago, but he had a few more things to check on before he was going to inform you of his discovery."

"Do you think he had the monstrance in his possession?"

She shrugged. "It was my impression that he did not. In fact, from what he told me, I gathered that retrieving it from where it's been hidden for half a millennium might involve some string pulling. But that's just my impression. We were supposed to meet at lunch for him to bring me up to speed on everything." Her voice began to crack.

They entered the public portion of Siddley. It was not her first time there. During her first month in England, she had paid her ten pounds and taken the tour along with all the other tourists, but her knowledge of the house exceeded that of those in her tour. In fact, the guide was so impressed that by the end of the tour, she was deferring to Antonia about Siddley's history.

Though this original section of Siddley lacked the elegance and grandeur of the part built in Georgian times, she thought she preferred this oldest portion. With its wooden floors and wood-beamed ceilings—even though they rose to extravagant heights— it had a homey quality. She supposed it was because of the wood's warm patina. It was easy to imagine the Sir Percy who had built Siddley gathering around one of the massive hearths with his nine children. It was the kind of house where one would want to raise children.

Lord Rockford shook his head as if in disbelief. "I had no idea what Ellerton was going to tell me was so significant."

The earl paused just inside the doorway to Siddley Hall and faced her. "Have you been in the main house before?"

"I took the guided tour about six months ago."

"Then you would have seen the chapel."

She nodded. "I fell to my knees in homage."

He cracked a smile. Yes, he did have very nice teeth. Even and white. Wonder of wonders. "You wouldn't have seen the Holbein. I just had it moved there from the private family dining room. I felt it belonged in the chapel."

It was almost incomprehensible to her that he could refer to his family's Holbein as casually as he would refer to the laundry.

She happened to know that the last time a Holbein came on the market, it fetched three million pounds—five million in US dollars—and it was a little bitty thing.

She and the detective chief inspector followed Lord Rockford along a wooden corridor lit by iron wall sconces that had been electrified. "I say, Patel," he said, halting, "why don't you allow Miss Townley to wash up? There's a loo right here."

Patel's gaze darted to her bloodstained hands. "Sorry. Do let's stop and have you wash."

Her eyes locked with Lord Rockford's in silent gratitude, then she entered the restroom, leaving the door open. It wasn't as if she were actually going to pee. Or was she? Now that she thought about it, she did have to go. She went back and closed the door.

How incongruous it seemed to have a 1930s-looking deco bath in the Tudor wing of this ancient house! Well, it wasn't really a bath. The anteroom had a toilet, and the small entry chamber featured a vitreous porcelain sink on a pedestal of the same material. For hours she'd been wanting to wash poor Mr. Ellerton's blood from her hands, but just looking at it made her queasy.

After she pottied, she lathered up. Industrial-looking soap and paper towel dispensers were mounted on the wall. Her mind fastened on the aristocrat who was kind enough to notice her distress. Chalk up compassion to the man's lengthy list of attributes.

She met them back in the hall, and they walked a short distance to its end, where there was a wide timber door. Its top pointed in the shape of a Gothic arch.

Lord Rockford opened the door to the chapel. There were four wooden pews on either side of the nave, each of which could accommodate eight to ten persons. Stained glass windows lined three walls to fill the somber place with diffused light.

The earthy materials used in the rooms they'd just passed had been abandoned here. Only magnificence would do for the house of the Lord. The floors here were of still-flawless Carrera marble, the crucifix above the marble altar appeared to be of sparkling gold, and lovely heavily gilded frescoes of celestial scenes adorned the ceilings.

She looked at the front wall of the chapel. "It's a shame the original statues had to be removed during the Dissolution."

"You remembered about those?" Lord Rockford's deeply honeyed eyes shone down at her.

"You may not know, my lord, but your family is one of those I'm studying for my dissertation. I believe I could go head-to-head with you on Percy family trivia."

"How fascinating! I shall be happy to take you up on the matter..." he eyed the DCI, "later. Now, if you will turn around and behold the wall behind us."

The large, gilt-framed painting on that wall was almost life-size. It featured four subjects: two men, one woman, and the monstrance. The cardinal in the center held up the Percy Monstrance, which was the focus of the painting. Kneeling on either side in the foreground were a man and woman dressed in typical Tudor style.

The woman wore an elaborate headdress that crested to a diamond shape and also looked to have several diamonds embedded in it. Antonia's guess was that the kneeling man was the baronet who built Siddley, Sir Harold Percy, who was also the man who commissioned the monstrance. The sole woman must be his wife, Mary, daughter of the Duke de Quincy.

As Antonia stared at the distinctly Holbein painting, she recognized the colorful Nativity in the stained glass window behind the cardinal and realized the painting had been executed in this very chapel.

The monstrance was a beauty. England had so few of these. The really great ones were in the Vatican Museums, but nothing in the Vatican could rival this. Its base and stem were of heavy, shiny gold and were encrusted with rubies, emeralds, and sapphires. The circular receptacle was faced with glass and framed with a gold-and-diamond sunburst. In the center of the monstrance was a circular white Host that was half again the size of a US quarter.

"That, Chief Inspector," she announced, "is the Percy Monstrance."

As she peered at the painting, another revelation slammed into her. She whirled at the earl. "Good lord! Is that Cardinal Wolsey?"

"Indeed it is. Which I would say would increase the provenance of the monstrance considerably, providing the Percy Monstrance *is* still in existence."

She continued to stare at the painting. "I suppose there are those who would murder to possess such a thing."

"When was this painted?" the detective chief inspector asked.

Lord Rockford shrugged. "About 1500, I should say."

"It would have to be between 1515—when he became the only cardinal ever in Britain—and 1530, the year he died." Her pathetic brain was filled with reams of similarly useless information.

Which explained why she did what she did. Those useless bits of knowledge about dead Englishmen were of no help whatsoever in information systems analysis, which was what her father had encouraged her to study.

Lord Rockford looked approvingly at her. "I see you specialize in that particular area."

She shrugged. Ever since her mother had dragged Antonia and her sister on a tour of English stately homes when she was eleven, Antonia had lived and breathed English history. Her obsession over all things English even extended to her choice of novels. Only British authors enthralled.

"Because this painting establishes the provenance of the monstrance," Hard Ass said respectfully to Lord Rockford, "you're saying that increases the value of the monstrance?"

The lord of the manor nodded. "Significantly."

"What value would you place on the monstrance?" the detective chief inspector asked.

"Offhand, I would guess it would become the most valuable possession at Siddley—if it's at Siddley. I can call some of my acquaintances who are experts at such things and give you a better figure in a few days."

A semblance of a smile actually cracked across Patel's face. "I would appreciate that." He tucked his small notebook inside the breast pocket of his tweed sports coat, then eyed Antonia and spoke sternly. "I don't need to tell you that you're not to leave the country while this investigation is ongoing."

"I'm not going anywhere."

"Here's my card. Don't hesitate to call if you learn anything that relates to this crime." He left the pair of them in the chapel.

She just stood there for a moment. Something that she felt was significant flashed into her mind the instant Hard Ass said to call him, but as quickly as it came, it vanished. She'd been through so much that day, it was no wonder her thoughts were muddled.

Lord Hunkford looked at his watch. She did her best to determine what kind it was. She was pretty sure it was not a Rolex. After that, she was hopeless at identifying expensive luxury watches owned by the rich and famous. "I can't believe it's already past six. Did you ever get that lunch?"

She shook her head. God, she was starved. Maybe that explained why she was shaking.

"Fancy a bite and a pint at the local pub? I may wish to try my luck in that Percy trivia game with you."

"Fish and chips and bitters and Percy family trivia. Sounds perfect."

"I thought I knew about the Percy family," she said as they drove in his car to the Black Labrador, "but you were quite the surprise. I suppose you must be a bachelor?"

He eyed the traffic on the street he was turning onto and nodded. He was thankful she was intelligent enough to have figured out why he would not plaster his picture on Siddley's website and other publications. Verbalizing his abhorrence of being what his brother laughingly called a chick magnet, might make him sound a bit egotistical.

"Yes, that would explain the absence of your photos in the Siddley Hall booklets," she continued. "Do you know almost all the other great stately homes' booklets have a welcoming letter and picture of the lord of the manor or the manager of the family trust?"

"But they're all married."

"And don't have to worry about females swarming about, throwing their bodies in their paths."

"Well, I wouldn't know about that." Which was a lie. He knew all too well about women who would love to be mistress of Siddley Hall and call themselves Lady Rockford.

"I think you're being modest. I expect those swarms of females must be a real problem for you." She turned to face him. "I expect George Clooney has the same problem."

He could not look at her because he would not take his eye off the road, but he laughed. "I should have such problems."

"You're much more handsome than the average lord of the manor."

"And you're much lovelier than the average archival researcher." He couldn't believe he'd actually said that to her. It was one thing for her to say what she's said. She was an outspoken American. But what was his excuse? Trying to hit on a traumatized woman? He felt like an insecure adolescent. Clearly, he needed to change the direction of this conversation. "You must tell me about your research."

"For my doctorate from Oxford, my dissertation's on the five secret Catholic families during and immediately following the reign of Henry VIII."

"I've never heard of the five secret Catholic families."

"That's because it's my discovery."

"Indeed? I'm intrigued." He pulled the car in front of the Black Labrador. It was close enough to Siddley that they could have walked, but he knew she needed to eat as soon as possible. As he walked around to her side of the car to open her door, she looked at him. "The Percys are one of the five families."

"Then I would say they did very well at keeping their Catholicism a secret."

She stepped from the car and fell into step beside him. "It was not only politically expedient, it was a matter of keeping one's head, I would say."

Inside the dark pub, he led her to the quietest corner, where an upholstered bench formed an L. On the opposite side of the rectangular room, several groups were watching soccer on a television suspended from the ceiling, and at the bar a number of men in business suits gathered with friends and a pint after a day's work. "So it will be bitters and fish and chips for you?" he asked, still standing as she scooted across the black velvet seat.

She nodded, then he went to the bar, placed the order, and returned a moment later with two pints. He set them on the tiny round table, then came to sit beside her. "Who are these five secret Catholic families?"

"They're all related to the last baronet."

"So let me guess. His eldest daughter would have to have been one. I understand the bond between Sir Harold Percy and his first daughter was very close."

"Bingo! His daughter Katherine, who married John Farr of Castle Paxton, was one of the secret Catholics, as was her husband."

"What about Sir Harold Percy's wife? Wasn't she the daughter of the Duke de Quincy?"

"You may go to the head of the class. Just today I found a letter in your archives from the Duchess de Quincy to her daughter. It proves that both families were secret practicing Catholics."

"I should love to see it."

She sighed, and her eyes glistened. "I was coming to show it to Mr. Ellerton—"

He put his hand on hers. And once again felt like an adolescent holding hands with a girl for the first time—even though they weren't holding hands. "It's all right. You don't have to talk about it. I know it was beastly bad business finding—well, let's not discuss it."

When she looked up at him with those big, dark eyes, he felt an overwhelming urge to protect her. "Do you think Detective Chief Inspector Hard Ass really thinks I'm the murderer?"

He burst out laughing. "I admit that's a jolly good description of the DCI, but I expect he's just doing his job. I don't see how he could possibly think you committed murder."

"Thank you, my lord." She dabbed at her eyes.

"No need to use my title. My friends call me Rockford. No lord." He gave her a crooked grin. "But I shan't answer to Rocky."

She giggled. "You're not exactly the Sylvester Stallone type."

They were silent for a moment, which proved to be long enough for her to grow solemn again. "I can't believe anyone would harm Mr. Ellerton. He was such a nice man."

"I feel the same." He could not express to her how he felt such a deep chasm. He would never again find someone who could replace Ellerton, never find someone who knew all the little discoveries they'd shared these past nine years. No one else would ever possess Ellerton's affinity for Siddley...

Then he remembered the e-mail Antonia Townley had sent to her sister, and he could not deny that she just might have the qualifications to replace the slain man. Though this was neither the time nor the place to bring up such a subject.

"I still have a hard time believing I heard his final words correctly," she said. "They seemed so out of character."

"Exactly! Is there anything else it could have been? Someone's name that sounds like...*shit*?" It was extremely distasteful to him to use that word at the dinner table.

Her eyebrows scrunched down. "Pitt? Slit? Witt? Britt? De Witt? She it?" She gazed up at him and shrugged. "Anything ring a bell?"

"No." He took a swig. "Enough discussion of Ellerton. You've been through a lot for one day. Let's return to those five secret Catholic families."

But before they could, a skinny young fellow with an apron delivered their warm plates.

"I decided to order what you did," he said. "I'm normally a carnivore."

She wrinkled her nose. "Not so much, here." She began to remove the golden crust from her cod.

"Hey! That's the best part. You aren't eating it?"

"I avoid saturated fats whenever possible."

"Oh, I see. If it comes from a cow, it can't possibly be good for you?"

"Exactly."

"So you're saying ice cream's not good for you?"

She shrugged. "If you were a thirteen-year-old boy who was trying to fatten up, I might suggest the consumption of ice cream."

"Are you telling me you don't eat ice cream?"

"I'm telling you I know I shouldn't eat ice cream. It's loaded with saturated fat." Those long, dark lashes of hers lifted, and a smile lighted her face. "But on occasion, I succumb."

"It's good to know you're human." And what a human! Very pretty. And smart. He stabbed at the crunchy bits she'd pulled from her fish. "Mind if I help myself?"

She shrugged. "It's your heart attack."

"I'll start worrying when I hit forty."

"I do remember reading in *Debrett's* what year you were born, so forty is six years off?"

"Correct. Which I would guess is a decade older than you."

"Close. We're the same age difference as Winston and Clementine. I wonder if that's of any significance?"

He began to chuckle. "It appears you're in possession of a photographic memory. You not only memorized my entry in Debrett's, but you know the exact age difference between Winston and Clementine Churchill."

"I wish I *did* have a photographic memory. Then I wouldn't have to always be taking copious notes."

She was far too humble. "So you study the current *Debrett's*, too?"

"I didn't buy a subscription or anything, but I can log in from my Oxford account. One of the best perks to doing graduate work there is the research that's available to me at my fingertips—and I don't have to pay anything for it."

"Now that I do what I do—you know I manage the Percy Family Trust?"

She nodded. "It wasn't in the Siddley booklet. I learned it from Mr. Ellerton."

He found himself trying to recall what was in the Siddley booklet. This girl probably remembered every word. "I wish I had studied history as you are. I had thought a degree in art history would serve me well."

She nodded. "Because of your family's art collection, yes, I suppose it would."

His cell phone rang. He yanked it from his pocket and looked down at the caller ID. "The Metropolitan Police," he told her. "Hello?"

"This is Detective Chief Inspector Patel. Can you tell me why Ellerton's phone conversations were being recorded?"

"I had no idea they were."

"Are you with that American?"

"Yes, I am."

"May I speak with her?"

Frederick handed the phone to Antonia.

"Yes?" Her eyes narrowed. "Of course I don't know anything about that!" Her dark eyes flashed angrily as she listened. "I told you already. I'm not leaving the country! You want to put a GPS on me?"

She terminated the call and shoved the phone back at him. Her hands were shaking.

"So what do you think?" he asked.

"I think someone else knows about the monstrance, and I believe that's why that poor man was killed. Don't you see, it's significant that he was killed *before* he was to reveal its existence to you?"

"You are brilliant!"

Nibbling at her lips and lost in thought, she ignored his comment. "Would the monstrance belong to you?"

"Not necessarily. If it's found at Siddley, then, yes, it would become the property of our family."

"So it's the old thing about possession being nine-tenths of the law?"

"Something like that."

"If it were at Siddley, where would it likely be hidden?"

"I quite honestly don't see how something like that could be hidden. And it's been five hundred years. Surely if it were here, it would have been found by now."

"It could be buried."

"Then I shall launch a metal detection investigation."

She cut up the remainder of her cod and began to eat it, piece by skinless piece. "It occurs to me I don't know about any graveyards or crypts at Siddley."

"That's because there aren't any. All the Percys were laid to rest in the parish church on the outskirts of Siddley."

"I guess that rules that out." She took a stab at her last bite. "If the Percy Monstrance were found at, say, the de Quincy family's Blyn Court Castle, the monstrance would belong to the de Quincys?"

"I expect so."

"I wonder what the monstrance would be worth in today's pounds."

He looked at his wristwatch. "Since it's Friday, the V&A is—"

"—open until ten tonight."

"I rest my case. You are the uncrowned queen of trivia." He punched in a single number, and while he waited for it to connect with Nigel, he turned to her. "I've an old professor who's something big at the V&A Museum. If anyone knows the value of an artifact like the Percy Monstrance, it'll be him."

A moment later, Frederick was filling Nigel in on the background of the monstrance. "And how's this for provenance?" Frederick said. "We've a Holbein painting of the thing with none other than Cardinal Wolsey himself holding it."

"Good lord, Rockford! That makes the thing practically priceless. As much as I'd like to bid on it, I suspect the Vatican would outbid us. Can you send me a snapshot of the painting?"

"I shall do so tonight. Thanks ever so much, old chap. Oh, and if the thing proves to be in our family's possession, I would be delighted to *give* it to the V&A. Got to keep it in Jolly Old England, don't ya know."

As soon as he ended the call, she asked, "What did he say?"

"I expect he'll have a value on it after I send him a photo. Probably tomorrow."

"I bet he thought it was pretty valuable."

He nodded. "He did throw out the word *priceless*."

"Definitely worth murdering for. I have the feeling that if we could find out who knew about the monstrance, we might know who killed that sweet man. It wasn't like he pranced around announcing his discovery to everyone. He hadn't even told you yet, and I know you and he had a solid partnership."

"I wonder if Alistair knew about it—not that I'm accusing the lad of murder."

She rolled her eyes. "I cannot imagine why Mr. Ellerton tolerated Alistair Bumbler. He's an immature child."

"Alistair's last name is Pen—oh, I see. Another of your little nicknames, like Chief Inspector Hard Ass. I wonder what name you've attached to me."

A wide grin brightened her face. "I'll never tell."

"I can tell you why Alistair was hired. My cousin Richard, the Earl of Bessington, asked me to hire the lad as a personal favor to him. Alistair is some relation to him on his mother's side. I take it he's not especially bright. Didn't make university but liked being around books. Musty old libraries and the like. Since the Bessington family archives were sold to the University of Portsmouth, my cousin had nothing to offer Alistair at Chumley Manor."

"The Bumbler may be interested in musty old libraries, but he's pretty clueless."

"He's young."

"I'll say! I'm not even certain if he shaves yet." She shrugged. "I suppose he does need a bit more training. He is awfully courteous, and he tries to be helpful." She scooped peas onto her fork. "It has just occurred to me that the murderer may not be in possession of the Percy Monstrance."

"What makes you think that?"

"It's only a hunch. It's a given they would have committed murder to get the monstrance from Mr. Ellerton if he had it, but there's also the possibility that they would have killed him to keep him from telling you about it. They may believe they can discover its whereabouts on their own."

"I see what you mean. If he told me about it, they may have feared I would take possession of it, and they'd never get it."

"It's one possibility. There is also the possibility they found out from him where it was before they killed him."

"What's to prevent us from accusing them of murder when they turn up with it, then?"

"I don't suppose it's the kind of thing one could secretly sell?"

He shook his head. "No. It definitely would belong in one of the world's great museums."

"I think it belongs at Siddley."

"I dismissed that idea because we've been Protestants for so many centuries, but I suppose you're right. Especially if you have proof we were secret Catholics." As he watched her, he realized that she looked incredibly tired. "Don't tell me you've come to Siddley from Oxford?"

She nodded. "I left my flat in Oxford at six thirty this morning."

"You drove?"

She shook her head. "Not here—on the wrong side of the road!"

"But I have it on great authority *this* is the right side of the road."

They both laughed.

"You came on the train?"

"Yes. I go everywhere by train. A most efficient rail system you've got here."

"Any number of efficient things occur in a country where capitalism merges with socialism." He looked at his watch. "I regret to tell you that you've missed the last train of the night."

Her eyes rounded.

"Don't worry. I think there's a possibility we might be able to find a room for you at Siddley."

"I expect you could somewhere in those three hundred sixteen rooms, and I appreciate the offer, but I'll need my nightie and toothbrush and clean clothes for tomorrow—even my makeup is at my flat."

"Then I'll take you home. In my car, it will only take an hour."

He had waited until he was quite alone. No one around. Then he'd called his associate. It was a call he'd been dreading. Though they had discussed the possibility they might have to commit murder in order to get the monstrance, his partner had stressed murder was a last resort.

As soon as he heard his tone, his breath swished from his lungs in relief. His associate didn't sound angry. Thank God! This wasn't a man he wanted to cross.

"It's all over the television. I know you wouldn't have done it unless you had to."

"He was going to tell Rockford. I had to stop him."

"Of course you did. Under no circumstances is Rockford to find out about the monstrance. You did find out where it was before you killed him?"

He felt like he'd been kicked in the gut. "No. But I think the girl might know."

"Shit!"

"Don't worry. I managed to put a GPS chip in her bag. Wherever she goes in search of the monstrance, we'll be able to follow."

"And what about Ellerton's tapes? Was there anything on them?"

Now he felt like he could throw up. "I...wasn't able to get them. As soon as I knifed him, the girl came knocking on his door. I had to get the hell out of there."

"Do whatever you have to do tomorrow to get those tapes. Do you understand?"

"I'll get them."

"Let's hope they have the monstrance's location. You know what to do with the girl if she gets them before you?"

"I know what to do."

"They say the second time's easier."

EPISODE 2

CHAPTER 3

Like a gentleman, he kindly put up the top on his sports car so her hair wouldn't blow to smithereens on the M4. She might not be able to identify the watch he wore, but she certainly had heard of Aston Martin cars, though the vision of the aging Prince of Wales tooling along in one held no appeal.

They had been driving on the motorway a few minutes when she said, "So this is the same kind of car James Bond drives?" Which *was* really cool. It certainly beat riding in standard class on a packed train.

"Actually, he's a fictional character."

"Thank you, Sherlock."

A slow smile made its way across his very satisfactory face. "You haven't finished telling me about those five Catholic families. There was Sir Harold Percy; his wife's parents, the Duke and Duchess de Quincy; and his daughter, Katherine Farr. I can't think who the two other families would have been."

"His sister..."

"Oh, yes. She married Sir Thomas Montague of Monlief Hall."

"Very good, my lord."

"You're not to address me as your lord." His tone sounded like Simon's.

But it was OK for Lord Rockford to sound lordly because he *was* lordly. Unlike Surly Simon. "I don't feel right calling you Rockford. It's something a guy would call another guy, and I'm not a guy, in case you haven't noticed."

"Oh, I've noticed all right."

Just the way he said that made her feel the same way she'd felt when she was thirteen and Justin Manzanolli asked her to the school dance. (Never mind that Justin wasn't the prize she'd thought him. She would just as soon forget the part when Justin tried to feel her up in the backseat of his parents' SUV. With his parents in the front!) "May I call you Freddie?"

She watched his profile. His straight nose was as perfect as his teeth. God, just riding in the car with this guy felt like she'd hit a jackpot in Vegas. Even before he'd said what he'd said about noticing she was a female.

"No one calls me Freddie." Now he sounded like Hard Ass.

"What do your sisters call you?"

"You would know my entire family history," he mumbled almost under his breath. He accelerated. This guy liked speed.

She didn't.

"I suppose there are some things at which I do have a bit of a photographic memory. Your parents' firstborn was Harriet, who's married to Robert Haddley, third son to the Duke of Richland, and your other sister, who's a year younger than you, is named Barbara, and she works on Wall Street."

"You should go on a quiz show."

She was determined not to act like a wuss and comment on his fast driving, but she couldn't help gripping at her seat like a scared child. And she kept watching the speedometer, but she'd never quite gotten the hang of kilometers. She did know he was going really, really fast. "The rub is that my sphere of knowledge is extremely limited."

"Let me guess. Your hobby is studying the old noble families of England."

"And their residences. I have a thing for the houses, too. I have now visited twenty-seven of England's finest stately homes."

"And Siddley really is your favorite?" He let up slightly on the accelerator.

"Oh, yes!" Was she commenting on his driving or his house?

"But it's not grand like Blenheim, and it sits on a rather reduced piece of property. Nothing like Chatsworth."

"True, but I love the way it was added on to willy-nilly over the centuries without some aesthete pulling down or covering up the old so that it would all have the same architectural style."

"You have just perfectly described Siddley Hall."

"I think, too, it's useful that Siddley is so close to London and so central to the country."

"Yes, it is very useful." He took his eye off the road just a smidgeon so it looked as if he was facing her. "You never have disclosed to me that last Catholic family."

"I'll give you a hint. You mentioned to me tonight the name of the home of that last Catholic family."

His foot came off the accelerator. "Chumley?"

"Yes, even though it has passed out of the Earl of Godwin's family. Sort of."

He was nodding. "If I recall my family history, the first Earl of Godwin's wife was sister to Sir Harold Percy's wife. They were both daughters of the Duke de Quincy."

"I can see you're going to be stiff competition in that trivia contest. The sisters, I gather from their letters, were very close."

"I should love to see their letters."

"Some of them are in your archives. I'd be glad to show them to you. I've also transcribed all the ones I've found all over England and keep them in my notebooks."

"I don't need to see the originals. I'm sure I'd find your notebooks fascinating."

Though Simon seldom complimented her work, he had thought her notebooks should be published. It was something to consider.

And thinking about it took her mind off his heavy foot.

"I'm unclear," she said, "how the present Earl of Bessington came to possess Chumley."

"The Earl of Godwin's title went extinct, so Chumley Manor passed down through the female line. It's been in the Earl of Bessington's family, I believe, for over three hundred years."

"So this cousin Richard of yours also inherited young, or is he much older than you?"

"We're close in age, and he only recently succeeded. Why do you ask?"

She shrugged. "Idle curiosity, I expect. Chumley is the only one of the five family homes I have yet to see."

"If you'd like, I could take you there and see that you get a proper tour of it by Richard himself."

Had he just asked her for a date? Even if Justin Manzanolli was the most popular boy in the whole junior high, she hadn't been this excited when he'd picked her over all the other girls. Her heart was beating ninety to nothing, but she had to act calm. "I would love it!" Had she sounded too excited? Of course, this wasn't like a real date. He was probably just being nice.

Her cell rang. Her cell phone never rang. She had no friends in England, and she and her sister typically communicated by e-mail because of the time difference between San Francisco and England. Her insides did that elevator thing as she went to answer it, then she saw Simon's name. Why in the heck was he calling her this late at night? She slid the screen to connect. "Simon?"

"Good Lord, Antonia, I've been worried sick about you ever since I heard on the news about the murder at Siddley." Now, this did not sound like the obnoxiously superior scholar who smothered her with his so-called mentoring—and criticism. Simon worried? No way.

"Why would you be worried about me? It's not like I was the one who got plunked in the chest with that dagger." She really hated being so flippant about poor Mr. Ellerton's brutal death. It's just that Simon always brought out the worst in her.

"But you're the one who found the body. What a terrible thing for a sensitive woman like you to discover."

Simon thought her sensitive? Maybe there was a side to Simon she'd failed to see before. Maybe he wasn't so God Almighty superior. "It *was* beastly. And you won't believe this, Simon, but the detective chief inspector of the Metropolitan Police—"

"Thinks you did it."

She felt like she'd been hit by a moving vehicle. "They said *that* on the news?"

"Well, not actually, but I could easily pick up on the subtext."

That was better. Now he was back to talking like the Simon she knew. She exhaled. "You just scared the crap out of me."

"I'm sorry, Antonia."

That sweet tone didn't sound like Surly Simon. "It's been a long, terrible day."

"And you're still not home. I just called your flat."

"No, but I'm on the way."

"Why don't we meet in the morning for coffee?"

"I've got to be back at Siddley in the morning."

"You can't be serious."

"But I am."

"You're not afraid to return to the scene of the crime?"

"Why would anyone want to kill me?"

"Why would someone kill Ellerton? I've never known a nicer or more honest man."

"You've got a point there, but I'm still returning to Siddley tomorrow."

"Then I'll visit you there. You need a man around."

Simon, a man? She'd never thought of him as anything but a thorn in her side. "I happen to be with a man right now."

There was a long silence on the other end, then he said, "Oh, really? I didn't know you had a fellow."

"I don't." She wasn't sure if she wanted Simon to know about Lord Rockford. Or Frederick. Her heart fluttered when she thought about addressing Lord Hunkness by his first name.

"OK. Then allow me to drive you to Siddley in the morning. I know you don't drive in England."

"Sure. That'll work."

"If you need anything, you've got my number."

"Right here in my trusty iPhone."

"I'll be at your flat at seven thirty. And I'll bring coffee."

She was practically dazed as she put her phone back in her purse. Why was Simon being so darn nice?

They drove through the inky darkness in silence for a few minutes. This was the first she'd been aware that music was coming from Lord Rockford's car's sound system. Sultry jazz. She liked it.

Finally, he spoke. "I take it your boyfriend just heard on the telly about the murder."

She needed him to know she was available. "I don't have a boyfriend." *But you can fill the position anytime.*

He drove on in silence for another minute. Then he said, "I'm glad."

Her flat was located in the old town of Oxford on a narrow, out-of-the-way street where there was no place for him to park. The street was poorly lit, too. He did not feel comfortable just dropping her off as if she were a piece of Royal Mail.

"I can get out here," she said as his car slowed in front of the dark three-story building.

"No, you can't." His foot pressed on the accelerator.

She whirled at him. "What are you doing?"

"I'm going to find a car park, then escort you to your flat. That street's entirely too dark."

"Surely you don't think the murderer is lurking there to kill me?"

"I honestly don't know what to think, Miss Townley."

"Please, call me Antonia."

He nodded. "I'm sure when this day started Ralph Ellerton never dreamed he'd be murdered, but someone wanted him silent. You know about the monstrance; someone may wish to silence you, too."

She was silent for a moment. "Now I'll be scared of my own flat."

"Until the murderer is discovered, you need to be scared."

He parked in a car park four blocks away, then went and dropped his coins into the slots while she stood beside him. He was conscious of her long, slim legs clad in faded blue jeans and looking even longer than they were because of the high-heeled boots she wore. He found the way her long, dark hair slid over her face as seductive as a striptease.

They started to walk along the dark, quiet street. "It's certainly nothing like London," he said. "This town must shut down at ten o'clock."

"We Oxfordites—is that a word?—gotta hit the books, and I did specifically select this part of town because it's more somber."

"I'd feel better leaving you at a flat in the middle of Party Central. Listen, Antonia, if you're scared, you can just collect your things now, and I'll take you back to Siddley."

"I appreciate the offer, but here I'm surrounded by all my notebooks and books and stuff...and Simon's coming—"

"Oh, I don't mean to interfere with you and this Simon chap." Why did Frederick have the urge to slug that Simon chap right in the face? He'd never even met the bloke.

"Simon will be here at seven thirty in the morning. He's offered to drive me to Siddley."

"Right-o." He was really glad he was seeing her safely home. There were any number of darkened doorways where danger could be lurking. *But what the hell would I do if I confronted an armed man?*

She stopped in front of a closed door. It opened into a stairwell that was lit by a single dim bulb. "You didn't even need a key?" he asked, incredulous.

"Not for this door. Of course, my flat stays locked, as do the others here." She began to mount the stairs, then turned back and spoke in a low voice. "You're welcome to come in for…a glass of wine? I think I've got wine. But you don't have to see me all the way to the door. I'm on the third floor."

His brows lowered. "Is there not a way you could lock that door to the street?"

She shrugged. "It's always been left open."

He followed her up the first flight of stairs. "You don't have to offer me a drink. I just want to ensure that you get safely to your door." It got increasingly darker as they climbed to the top floor. The fact that her door was the last one on the darkened corridor made him uneasy. For her.

She stood in front of the door and began to search in her large, soft leather bag for her key.

"Is that a bag or a suitcase?" he asked, his voice lowered.

"It's my everyday purse. Sir Paul would not approve. It's made of real leather."

"Sir Paul would definitely not approve of my carnivore preferences, but then it's not likely I'll be at the same functions with Paul McCartney."

She was smiling as she found the key, inserted it into the lock, and opened the door.

Then she screamed.

CHAPTER 4

Someone had been there! Searching through her stuff. Her flat was in chaos. Desk drawers had been flung to the floor. Her metal filing cabinet had been emptied, its contents heaped onto the floor, too.

Even though Lord Hunkness was standing there beside her and the overhead light now shone brightly in her living room, she stood at the threshold to her flat, afraid to step in. Her petrified gaze swept over the hundreds of papers dumped on the floor. This had to have been done by the same person who murdered Mr. Ellerton.

And the murderer might still be there. She was shaking like a jackhammer, and tears pricked at her eyes.

"Good lord!" Frederick brushed past her as he strode into the room with a commanding air. "The bastard's been here! Thank God you didn't come alone." His gaze circled the normally tidy room, then came back to rest on her. She was still frozen in the doorway. "I'll check the other rooms, make sure he's not still here."

How different her little living room looked now. With its hodgepodge of styles, it had never been visually appealing, but now it looked—as her daddy would say—*bone-ass ugly*.

The scratched-up mahogany kneehole desk looked as if it had been used for well over half a century. Incongruously, the armless black leather sofa and its accompanying glass-and-chrome tables were modern, as did the flat-screen TV on the stark white walls. Paisley draperies in varying shades of red provided the room's only color.

Had she known a peer of the realm was going to be poking his handsome nose in her flat, she would have at least purchased a couple of red throw pillows for the sofa or hung meaningful wall art, like a watercolor of Siddley.

She cringed at the one piece of wall art that had come with the flat: a print of tacky liquor bottles labeled in an unrecognizable foreign language. She cringed, too, that she'd gotten the cheap, two-drawer metal file cabinet instead of one that looked like a piece of wood furniture.

Behind her, doors flew open and questions flurried. Several of her neighbors in varying states of undress rushed into the darkened hallway, obviously awakened by her scream.

"Someone broke into my flat," she told them.

"Oh, luv, how terrible!" elderly Mrs. Maguire uttered. The others stood behind Mrs. Maguire, gawking into her living room.

Antonia turned so one half of her faced the gathering crowd and the other half tilted toward her flat as she nervously watched for Frederick. "Did any of you see anyone enter or exit my flat?"

Nothing but solemn head shakes answered her.

The other rooms in her flat consisted of a bathroom that was only slightly larger than a refrigerator, a teensy bedroom that was mostly all bed, and a hallway her landlady referred to as a kitchen but that hardly qualified as a kitchenette with its single burner, miniscule microwave, and an appliance Antonia referred to as sawed-off refrigerator. She estimated it would take him fifteen seconds max to search the whole flat.

In less than that time, he was back in the living room, reassuring her. "It's OK, Antonia. He's gone. Come on in."

"None of these neighbors heard or saw anything."

He nodded at them as he came to close the door. "If any of you remember seeing anything suspicious, we'd appreciate knowing about it. I'm Lord Rockford," he said, reaching into his billfold, extracting his cards, and distributing them to each of the eight who had gathered.

Her gaze swept to a long, narrow credenza-like table abutting her desk. When she'd left this morning, her notebooks had been lined up there like birds on a wire. Now it was empty. The discovery brought instant nausea and a gush of tears. Sixteen hours a day, seven days a week for the past six months she had slaved over those precious notebooks.

Now they were gone. All of them.

"My notebooks!" Her voice sounded hysterical. Which she pretty much was as she tore into the room. Like a deranged bag lady, she started rummaging through the pile of papers fanning across the cheap beige carpet around her desk. Travel documents. Rental agreement. Oxford matriculation. All that kind of paper-work was still there, as were various booklets she had collected from the stately homes she had toured throughout England.

But what she liked to think of as her life's work was gone. Stolen.

She sprang back up and raced through her apartment. She knew it was useless, but she looked in her skinny closet, under the bed, in the trash cans. Nothing.

Back in the living room, she met Frederick's sympathetic gaze. And burst into sobs.

He came to her and drew her into his arms. "At least you're OK. It's going to be all right." His voice was incredibly gentle as he continued to hold her, tracing sultry little circles on her back.

Slapped against his solid chest, she gratefully clung to him. Despite the reality that she'd yanked a bloody dagger from a dead man's chest, despite the fact that a murderer had invaded her home, despite the theft of her precious notebooks, this moment she actually felt safe.

Her shoulders shook as she wept. "No, it's not OK. All my notebooks are gone!"

He held her at arm's length and looked her in the eye. "But you're unhurt. You can replace the notebooks. It will take a long time, but it's doable."

A lock of his dark-blond hair flicked over his brow. She fought the urge to stroke it back into place, to run her hand along the square planes of his aristocratic yet manly face.

"I think…" Sniff. Sniff. "I can use that glass of wine I offered you."

"Sit down. I'll get it for you."

"First, I need Kleenex." She found some, blew her nose, grabbed extras, and went to sit yoga-style on her leather sofa. The tears wouldn't stop coming. "Do you know how many hours I spent on those things?"

He came to stand before her, offering the glass of wine. "I don't suppose you backed up on a laptop or iPad or something?"

She shrugged. "Generally, I transcribed the historic letters right into my spiral notebooks. I had different spiral notebooks for each branch of each of the five Catholic families. Much of the other research I have saved electronically." She took a sip of the red wine and watched him as he came to sit beside her. "I also had some three-ring notebooks filled with photocopies of documents and other assorted research. They're all gone, too." She started sobbing again. "Every la-a-a-s-st one of them is gone!"

He settled a firm but gentle hand on her shoulder. "Obviously, someone thinks you may know where the monstrance is. Can you tell if anything else has been nicked? What of your laptop?"

"I left it at Siddley. Normally, I bring it back and forth each day, but today was not a normal day."

"I'm frightfully sorry." He reached for the telephone on her desk. "I'm going to ring the police."

"What help will that be?"

He punched in nine-nine-nine. "Perhaps he left fingerprints, and—" He stopped and listened. "Yes, I'd like to report a break-in." He looked back at her. "What's your address here?"

"One-twenty-two Chaucer Way, flat six."

He repeated the address, then spoke in an authoritative voice. "I'm Frederick Percy, Lord Rockford. This may not sound like a priority case to you, but it's connected to a murder case being investigated by DCI Patel of the Metropolitan Police. He will need to be apprised of this crime."

She admired the way Frederick threw out his title when it could be useful.

He listened for a moment, then set the phone back into its cradle and faced her. "The information will be passed to the proper department."

"Will you stay until they come?" Her voice sounded pathetically needy.

"I'm not leaving you." He saw that she'd gone through her handful of tissues, got up, and brought her more. He waited patiently while she cried herself out. She was so humiliated. Just a half hour earlier she'd been on top of the world, riding along in his 007 sports car, feeling flattered that he'd noticed she was a she, and now her eyes were all red and her nose was red from blowing it like some foghorn, and she was acting like a Gypsy wailer.

So much for him ever wanting to take her to Chumley Manor now.

A half glass of wine to Antonia was like a syringe of Valium to another person. Her woes drained away, leaving her mellow as she peered into Frederick's amber-colored eyes.

Her heart flipped when he somberly met her gaze and tapped his glass against hers. "Shall we drink to the restoration of your notebooks?"

She practically devoured him with her simmering gaze as they clinked glasses and drank.

He looked away first. "I'd help tidy your room, but I'd like the police to see it as it was left. I'm hoping they can get prints."

She nodded. "I know how he carried out my notebooks."

He gave her a questioning look.

"In my own kitchen trash bags—what you guys refer to as bin bags. He left out the box in my kitchenette."

"Let's hope CCTV has footage of a chap toting a plastic trash sack."

A moment later, his brows lowered. "You're sure Ellerton never said anything to you to indicate where he thought the monstrance was?"

She nodded.

"But didn't he comment to you that your research was helping him to locate it?"

"He did, but he wasn't specific. Obviously, something I shared with him that I had learned from one of the five families was helpful to him."

"But you don't know which family or which document he found useful?"

"I haven't much of a clue. Well, I know which pages I scanned and sent him—"

His dark-blond brows shot up. "You sent them electronically?"

"Yes!" She felt like giving him a high five. "They'll still be on his computer!"

"See, all's not lost. Some of your papers can now easily be replaced."

"And maybe if we study those same papers, it will trigger something to either you or me—something that may lead us to the monstrance."

"We've learned something important tonight."

"Yes, we now know the murderer doesn't have the monstrance."

Within fifteen minutes, a chief inspector was in Antonia's flat. Burglary to a habitat in a university town would not normally summon such a respectful response. Frederick's father had taught him well that the squeaky, well-heeled peer always got greased first, and it was a lesson Frederick had no qualms about invoking whenever it could be helpful.

Especially when it could be helpful to a distressed female.

Frederick could not help but compare this Oxford chief inspector to television's tall, slender Hathaway on *Lewis*. They were total opposites. This Mr. Ranleigh was shorter than average and on the portly side. Frederick took charge and explained the connected, more serious crime that had occurred earlier in the day in order to stress the significance of apprehending the person who stole Antonia's notebooks. "I have little doubt that the person who did this is a murderer," Frederick said.

"It does appear there's a possible connection," the chief inspector said. "I shall be in communication with DCI Patel of the Metropolitan Police."

Antonia's phone rang. Frederick's gaze followed her. Her brows dipped as she reached for the phone. Who in the hell was calling her at midnight? He stiffened. It was probably that Simon chap.

Even though he was in the midst of a conversation with the young inspector, Frederick stopped and listened to Antonia.

"Yes, I've been crying. Someone broke into my flat and stole all my notebooks—even the sisters' letters we'd talked about publishing."

She listened a few seconds, then said, "No, no. I'm fine! No, really, you don't have to come. I'm not alone. The police detective's here, and so is the person who kindly gave me a lift from Siddley."

This was definitely one of those times Frederick would like to have heard his title used. Why wasn't she telling Simon about him? There must be something between her and that damn Simon. Even though she'd told Frederick she didn't have a boyfriend. She must want this Simon chap to be her boyfriend.

"Listen, Simon, I'm going to have to let you go—oh! I won't need a lift in the morning after all. I've decided to go back to Siddley tonight."

Yes!

She rolled her eyes. "All right. I know it's not technically night anymore. It's a new day." She went to terminate the call, then listened some more, rolling her eyes again. "It's not necessary…" Seconds later, she finally ended the call. "If you insist. See you tomorrow."

The inspector used his cell phone to order personnel to dust for prints, and he told Antonia that on the following day they'd interview those who lived beneath her and would check CC television of the area. Antonia gave the inspector her spare key so the police could come and go when she wasn't there.

"Can you narrow down the time frame we'd be looking at?" he asked Antonia.

"I left at six thirty this morning and returned an hour ago."

"I should think," Frederick added, "that this crime likely occurred after Ellerton was slain at noon."

Antonia faced him. "Simon informs me we mustn't refer to it as *this* morning. It's now yesterday's tomorrow."

That Simon sounds like a total prick.

"And can you tell me, Miss Townley, exactly how many notebooks are missing?" the detective continued.

"There were four three-ring notebooks." She started mumbling to herself, counting on her fingers and nodding until her tally was completed, then her gaze returned to Ranleigh. "And eleven spiral notebooks." She teared up again. "And I'd give everything I own to have them back."

"I'm terribly sorry," the inspector said.

Frederick found himself wondering if Antonia would attach one of her monikers to this public servant. He was completely different from Hard Ass Patel. This guy was tripping all over himself to be attentive and considerate toward Antonia. The more Frederick watched him, the more he thought any nickname this man would elicit would have to pertain to his weight.

After he left, Antonia peered at Frederick with those big brown eyes, still beautiful without any makeup. "Are you sure you can find a room to put me up in tonight?"

"I'll put you in the one nearest to me—my brother Bagsy's." He thought she might need the reassurance of being close to him.

Her eyes widened. "You call your brother Bagsy?"

He shrugged. "A nickname he picked up at school. It came from Percy being associated with a lady's purse and from there morphed into Bagsy. Now all of us in the family call him that. Except for Mother." He eyed Antonia. "And I'll wager you can tell me his Christian name and what year he was born."

"Of course, though I don't know if Upton is actually a Christian name. Your brother is two years younger than you." She started for the bedchamber. "Speaking of bags, I believe I'll pack mine."

The return journey to Siddley took even less time because there were few cars on the road this time of night. And because of that, he drove as fast as he dared.

Antonia spoke little. Poor girl. She could live to a hundred and never again experience a more beastly day than this past one had been. He was glad she was going to be under his roof. He somehow felt responsible for her, and having her close would give him one less thing to worry about.

Despite her brilliance, she was incredibly vulnerable. He not only wanted to protect her, he also wanted to free her mind of depressing thoughts. "So we've established that the murderer not only does not have the monstrance," Frederick said, "he doesn't know where it is."

"And we've established that something in the e-mails I sent to Mr. Ellerton may have helped Mr. Ellerton discover its location."

Nodding, he kept his eyes on the road ahead as his headlights sliced through the darkness. "Tomorrow, we'll look through those e-mails together. I think, too, we should give a proper search to Ellerton's office. There may be something there that will point to the monstrance's location."

"Are we looking for the monstrance or the murderer?"

"I suppose both—not that I want either of us to actually come face-to-face with the despicable person. It occurs to me, though, that if I can reveal the whereabouts of the monstrance, that should keep you alive by eliminating the murderer's quest."

"If you get it, he might kill you for it."

"I assure you, I'll have Patel advised of it the minute we find the thing."

"We?"

"I don't like to endanger you, but I can't do this without you. I perfectly understand if you want to pack your suitcases and return to the States."

She shook her head. "No, not that! I always finish what I start. I do feel better knowing I'm not alone."

She made him feel like a superhero. If there were such a thing. "So where in the States are you from?"

"California." ·

Why isn't she in movies? "I wonder how many California girls get doctorate degrees from Oxford."

"Probably not too many. I did come by way of Harvard. I took a bachelor's from Stanford and got a master's from Harvard. I think my master's thesis on the Duke de Quincy's family is what got me accepted at Oxford."

"I should love to see it."

Her hand flew to her mouth. "They got that, too! It was with my notebooks." She shrugged. "Simon has a copy."

The mention of that damned Simon clamped shut Frederick's lips.

When they reached Siddley, he wondered how in the hell he was going to be able to get a minute's sleep knowing that she lay in bed in the very next room. He had never desired a woman like he desired Antonia Townley.

CHAPTER 5

They were both exhausted by the time they returned to Siddley. He showed her through a maze of dark corridors until they came to his brother's bedroom. "Sorry that it's not a lady's room, but since Bagsy was the last one here, I know the linens have just been freshened," he told her as he opened the door and turned on the light.

Because she wanted to project a sophisticated image, she refrained from oohing and ahing over the sumptuous room. She tried to look like sleeping in a room with sixteen-foot-high ceilings, a marble fireplace, and a beautiful canopied bed draped in silk was an everyday occurrence. "It's perfectly lovely."

"There's also an adjoining loo, so everything you need should be right here. And I'll be just next door—" He pointed north. "If you should need…anything. Anything at all."

"Thank you."

"If it's all right with you, I'll tap at your door at eight in the morning to escort you to the breakfast room."

"That would be lovely."

"Don't expect to get the guest house treatment here, though. I'm afraid breakfast is rather a serve-yourself affair."

"That's what I'm used to."

Alone in the chilly room, she kicked off her boots and began to explore the lofty chamber as her toes sank into the plush gold carpet. Because this wing of Siddley dated to the Georgian era, everything here was elegant: the Carrera marble fireplace, the tall windows draped in striped silk of royal blue and red beneath shiny brass cornices, and the magnificent bed.

It wasn't as wide as a king-size bed but would easily accommodate two people. She was almost afraid to mess it. More of the blue-and-red silk swathed the bed in its curtains and on the spread, and mounds of gold-tasseled, solid-colored pillows lined up against the carved wood headboard.

From the bed, she went to investigate the bathroom, passing through a dressing room that held an assortment of men's clothing ranging from parkas to dark-colored suits. The bathroom itself would not compare favorably to those humongous ones in new American houses with their garden tubs and separate showers and meandering vanities. This appeared to have been constructed in the early to mid twentieth century and had the shiny glazed ivory tiles to prove it. It was small but did have one of those luxuriously deep tubs she only found in Europe. If she weren't so tired, she would have given herself a long soak. But it had been a long, harrowing day. Wash her face, brush her teeth, and off to bed it would be.

Five minutes later she was snuggled in the bed in near total darkness. Unfortunately, the dark invited disturbing thoughts. She pictured poor Mr. Ellerton with that dagger protruding from his chest. She also recalled how terrified she'd been when she opened the door to her flat and instantly knew someone had been there, knew that someone was probably the murderer.

As much as she liked staying in Bagsy's room, she knew she couldn't infringe on Frederick's kindness indefinitely. Nor could she go back to her flat in Oxford. She needed to find a new place to live—and keep its location secret.

She tried to quell her fears with logic. Why would the murderer come back to her flat? He'd taken everything she had that could possibly link her research with the location of the monstrance. *Wicked, evil, despicable murderer! And thief!*

She was pretty sure nothing in her notebooks would lead him to the Percy Monstrance. When the murderer came to the conclusion that her notebooks were useless to him, would he then come after her, thinking she might know something that would help him find the monstrance? Wouldn't he realize that if she knew, she would give that information to Frederick or to Detective Chief Inspector Patel?

Despite all she'd been through, she felt safe now. Ever since Frederick had hauled her into his arms, she had felt invincible. He worried about her. He wanted to protect her. He wanted her close by. Without any real intimacy having occurred, she felt unbelievably close to him.

And incredibly attracted to him.

I'm glad. She remembered how happy she had been when he'd said he was glad she didn't have a boyfriend. *I'm glad*: the two sweetest words she'd ever heard. With a smile on her face, she drifted off to sleep.

He hadn't slept well. It was beastly to lose someone like Ellerton. They had gotten along rather well for rather a long time, and he'd miss him like hell.

Antonia also dominated his thoughts. Why had he felt such a compulsion to protect her? No other woman had ever affected him in such a way. There was the fact that he'd never before known a woman—a beautiful woman, at that—who'd found a man murdered. *The poor girl.*

It was a good thing he *had* taken her home. He hated to think how frightening it would have been for her if she had faced her ransacked flat alone in the solitude of midnight.

He hoped, too, he could count on the Oxford police to work hand in glove with Scotland Yard. The sooner the culprit was apprehended, the better they'd all sleep.

At six, he left his bed, showered, shaved, and dressed. He went to the small family kitchen, put on the coffeepot, and sat down to read his morning *Guardian*.

He cringed when he saw Ellerton's murder featured on page one. He quickly read over the article, hoping there were no inaccuracies. There were none.

He hoped to God the murder wouldn't scare off tourists. The ten quid per person went a long way toward repairing roofs and guarding against dry rot. Not to mention the staggering costs for grounds upkeep and various sprucing up of the interiors. Just the curtains for two rooms last year cost fifty thousand pounds. The rooms were very large, and the silk was very dear.

At seven thirty, his cell phone rang. Who in the hell was calling at that hour? He looked at the screen. *Mother.* He knew immediately someone had read the *Guardian* and called her. His mother was never awake this early. And she couldn't get the *Guardian* in Italy. Unless she read it online, but his mother refused to even own a computer.

"Hello, Mother."

"I just heard about Ellerton's murder."

"I'm guessing Aunt Essie rang you."

"Yes, my sister sees that I'm informed, even if my firstborn son does not."

"I doubt there's much you could have done from Lake Como."

"Tell me you did *not* find the body."

"I did not find the body."

"Did you see the body?"

Why all this interest in so gruesome a topic? "He'd been carried off by the time I arrived."

"Oh, that's right! You and Upton were playing golf in Scotland. Thank God you've got an alibi!" His mother was the only person in the United Kingdom who still called his brother Upton.

"I seriously doubt I was under suspicion."

"No, I don't suppose you were. I should say a knife indicates it definitely was a crime of passion, though I cannot conceive of Ellerton as either passionate or promiscuous. Was he married, do you know? I can't conceive that any woman could be attracted to him, even though he is—or was—excessively nice *and* excessively intelligent."

"He was not married, except to his job. I would be hard pressed to ever find a more dedicated employee."

"Darling, you must tell me, who is this Antonia Townley the paper mentions?"

Her name evoked a mental image of her. Now that he pictured her, he realized that the name Antonia perfectly suited her. She looked rather Italian. Even if she was from the States. "She's a doctoral student at Oxford. She was doing research in our archives when she discovered…" He really hated talking about poor Ellerton in such a way. "Ellerton's body."

"How terrible for the poor girl! I don't suppose she might be responsible—"

"Absolutely not!"

"What does Caroline say about all this?"

"How should I know?"

"Do you mean she will learn about it the same way I did?"

He shrugged. "It's really not her business, and I doubt that Aunt Essie is in communication with Lady Caroline Hinckley."

"You are being obtuse. I just feel that as the future Countess of Rockford, Lady Caroline should know about this nasty business."

"How many times do I have to tell you? There's no understanding between Caroline and me."

"But she's so perfect for you, and you can't tell me she doesn't think there's an understanding between you two."

Why was it marriage was always on women's minds? He planned to cling to his freedom for as long as he could. Even if Caro was perfect for him. "Be that as it may, Mother, I'm not actually in the market for a wife at present."

"Tell me about this Antonia. I suppose she wears very thick glasses and orthopedic shoes?"

"Nothing could be further from the truth."

"Oh, dear. Do you mean she's pretty?"

"Very."

"Caro won't like that. I would advise you to see that she never sets eyes on your little doctoral student."

"She's not my little doctoral student." And he hoped she wasn't Simon's.

"I don't suppose Ellerton had any dying words?"

"Actually he said one word, but it does not appear to be significant."

"What word was that, darling?"

He really did not want to repeat it. It seemed somehow disrespectful of Ellerton. "I told you, nothing significant."

"I will not hang up until you tell me what the poor man said."

Frederick gritted his teeth. "Shit."

"Frederick! How dare you talk to me like that!"

"That, Mother, was Ellerton's last word."

She was silent for a moment. "Oh, I see what you mean," she said weakly. "What do the police think is the possible motive?"

"There's actually a possibility that Ellerton was able to locate the Percy Monstrance."

"The Percy Monstrance! I thought that was melted during the Dissolution."

"So did I, but apparently Ellerton discovered that the Percys—who were secret Catholics—kept it."

"How utterly fascinating! Do you have any idea how valuable that would be? Goodness, with the Holbein of Cardinal Wolsey, the fact it's been hidden half a millennium, so many factors make it extremely valuable."

"I shall have an estimate of its value today or tomorrow."

"Then you have it!"

"Oh, no. I have no idea where it is. It's likely Ellerton was killed so that he couldn't tell me what he'd discovered."

"Then how did you find out about it?"

"From Antonia Townley."

"It's really too shameful we no longer have the death penalty in England. Ellerton's deranged murderer certainly deserves to be hung."

"That deranged murderer hasn't been caught."

"Oh, my darling, I don't like him running loose. Perhaps you should engage a bodyguard."

"I'm not getting a bodyguard."

"I do wish you would. I won't have a moment's peace. In fact, I might just have to hop on a plane and come home to take care of you."

He started to laugh. His mother had never been the hovering type.

"I did not call to be laughed at. I shall ring you later and hope to be better treated."

He was still laughing when she hung up on him.

He went back to the north wing where the family's rooms were so he could escort Antonia to breakfast.

Immediately after his knock, she opened the door. And almost took his breath away with her stunning beauty. That long, vibrant hair the color of coffee beans swept over a third of her face. Did she have any idea how sexy it was when those slender fingers of hers pushed the swath of hair behind her ear?

She wore well-cut jeans again, as well as leather riding boots. A simple, crisp white blouse completed her wardrobe. He smiled when he remembered his mother's allusion to the thick glasses and orthopedic shoes. She did look much better suited to Hollywood than to musty archives in cold English basements.

"You look fresh as a daisy," he said.

She joined him in the corridor. "I feel fresh. I'm ashamed to say I slept wonderfully."

"Why does that make you ashamed?"

"Because I should have been more distressed over poor Mr. Ellerton."

"You were. Yesterday. Now let's not discuss him first thing this morning."

They came to the end of the corridor and went down two flights of stairs, her hand skimming along the iron banister. "This looks rather different in daylight."

"I hate that your first glimpse of it was in the dark. This is my favorite portion of the house."

"It's Palladian. You must have an affinity for Georgian architecture."

"I do, actually."

"Then you admire Robert Adam?"

"Very much."

"I remember that while he did not have a hand in Siddley, various members of your family managed to acquire a lot of his furnishings and accessories. A number of his mirrors, as I recall. Personally, I think he was too symmetrical, too perfect."

He laughed. "How can you be too perfect?"

"I suppose I'm a bit like Artie Shaw."

His eyes narrowed. "The 1940s bandleader?"

She nodded. "Yes. He was interviewed on Ken Burns's series on jazz—"

"I saw that! Great program."

"I love everything he's ever done, but back to Artie Shaw, do you remember what he said about perfect music?"

He did not even remember Artie Shaw being on Burns's series. It was a long time ago when Frederick had seen the program. "No, but I'm sure you'll tell me."

"He didn't care for flawless music. That was his big criticism against Glenn Miller."

"And I thought Tudor history your specialty."

She met his gaze, and they both laughed.

When they entered the family's private dining room, he tried to evaluate the room as would one seeing it for the first time. Even though it was used for extremely casual dining, the room had a decidedly formal air. Lovely faded Persian carpets covered the smooth wooden floors. The lone marble chimneypiece dominated the wall nearest the head of a gleaming mahogany table, and on the opposite wall, a series of identical tall windows afforded a view of Siddley's man-made lake. Assorted portraits of long-dead Percys hung above the mahogany sideboard, upon which a modern cof-feemaker sat. He invited her to sit at the mahogany table, where two modern placemats in a floral green marked their places. He had already opened the emerald-green silk draperies here to give them a view of the lake. "I made a pot of coffee earlier."

"Then you got up early? Did you not sleep well?"

"Not very." He went to the sideboard and poured her coffee. "Cream and sugar?"

"Neither."

"Of course. I should have known. Nasty stuff from cows and that demon sugar." He brought the mug to her. "Now I'm going to dazzle you with my culinary prowess." He left her, went to the small kitchen, and returned to the breakfast room with a box of cereal tucked under his arm, two bowls and a pair of spoons in one hand, and a quart of milk in his other.

She eyed him with skepticism. "Corn Flakes?"

"I thought an American would approve."

She smiled. "I am a cereal person. Normally I shy away from refined wheat and corn, but I'll make an exception today."

How could she tell from looking at the box that this was refined corn, whatever that was? "What's wrong with refined wheat and corn?"

"Whole grains are preferred."

Why in the hell would whole grains be preferred? He set everything on the table and came to sit across from her. "I'm surprised you drink coffee. Caffeine and all."

"The newest studies demonstrate that those who drink caffeinated coffee are less likely to suffer dementia as they age."

He lifted his mug for a toast. "To the preservation of clear thinking." Their mugs tapped, and he took a long swig of coffee.

"One of the first things we need to do is to draw up a list of who may have known about the monstrance and give it to Patel." He handed her the Corn Flakes box.

She poured the cereal in her bowl, then picked up the milk carton and read its label. He fully expected her to chide him because there was actually fat in the milk, but she remained mute on the subject. "My name is the only one I could give you. Mr. Ellerton specifically discussed the monstrance with me."

"And he didn't with me." Frederick filled his own bowl. As he spooned sugar onto his Corn Flakes, he noted her dumping a packet of sweetener onto her cereal. "Think, Antonia, could you have told anyone? What about that Simon chap?"

Her eyes rounded, and her hand flew to her mouth. "I believe I may have mentioned it to Simon! I didn't know it was anything secretive, or that someone would kill to obtain it."

Ah ha! Simon was suspect number one. "Anyone else you may have mentioned it to?"

She sat there in deep contemplation, her long lashes sweeping down to her cheeks. "I'm almost certain I never mentioned it to Alistair. I wonder if he knew about the Percy Monstrance."

"Good question. I suppose it's possible the lad could have mentioned it in front of the wrong people, people who would kill to get their hands on it."

"I have difficulty even picturing Alistair in a pub."

"I shall ask him about it this morning."

"And you can go on from there. If he knew, did he tell anyone? And so forth."

He nodded. "I have already looked into getting some metal detectors today. I'll have my groundskeepers go over the property. First, I thought you and I could go through Ellerton's office, see if anything there seems significant to either of us."

"Thank you. I really didn't want to go into his office alone. I'm such a wuss."

"Who wouldn't be after all you've been through these last twenty-four hours?"

He finished his Corn Flakes before Antonia, and he was staring out the window when he saw a Mini Cooper go speeding along his driveway. He doubted it was Alistair because, like Antonia, Alistair said he didn't drive. He, too, used public transport. It couldn't be Siddley's head gardener because he lived on the premises, and the car choice somehow didn't seem like something the undergardeners would drive. It was too early for either the guides or the tourists since tours didn't start until nine thirty.

She finished her cereal and looked at her watch. "I suppose we should go start on Mr. Ellerton's office."

Before he'd taken her to the pub the previous night, he'd checked with Patel to get approval for his night custodial staff to clean Ellerton's office. He sprang to his feet. "Yes, let's."

They went through the front door of Siddley and began to walk along the gravel driveway. "Do you know who that car belongs to?" he asked Antonia as they drew near the Mini Cooper.

She squinted toward the two-tone red-and-white vehicle. "Oh, that's Simon's. He certainly is the early bird."

"How did he know where to go?" Only a handful of people in the world knew where the archivists' offices were located within Siddley's sprawling three hundred sixteen rooms.

"I expect he's been here before. He and Mr. Ellerton were colleagues."

Frederick cleared his throat. "So, what does this Simon chap do?"

"He's Dr. Simon Steele of Oxford, specialist in medieval and Tudor studies and my doctoral supervisor. He and Mr. Ellerton have shared research with one another for many years."

Why in the hell didn't she call him Dr. Steele? Why in the hell was the man calling her at all hours on her mobile phone? Why in the hell was he poking his nose in Siddley's business?

When they reached the easternmost wing, where the archives were located, he and Antonia came upon Alistair and an older man standing near the exterior entrance to the wing.

"There you are, Antonia!" a fortyish man greeted her.

Frederick took a long look at the fellow. His height and weight were both average. He was not more than three inches taller than Antonia. His cork-brown hair—what there was of it—receded from his pale brow. Rimless glasses. Typical professorial dress consisting of tweed pants, V-necked sweater-vest, rumpled shirt, and scruffy brown leather shoes.

He was far from handsome, but Frederick supposed that to an intelligent woman like Antonia an attractive appearance in a man was not as important as a brilliant mind. The bloody don was bound to be seriously smart. Damn him.

And look at the way he was fawning over Antonia!

His hands firmly gripped her shoulders as he peered at her, his face etched with concern. "How are you today? I don't see how you could have slept after all you went through yesterday." *He's in love with her.*

"I'm fine."

"How fresh you look! I pictured you sleeping in a chair in your office." Simon then seemed to become aware of Frederick and gazed warily at him.

If Frederick were a feline, his hair would have been standing straight up as he watched Dr. Steele through narrowed eyes as the man acted like he had some kind of claim on his pupil.

The men's cold eyes met and held.

This was naturally one of those times Frederick would like to assert his aristocratic identity, but he did not want to come off sounding like some pompous ass. Finally he stepped forward. "Hi. I'm Rockford."

Antonia turned to Simon. "This is his place, Simon."

Simon's gaze pored over Frederick, and he gulped. "You're Frederick Percy, the Earl of Rockford?"

"Yes, but feel free to call me Rockford. That's what I usually answer to." Should he insert another comment, one that would be sure to offend the professor? Oh, hell, why not? "Only Antonia prefers calling me Frederick."

Simon did not look happy. "I…I expected someone older."

"If you read the current *Debrett's*," Antonia chided, "you'd know all about his family."

"It appears I should thank you, my lord, for giving Antonia refuge."

The educated weasel acted like Antonia was his own personal property! "How nice of you to adopt so fatherly an interest in your student who's so far from her own shores."

Simon stiffened.

Antonia smiled at Frederick and put hands to her hips. "As a bachelor who's just four years older than you, Simon won't appreciate the *fatherly* reference, but I can attest that he cares for all his students. Now, let me properly introduce you to Dr. Simon Steele."

Frederick offered his firm handshake. "Perhaps I can assist you in the matter that's brought you here today."

Simon glared at him. "I've come to offer my assistance—and to be here for Antonia."

Antonia frowned. "And I told you it wasn't necessary."

"I had to see for myself that you were OK."

"Such a dedicated teacher." Frowning, Frederick turned to Alistair, who had been standing there politely quiet as the rest of them spoke. "You don't have a key?"

The young fellow shrugged. "I've never needed one. Mr. Ellerton was always here when I arrived each morning."

"I shall have to get you a key." With a thud to his heartbeat, Frederick realized he could probably give Ellerton's key to the lad.

"Now that you're here," Antonia said to Simon, "I'll be glad of your help. We're going to look through Mr. Ellerton's things for clues about the…well, I'll explain when we get inside."

They stood back as Frederick slid his key into the lock. He opened the double-bolted door, stood back, and gallantly waved in Antonia first.

She began to stroll to Ellerton's office, talking to them as she peered over her shoulder. "Simon, I did tell you about the Percy Monstrance, didn't I?" She came to stop in front of Ellerton's office, and she drew in a deep breath.

Frederick thought of the last time she'd opened that closed door. He brushed past the others to be next to her, a reassuring presence, he hoped. His hand coiled around her forearm, and he spoke in a tender voice. "It's OK. I had everything cleaned."

She nodded and opened the door.

Then she screamed.

EPISODE 3

CHAPTER 6

This was not the kind of déjà vu Antonia liked to experience. Once again she stood statue-still at the threshold to a ransacked room. Once again she struggled to hold back tears. And once again it petrified her to realize the murderer had boldly returned to the scene of the crime.

While Mr. Ellerton's office today was not as horrifying as it had been the previous day, the culmination of three terrifying events was almost too much for her. She kept thinking that the murderer had been here probably as she slept in the connected house. The thought sent a chill spiking along her upper torso.

Like at her flat, the floor here was littered with papers and scads of printed matter like directories and reports. The drawers on the desk and file cabinets gaped open. The second she realized the most important thing in the room had been stolen, she yelped. "His computer's gone!"

Frederick stood just in front of her. "Bloody, bloody hell." His gaze fanned over the room's chaos, then reconnected with hers. "Good lord! I hope he didn't get yours, too."

Her heartbeat thundered. Why hadn't she taken it when she left Siddley the day before? She and Frederick quickly pivoted and began to race toward her temporary office at the opposite end of the corridor.

As they drew near and she saw the door to her skinny office open wide, she knew her laptop was gone too. A quick glance at the barren desktop confirmed her fears. She and Frederick skidded to a halt and faced each other. Neither spoke. There was no need since each knew exactly how the other would react to the disappointing discovery.

Simon and Alistair drew up behind them. "What in the bloody hell's going on?" Simon asked.

Antonia faced him. "My laptop's gone—and with it, all of my communication with Mr. Ellerton."

Frederick nodded at her professor. "We had hoped something in their back-and-forth e-mails would lead to the monstrance."

"You refer to the heavily bejeweled Percy Monstrance?" Simon inquired as he haughtily raised a brow.

Why did she find Simon so irritating? Anyone else would have just asked about the Percy Monstrance without providing a description of the darn thing. Simon was of the school of thinking that it was better to say in ten words what others said in five. "I did tell you Mr. Ellerton thought he could prove the Percy Monstrance was never melted, didn't I?" she asked Simon.

"Yes, you did. Is that why he was killed?"

Frederick frowned. "We know nothing at this point." He spun to Alistair. "Had Ellerton spoken to you about the Percy Monstrance?"

If it were possible to look more dim-witted than he already was, Alistair hit pay dirt with the blank look he gave his employer. The nose on his lightly freckled face screwed up, and his pale-green eyes squinted into the lenses of his glasses. "What's a monstrance?"

Frederick impatiently waved him off. "Never mind. I'm calling Patel." He yanked his cell from his pocket.

Anticipating his next need, Antonia whipped the detective chief inspector's card from her purse and handed it to him.

While Frederick punched in the number and spoke to an apparent succession of underlings, Simon came up to her, setting his hand at her waist and speaking in an un-Simon-like voice. There was nothing arrogant about him when he said, "I'm frightfully sorry you have to be exposed to all this sordidness. I feel so responsible for connecting you with Ellerton in the first place." Simon's voice was uncharacteristically tender. "I'll do everything I can to help you replace all the work you've lost."

It sounded like a sweet gesture, but Simon of all people had to understand almost all the research she'd lost was original. It wasn't like he could whip out a book and scan it.

Useless Alistair sidled up beside her and Simon. "Did you leave your laptop here?" he asked.

She nodded.

"I take it it was nicked."

"Yes. Maybe you should check to see if yours is still here," she suggested.

Off he scrambled to his office, while Antonia calculated that only a moronic, murdering madman would think Alistair's computer contained anything of value.

That the door to his office, which was midway between her office and Ellerton's, was closed told her it had not been disturbed. Her attention returned to Frederick. It sounded as if he'd actually gotten connected to Detective Chief Inspector Hard Ass.

As Frederick listened and nodded, he met her gaze. "Yes, Miss Townley will be here all morning." He nodded again. "Cheers." After terminating the call, he told the others to stick around until Patel returned.

"I suppose we should go to Mr. Ellerton's office to see if there's anything salvageable there," she said. She tuned to Alistair, who had returned from checking his office.

"Nothing disturbed in my office," he announced.

"That's because the murderer-slash-burglar-slash-thief must know you didn't know about the monstrance," Simon said.

That Simon was likely right disturbed her even more. Who else could know? Was it possible someone close to them was the murderer? She remembered that Mr. Ellerton's telephone had been tapped. Was someone spying on them? It was a horrifying prospect.

But not as horrifying as the thought that the murderer could be someone she actually knew. She tried to think who else could have known about the monstrance. Simon might be an arrogant megalomaniac, but he was no killer. Her circle of other personal contacts was almost nonexistent. It wasn't as if she'd strike up a conversation with Mrs. Maguire while carrying out the garbage. "I say, did you know we might have located the Percy Monstrance?" The murderer had to be someone Mr. Ellerton had told.

As Alistair returned to his office, he muttered under his breath, "I wish someone would tell me what a bloody monstrance is."

"A moment, Alistair, if you please," Frederick said.

Alistair turned, cocking a brow. "Certainly, my lord."

"Are you acquainted with Mr. Ellerton's work habits? What I mean is, do you think it was his practice to save things on his computer, or did he tend to print things out?"

Boy, was Antonia kicking herself because she hadn't been one of those people who endlessly backed up things on her computer and flash drives. As it was, she loved compiling her silly notebooks. Why couldn't she have just kept folders on her laptop? She'd always been a bit of a techno moron. Her Silicon Valley daddy would shake his head in disgust.

The simpleton had to ponder Frederick's question for a moment. "I expect I haven't been employed at Siddley long enough to have learned Mr. Ellerton's work habits."

Alistair's explanation seemed credible to her. It wasn't as if he and Mr. Ellerton were actually colleagues. As far as she could tell, Alistair's job was to assign dates to each box, and this sometimes involved the transfer of documents from one box to another.

Even a simpleton like Alistair was capable of reading a date. And, to Alistair's credit, he was always punctual—and extremely courteous.

Frederick nodded. "What time did you arrive today?"

"Eight forty-five—the same time as this gentleman." Alistair glanced at Simon.

"Did you see anything suspicious when you arrived?" Frederick asked.

Alistair shook his head. "Nothing at all."

"Carry on," Frederick said.

The other three returned to Mr. Ellerton's office. "It occurs to me that even though our first order of business this morning was to search through his office," Antonia said, "we might want to wait on the detective chief inspector."

Frederick looked disappointed. "You're right."

"Do you have a laptop?" she asked Frederick. "Or any computer, I suppose?"

"Certainly. Why do you ask?"

"I just realized I've got my flash drive in my purse. Though my father tried to teach me to back up my computer, I'm not very good about doing it, but I may have backed up some of the stuff I sent to Mr. Ellerton."

"Antonia's father is one of those Silicon Valley computer gurus," Simon explained with the same authoritarian tone he would use were he standing in front of a lectern.

"Pity you didn't take after him," Frederick lamented, his voice lowered to where he wasn't really addressing her. "Why don't we carry on to my office?"

The notion of a lord of the manor having an office seemed wildly incongruous to her. She was so steeped in the history of Britain's powerful aristocratic families, she could easily picture Frederick surrounded by a bevy of servants vying to wait upon him hand and foot.

How glad she was that times had changed! Had she lived in olden days, she would probably have been the poor chambermaid the aging lord wanted to bed but never wed.

The very idea of wedding one certain lord sent her pulse skittering—which was totally unexpected, given her long-standing resistance to marriage. She had sworn she would not marry until she was nearing the expiration date on that biological clock.

They climbed the dark interior stone staircase—something she'd never done before—and she learned that the office from which Frederick managed Siddley was located directly above Mr. Ellerton's.

"Did you hear anything yesterday morning just before noon?" she asked Frederick.

"Other than the radio in my car? Remember, I was returning from Scotland at that time."

She thwacked her forehead. She'd completely forgotten that he hadn't arrived until a few hours after the murder had been committed.

"Antonia's not herself," Simon said sympathetically. My God, but he *was* acting fatherly!

Frederick's office was the same size as Mr. Ellerton's directly below, but that's where the similarity ended. Her gaze fanned from the walnut-paneled walls to the rusty-colored Persian carpet to the stately-looking desk with masculine empire-style legs.

Even though the room looked perfectly like one in a five-hundred-year-old manor home, the desktop was pure twenty-first century. Cordless computer. Cordless, humongous slim monitor. Cordless phone system like something the operator at an upscale Zen hotel might use.

As Frederick booted up his computer, she gave him her flash drive, then the three of them gathered around to peer at the screen. "I suppose I'd better control the mouse," she said, plopping into the big red leather desk chair.

While she was poking around, Frederick called someone on his staff, asking to be notified as soon as Detective Chief Inspector Patel arrived.

Sadly, most of the information that had been in her notebooks was never put on the computer. She kept opening up files, looking for anything that connected her to Mr. Ellerton, and she finally came to a file of her e-mail inbox. She clicked on it and began to scan for posts from the slain man.

She was just about to open one when Frederick's cell phone rang. He answered and immediately nodded. "Cheers." He disconnected, then looked at her. "He's here. You better come too."

Patel had driven straight to the rear of Siddley, where he waited for them at the entrance that Ellerton had used. Frederick strode up to him, extended his hand, and offered a greeting. "I say, have you been in communication with the Oxford police?"

A frown on his pensive face, Patel nodded, his gaze flicking to Antonia. "Nasty business. They found prints, but we'll have to eliminate Miss Townley's and any of her friends."

"I live alone. No one else's fingerprints should be on my stuff."

The detective chief inspector nodded. "I've looked at the list of what's missing from the flat, and this does seem to corroborate your theory that someone thinks you and Ellerton may have had information that would lead to something valuable like the monstrance."

"I thought," Antonia said, "that my laptop might have all the e-mails I'd sent to Mr. Ellerton—which might allow us to see if there was something in those communications which might have helped Mr. Ellerton find the monstrance…" She paused, her voice cracking. "But my computer was stolen in last night's break-in here."

"Break-in?" Patel's brows lowered. "You have evidence that someone broke into Siddley?"

"No. At both Siddley and at Antonia's flat, there was no sign of a forced entry," Frederick said.

Patel addressed her. "Who has a key to your flat besides you?"

"I told you. I live alone. No one has my key but me."

Why was Frederick so glad to hear that?

"And who has Siddley's keys?" Patel asked Frederick.

Frederick tried to calculate, but with a hundred employees, it was difficult to say right now. "I try to be judicious in determining who merits a key since we have so many valuable paintings. I shall compile for you a list of those who do."

The DCI faced Frederick. "When did you discover that Ellerton's office was broken into?"

"At eight forty-five this morning." As the group began to descend the stairs to the rear door of Ellerton's basement office, Frederick explained how they found the office and who was with him when the discovery was made.

Frederick paused at Ellerton's door, extracted his keys, and went to open the door. "It's not locked."

"That explains the point of entry, I should say," Patel said.

"I wonder if he—the murderer—had a key." Antonia's gaze met the DCI's.

He shrugged. "At this point, everything is conjecture."

They entered Ellerton's office. "Have you touched anything?" Patel asked.

"No, we wanted to wait for you." Frederick eyed the chaos.

"My men should be here any minute," Patel told them. "Can you tell what's missing?"

"His computer—as well as Antonia's."

Patel's gaze circled the floor, where mounds of papers were strewn. "What about papers?"

"I don't think either I or Antonia knows."

It was at this point the detective chief inspector questioned Simon. "And you are?"

Simon extended his hand. "Dr. Simon Steele of Oxford. Christ Church. I'm Miss Townley's supervisor as well as a colleague of Ralph Ellerton. It was I who put the two of them in touch with one another."

"Will you be able to judge if any of his papers are missing?" Patel asked.

"Oh, goodness, no." Simon eyed Antonia. "What about you?"

She shrugged. "I pretty much did my own thing. I suppose you could ask Alistair—though he seems pretty clueless."

Frederick's thoughts exactly.

"Rest assured, I'll question everyone." Patel's cell phone rang, and he answered it. "Patel." As he listened, he nodded. "You didn't miss anyone?"

A moment later, he terminated the call and addressed Antonia. "All of your neighbors have been questioned, but no one saw or heard anything."

"What about CCTV?" Frederick asked.

"They're on that now, but it will take a while." Patel turned to Antonia. "I understand you didn't sleep at your flat last night?"

She shook her head. "Lord Rockford was kind enough to offer me a room at Siddley."

"Surely, inspector," Simon said, "you wouldn't expect her to stay alone at her flat after such a terrifying ordeal?"

"No, I don't suppose any woman could—under such circumstances."

Frederick's cell phone rang again. He looked down at it and saw Caroline's name. "Hello." For some reason, he stopped himself from saying her name in front of Antonia.

"Oh, Frederick! I heard the beastly news!"

"It is quite dreadful."

"I just pulled into Siddley's drive."

He frowned. The last thing he needed right now was having to deal with Caroline. "Come all the way to the back, and I'll meet you there." After he disconnected, his gaze met Antonia's, and he felt guilty—even though he couldn't understand why.

CHAPTER 7

The elegant blonde with a condescending air held out her slender hand to Antonia. "Hello. I'm Lady Caroline Hinckley."

Antonia's gaze swept over the icy creature who'd just stepped out of a Range Rover. Except for the absence of jodhpurs and billed helmet, she looked as if she might have just dismounted from a dressage competition. She wore a brown tweed jacket with chocolate-colored suede patches on the elbows and the same Hershey chocolate color on the velvet collar. Her blouse was pristine white, her twill pants beige, and her tall riding boots were what Antonia's mother would have called saddle brown but what Antonia had learned to refer to as Oxford tan.

Lady Caroline's silvery-blonde hair swept back flawlessly into something far more elegant than a ponytail that fastened neatly into a tortoiseshell clip at the nape of her graceful neck.

Her skin was incredibly white, her eyes pale blue. Antonia was disappointed to acknowledge that she'd met still another English aristocrat with perfect teeth. Darn it. Why couldn't Lady Caroline's teeth be spaced willy-nilly in an overcrowded mouth? Instead, they were as perfect as Lady Caroline herself.

When her eyes met Antonia's, Antonia stepped toward Ice Princess. "Hi, I'm Antonia Townley."

The blonde squinted. "You're American?"

"Is that a problem?" Antonia quipped.

"No, of course not. I was just curious about your connection here." Her gaze flicked to Frederick. She spoke in that lazy, mumbly manner characteristic of aristocrats. Definitely upper class. Darn it.

"She's a doctoral student doing research in our archives."

Simon stepped forward, eyeing the exquisite creature.

"And this," Frederick said, "is Dr. Simon Steele, Antonia's supervisor at Oxford."

The blonde's pretty face brightened. "I'm very pleased to meet you."

"Likewise, Lady Caroline." Simon effected a mock bow. How cheesy could an old guy be?

Ice Princess immediately switched her attention to Frederick. "I've been so worried about you. How shatteringly beastly to have a man murdered right here at Siddley Hall!"

"It is rather." Frederick shrugged. "But there you have it."

Had Antonia heard Range Rover Girl correctly? Had she just used the word *shatteringly*? Antonia had never before heard anyone use that word. In fact, Antonia could not think of any reason why she would ever utter anything so silly.

She was beginning to feel a bit like a fifth wheel. If only she and Simon hadn't gotten so wrapped up in the conversation with Frederick that they just blindly followed him outside. Why hadn't she stayed with Patel?

"Go ahead and visit with your friend," Antonia said to Frederick, "while Simon and I go back to see if the detective chief inspector needs our help in Mr. Ellerton's office."

The Lady Range Rover gasped, her dainty hand flying to her mouth. "Detective chief inspector? Oh, my poor Rockford. Whoever would have thought you'd have Scotland Yard positively crawling over Siddley Hall?"

Rockford? Antonia was so out of her element with the English nobility, she'd thought calling him Rockford was something only another guy would do. In her circles, young women addressed young men by their Christian names. Obviously, though, aristocrats had their own peculiar practices.

Obviously, too, Lady Caroline and Frederick must go way back. Antonia wouldn't be surprised if their noble parents hadn't pledged them to each other at their respective christenings.

On Antonia's scale of annoyingness, Lady Shatteringly totally outranked both Detective Chief Inspector Hard Ass and Useless Alistair.

Even Simon was not as annoying as Lady Caroline.

"Don't let me keep you from doing what you need to do," Caroline said, gazing adoringly into Frederick's face. "I should love to meet your detective chief inspector."

Antonia glared at her. "He's not here on a social call."

Frederick's gaze flicked from Antonia to Lady Shatteringly. "I think what she means is the DCI won't appreciate another person getting into the muddle."

Though Antonia hoped Frederick would find his visitor as unwelcome as she found her, he was being awfully nice to her. Too nice for Antonia's taste. She felt betrayed. Why had he said "I'm glad" last night if he had Lady Range Rover waiting in the wings? Last night he was glad she didn't have a boyfriend, but he'd neglected to tell her he *did* have a girlfriend, a girlfriend with whom Antonia could never compete.

"If you want to be useful, why don't you chat up my siblings and assure them I'm fine and everything's under control?" Frederick's gaze locked with Caroline's. Antonia tried to determine just how close the two were, but Frederick's facial features were inscrutable.

Lady Caroline knew his siblings and likely had since birth. Which should be no surprise to Antonia. Then another thought slammed into her, leaving her sick inside. What if Frederick was engaged to her? That would explain why Caroline felt so compelled to be here with him today.

Antonia remembered the previous night. He had not placed a single call to Caroline, and Antonia felt pretty sure she would have known if he had, because she had been with him every minute from dinner until bedtime.

"I don't know if I *can* reassure them," Caroline said. "I've been frightfully upset over this. You know I adore Siddley above every property in England. This is going to tarnish its name."

So it now appeared Antonia and the "Range Rover Girl" had two common interests—only one of them of the two-legged variety. Her gaze followed Frederick's long legs, which were sheathed in faded denim and terminated at soft Italian leather shoes that were only slightly darker in shade than Caroline's expensive boots.

"You're overreacting," Frederick chided.

Antonia thought Frederick might want to be rid of the meddling lady so he could go back to Patel. "Lovely to meet you," Antonia said to Range Rover Girl before turning to Simon. "We'd best get back." *Now why did I go and tell her it was lovely to meet her?* Antonia's biggest fault had always been her brutal honesty. She never said things like *lovely to meet you* when she met someone who got up her hackles. Then she realized it was the kind of baseless comment Ice Princess was likely to utter, and Antonia realized she was merely poking fun at the intruder.

"Yes, lovely," Caroline said, attempting to smile at Antonia at the same time her simmering gaze studied the competition. "When do you return to Oxford?"

Antonia offered her a bright smile. "No time soon. I have much unfinished work here." *Slam dunk!*

Caroline's perfectly shaped brows lifted. "You're not terrified to continue on here—after such a brutal murder and all?"

"At this point, no. I do have Frederick and Simon close." *Frederick. How sweet!* She tapped Simon. "Shall we offer ourselves to the detective chief inspector?"

He, too, acknowledged how lovely it was to meet "Range Rover Girl" before following Antonia down the stairwell.

She strained to hear what Range Rover Girl was saying to Frederick.

"I had hoped to persuade you to come to Antibes with me. Our yacht's there, and I thought you'd need to get away."

Antonia was prevented from hearing Frederick's response because she had to open the door to Mr. Ellerton's office.

Inside the office, Patel stood near the desk, baby-blue rubber gloves on his hands, lifting the phone receiver. He eyed them. "It's probably safe to assume the killer came back last night in order to retrieve the listening device we found yesterday," Patel said.

Antonia nodded. "Did you guys find anything on it?"

"They're on that right now. Actually, I was hoping you might be able to listen to it, to see if anything might pertain to Ellerton's quest for the monstrance."

"I'd be happy to." Her gaze swung from him to Simon. "As can Dr. Steele, of course."

As Patel examined the phone, he nodded. "Yep, it looks like he tried to get the device out. See, he didn't put it back together."

"Oh, Simon," she said, "I'm going to go look for that de Quincy letter to show you, but you stay here in case the inspector needs any historical expertise."

In one of Siddley's storage rooms, she thought she could find the duchess's letter quickly, but it wasn't in the box where she'd found it originally. Had she put it in the wrong box? She searched a couple of adjoining boxes, and when she didn't find it, she went to her desk and looked for it there.

That's when she remembered she'd had it in her hand when she'd discovered Mr....she did not want to remember the horrifying sight. There was no telling where the letter was now. She'd been far too distraught to take care of a piece of paper when poor Mr. Ellerton was gasping his final breath. She must have left it in Mr. Ellerton's office.

By the time she returned to the office, she'd been gone for more than ten minutes.

Simon came strolling up to the office at the same time as she. She felt like scolding him for not having stayed with the detective chief inspector the whole time she was gone, but she suspected he'd had to visit the loo.

"Where's that letter?" he asked, peering at her empty hands.

She frowned. "I just remembered I was holding it when I discovered poor Mr. Ellerton."

As she and Simon reentered the office, she heard steps coming from the adjoining stairwell and turned to see Frederick enter the office. "Where's your friend?" she asked, her voice anything but friendly.

"Caroline's in my office making phone calls."

Antonia would have been far happier if Caroline had gone to Antibes. Or somewhere much farther south.

"The scene of a murder's no place for a lady," Simon said, scowling at Antonia.

"The murderer came back to get the phone device," she told Frederick.

Hard Ass gave her a hard look. "We don't know that the burglar and the murderer are indeed the same person."

"But it's probably a safe assumption," she answered. When his expression still did not lighten up, she said, "I know. Everything at this point is only conjecture."

Patel's cell phone rang. He talked a few seconds, then hung up. "My team's here. I'm going to have to ask that all of you get out of their way."

"Right-o," Frederick said.

The four of them then started to climb the stairs back up to the gravel drive where various municipal vehicles—and one very expensive Range Rover—were parked.

It was bad enough having to feel responsible for Antonia. He did not want to have to start bloody worrying about Caroline, too. She was so delicate and sensitive. He didn't like her anywhere around here with a murderer loose.

But how was he to get her out of here without offending her? After all, she was just concerned over his welfare. As he was about hers. He drew up alongside Antonia as they walked away. "We might as well return to my computer and your flash drive whilst we wait until the fellows are finished with Ellerton's office."

"It would be great if we found something to help Hard Ass with the investigation."

"Antonia!" Simon's mouth gaped open as he peered at her through narrowed eyes. "Are you disparaging that conscientious public servant?"

"I think it would kill Detective Chief Inspector Patel to smile."

Simon shrugged. "I must say, he was quite the poker face."

As well as being rather oblivious to a pretty girl, Frederick thought. That reprobate don certainly wasn't immune to pretty girls' charms. It was bad enough the way he chased after unsuspecting Antonia. His fawning over Caroline made him look ridiculous.

Once they were inside Siddley, Simon said, "Don't feel as if you have to be responsible for us, Rockford. Feel free to run off with your girlfriend. Antonia and I are quite capable of reading her files on your computer without any assistance from you."

Frederick's first inclination was to refute that Caroline was his girlfriend, but he wasn't precisely able to do so, seeing as they were a bit of a couple, he supposed. His second inclination harkened back to the previous night when he'd wanted to punch that insufferable Simon Steele in the nose—even though he hadn't yet met him. Now that he had met him, he disliked him even more. Simon's motives for wanting to be rid of Frederick were as transparent as clear glass. "I wouldn't think of missing out on all the fun."

Of course, there was nothing fun in exposing one more helpless female to danger, but how was he to be rid of Caroline? Perhaps if they continued to speak on research that was bloody Greek to her, Caroline would get bored and leave. That was one thing he understood about her. She was easily bored.

When they entered his office, the first thing he saw was Caroline sitting behind his desk, his desk phone at her ear, a smile on her face. "He wanted me to assure you he's perfectly safe." She sighed. "I wish I believed him. There was another…incident at Siddley this morning."

She was directly defying his instructions. "Here, Caro," he said with impatience as he stormed into the room, trying to snatch the phone away. "Let me talk."

"He's here now and wants to talk." Caroline handed the phone to him.

He didn't even know which sibling he would be addressing. "Hello?"

It was Harriet. "I've been waiting for your call ever since I talked to Mama this morning."

"Let me guess, she called you to inform you of the evil goings-on at Siddley?"

"She woke me at an ungodly hour. Dreadful about poor Ellerton."

"Indeed."

"Mama said Ellerton had found the Percy Monstrance. That is so utterly exciting! A priceless artifact hidden for half a millennium…"

"If he did find it, I don't know where it is—and neither does the murderer. Listen, Harriet, I'm frightfully busy just now but wanted Caro to call and assure you all is well with the eldest of your brothers. I'll ring you later when I have more time."

With the call ended, he put the receiver back and eyed Caro. "Would you mind if Antonia sits there? We were looking at some of her files on the computer."

Caro gave Antonia an icy glare. Good lord, was his attraction to the darker woman that obvious? Caroline—who made no secret she wanted to be the next Countess Rockford—must have sensed how Antonia affected him. Caroline certainly couldn't have known how tough it had been for him to sleep the previous night, knowing beautiful Antonia was lying in the next room.

Even though he had vowed not to marry before his fortieth birthday, the assumption that he'd one day marry Caro was tucked into the furthest recesses of his mind.

His mother, lamentably, was always right. Caroline *was* perfect for him. She was enough younger than him to still be in her child-bearing years when he was ready for marriage at age forty. She was reasonably intelligent. Since she was the daughter of an earl, her background matched his in every way. Which was good for a marriage. They knew all the same people and shared so many similar life experiences, particularly those of the privileged. And he could not ignore that she was beautiful. He was proud to walk into a room with her on his arm. Every man there took note of the incredibly attractive woman.

Against his will, he found himself wondering how it would feel to walk into a room with Antonia at his side. Every man in the room would lust after her. She wasn't voluptuous in any way, nor did she dress to appear sexy. But Antonia Townley could not conceal her enormous sex appeal were she to don a circus tent. Perhaps it was her habit of lowering her lengthy dark lashes so seductively that made her so vastly appealing. Or perhaps it was the way she pushed aside the thick tresses that often covered part of her right eye. Or perhaps her attraction had something to do with the way her perfect little ass and long legs looked in a pair of jeans.

He would be hard pressed to say which of the two ladies was the better looking. Both were beautiful—and completely different from one another.

He really shouldn't be thinking about Antonia with Caroline in the same room. Antonia, after all, was not the kind of woman a peer of the realm married. She was American, for God's sake! His grandfather would have disowned him for so traitorous a misalliance.

Antonia and Caro switched places. "I'll go in the next room to ring Bagsy," Caroline said, smiling brightly at him.

His gaze met hers. "Right-o."

Antonia began clicking at the mouse. Nothing came up on the monitor. She clicked harder. "I'm not getting anything." Her gaze went to the USB port where her flash drive was inserted. She yanked it out, then reinserted it. Nothing.

"Dear God, it's been erased."

CHAPTER 8

Her hands trembling so badly she could barely click on the mouse, she kept clicking over and over, and over and over nothing showed but a blank screen.

She was so upset she couldn't even begin to articulate the fears that pounded through every cell in her body. *Flash drives do not erase themselves.* The loss of her laptop and the flash drive she could live with, but the realization that the murderer had been in this very room in the last hour horrified her. It was enough to send her packing for the first plane back to the States.

She hadn't wanted to think someone she knew could be guilty. It was much easier to believe that someone who'd found out about the monstrance from Mr. Ellerton had perpetrated these crimes. Easier, but foolish. This wasn't the first time she'd thought the murderer could be someone she knew. This time, though, her suspicions were sharpened from foggy notion to horrifying possibility.

How much time had passed since they were last in Frederick's office? She looked at the time on the monitor. It had been about forty-five minutes. And in that time she had been separated from both Simon and Frederick, either of whom could have tampered with the flash drive, though she could not believe one of them capable of any crime. Hadn't Frederick even offered to *give* the monstrance to the V&A? He didn't strike her as a man who needed money—much less to kill for it.

She tried to consider other possibilities. The rooms could be tapped for sound. The murderer could be hiding somewhere on this massive estate, listening to their conversations and acting upon any threat to his goal. Perhaps it was a Siddley employee. They did have evidence that Mr. Ellerton's phone had been bugged. Perhaps they were dealing with an electronics genius with capabilities for concealed surveillance.

Still, regardless of the sophistication of the surveillance, a real person had to have been in this room tampering with this device. Which was a chilling thought.

Frederick stormed to the door and flung it open. "Caroline! Did you see anyone in my office or leaving my office when you entered?"

"No. Why? Is something wrong?"

He did not answer for a moment, and when he did, he spoke in a stern voice. "It appears a madman is running about Siddley. I'm walking you to your car right now, and you're not to come back until the murderer is apprehended."

If Antonia wasn't already deflated, she was lower than a snake's belly right now. Frederick's first concern had been for Ice Princess.

He came back and addressed Simon. "I'm taking Caroline to her car. Don't let Antonia out of your sight."

So Antonia wasn't totally persona non grata.

"In fact," Frederick said, his gaze swinging to Antonia, "I want you to punch my mobile number into your phone, and I'd like you to do likewise with mine."

They each entered the other's number into their cell phones, then Frederick left.

Before she even had a chance to put her cell back into her purse, it rang. It was Hard Ass. "Our audio expert is here now, and I was wondering if you could listen to the portion of Ellerton's tapes where there might be information about missing antiquities."

"Certainly. I'll be right down."

She filled Simon in, and he escorted her to Patel. As soon as she entered Mr. Ellerton's office, her cell phone rang again. This time it was Frederick. "Where are you?" His voice sounded panicked.

"I'm back in the basement with about a jillion cops."

"I'm coming."

She and Simon told the detective chief inspector about the corrupted flash drive.

He frowned. "I've more bad news. Ellerton's flat was also broken into last night, and his personal computer's been taken."

"This creep really gets around." She paused, then opened another line of inquiry. "Did Mr. Ellerton live alone?"

Patel nodded. "I was at his flat late yesterday. The neighbors said he was an exceptionally quiet tenant, and having seen his flat I can well believe it. There was no telly, but if there was a book on English history that wasn't in his flat, I'd be surprised."

There was one more thing she wished to ask about Mr. Ellerton—a thing she wished she didn't have to ask because she had liked him so much and did not want to disparage him in any way. "Were you able to determine if Mr. Ellerton was...straight?" She hoped the librarian might have had a gay lover who was obsessed over obtaining the monstrance. It was much better to think that than to think the murderer could be someone she actually knew.

He shrugged. "One of the neighbors said up until about six months ago, he had appeared to be sharing the flat with another man."

"We must find that man," she said.

"Not *we*, Miss Townley. This is *my* investigation, and I will find him."

"I hope you do. I can't tell you how upsetting all this is."

Simon came and put an arm around her. If he'd done that a week ago, it would have had great ick factor, but she did find it oddly comforting today. "You can imagine how the poor girl feels.

First, finding the murdered man. Then having her flat burglarized. And now her flash drive tampered with. It's as if the murderer himself is stalking her."

"Gee, thanks, Simon." She was peering into his bespectacled eyes when Frederick entered the office.

She turned to him, a grim expression on her face. "Mr. Ellerton's flat was also broken into last night."

"Bloody hell! I've got to get extra security." He grabbed his cell phone and started punching in numbers as he crossed the room and went into the corridor.

"If you could go into the next room, Miss Townley," Patel said, "the audio tech is waiting for you there. He doesn't think he'll need you for more than an hour."

"I'm coming with you," Simon said.

"Really, I don't need your help. The place is crawling with police. I'll be fine. I know you've got that panel you're supposed to be on this afternoon."

"Bollocks! I'd almost forgotten about that. Are you sure you'll be all right?"

She nodded.

Simon turned his attention to the detective chief inspector. "I'm counting on you to keep her safe."

"She'll be fine."

As she exited the room, Simon eyed her. "You're sure you've got my number on your mobile?"

"I've got your number on my phone."

Listening to Mr. Ellerton's cheery voice and knowing he lay dead in a morgue gave her an eerie, depressing feeling. As much as she admired Mr. Ellerton, Antonia had to say the man's phone conversations were about as exciting as getting new tires. The parts they wanted her to listen to were conversations between her and the dead man. When he'd been alive. Unfortunately, they had mostly talked about her research and his suggestions for further investigation.

In only one quick statement did he allude to the monstrance. "By the way," he'd said to her, "something I learned from your research awakened me to a possibility regarding the location of the Percy Monstrance."

He'd told her about the monstrance in an earlier e-mail. "Have you found it, then?" she'd asked, excited.

"I think I know where it is. I'll tell you all about it when you come to Siddley."

And that was that. If the murderer had gotten the tape, he would have been very disappointed.

It was nearly noon when she finished, and Frederick was waiting for her. "I thought we might grab some lunch from the tearoom," he said. She was gratified that he wanted to be with her, but not nearly as gratified as she was that Lady Shatteringly was gone.

Like most of the stately homes that were open to the public, Siddley provided a tearoom where one could purchase sandwiches or cream tea for five or six pounds. Siddley's was located at the rear, and it overlooked a portion of the estate's gardens. It was located in the former orangery, so the place was nothing but windows and was filled with light. On wet days, patrons could eat in and look out over the gardens that stretched as far as they eye could see.

This was definitely the kind of day that invited alfresco dining on the stone terrace. Frederick had ladled himself a large bowl of fresh leek soup, and Antonia got her usual cream tea spread, with extra clotted cream to slather on the freshly made scones. On her first visit here, she had been pleasantly surprised at how good the food was at Siddley's tearoom.

On this day, she enjoyed jaunting through there beside the lord of the manor while all the teashop's employees ogled Frederick. She almost allowed herself to feel like she was special to him, to feel as she had felt the previous night when he'd said *I'm glad*. She could still remember the satisfaction that had whistled through her as they had sped along the M4 late at night, the soft jazz music in the background, and she'd felt like they *were* special to each other.

Then, with a surge of crushing disappointment, she remembered Range Rover Girl.

Her teeth clenched as she made her way to the terrace. She sat at a little iron bistro table in a chair that faced the lawn fountain, and Frederick came to sit beside her. She could not understand why the other patrons chose to eat indoors when they could be seated out here beneath sunny blue skies. It was a bit windy, but she didn't care that the wind whipped her hair around pretty thoroughly.

With the peaceful sound of the fountain's trickling water, she just sat there for a moment gazing at the neaty clipped lawn and the twin rows of identically sculpted trees that lined the pedestrian path like giant green lollipops. The path led to the man-made lake, which could only barely be glimpsed from here—if one peered through a copse of trees of varying hues of green.

She didn't speak as she sliced open her scone and smeared humps of clotted cream over it. She could not purge Ice Princess from her admittedly jealous thoughts. *Are they engaged?* She should just come right out and ask him.

Only she didn't want to know it if they were. She wanted things to go back to what they'd been the previous night when he'd drawn her into his arms and murmured reassurances as his hands pressed into her back with almost unbearable tenderness.

The very thought of *Lady* Caroline caused Antonia's entire body to go rigid.

His brows lowered, Frederick eyed her plate. "I thought you didn't do clotted cream."

"Clotted cream is without a doubt my biggest weakness." She shrugged. "I don't allow myself to have it at my house—or flat—but I cannot resist it at a tearoom. And I confess, I go to a tearoom whenever I get the chance."

"And how does ours stack up?"

The way he observed her with such confidence indicated he had full confidence in Siddley's tearoom—or lunchroom, as the menu said.

She gave him a silly smile. "I'm not saying this because it's yours or because Siddley is my favorite stately home, but it's the best. Food's fresh and good, and it's hard to beat the view."

"Thank you. It was my idea to turn the orangery into the restaurant's seating area."

"Brilliant!" She took the last crumb of her first scone and dipped it into her little tub of clotted cream.

"I take it there was not success with the tapes."

She shook her head. "The murderer would have been gravely disappointed. The audio tech thought that someone was likely switching out the device every week or so."

"It's chilling to know a murderer is lurking at my house." His handsome face went pensive, his smoky-brown eyes somberly meeting hers. "I've hired night watchmen."

"As in plural?"

"Four, to be exact."

"It doesn't seem right that on top of everything else, this horrible business is hitting you in the pocketbook."

"Not me directly. The Percy trust will pay for it. But, yes, it will rob funds set aside for necessary maintenance and repairs."

As they spoke, a man in what she'd come to know as the khaki dress of Siddley maintenance staff began walking across Siddley's lawn, a metal detector directed at the earth. "That was certainly quick! I thought you'd just ordered the detectors this morning."

"I made it top priority."

"Obviously if the Percy Monstrance is found at Siddley, it will belong to you, and the murderer will slink away—not likely to ever disturb you again. But…how will you ever feel comfortable knowing Mr. Ellerton's killer is still on the loose?"

"I'll never know peace until he's apprehended." He swigged at his teacup, then set it down. "How well do you know Simon? Really know him?"

Her insides fluttered. Not in a good way. Obviously, Frederick suspected Simon, and to be honest, she'd had the same suspicion, but that's all it was: a suspicion. "I know he's not a murderer. You saw how sweet he was to me—how concerned he is over my welfare."

"He's nice because he's in love with you!"

She stiffened. It was impossible for her to deny that the same thought had occurred to her that very morning. "There is nothing between me and Simon!"

"I didn't say there was anything between you two more than as student to teacher." He drilled her with those penetrating eyes of his.

"Simon is a popular, well-liked teacher, and one of the reasons he's so highly thought of is the amount of concern he demonstrates toward his students."

"Especially if they're beautiful females."

He thinks I'm beautiful. She experienced a flickering sense of effervescence. "You've only seen him with me," she defended.

"And I've seen enough to know he's more than smitten." He set aside his soup and watched her.

"Simon is not a murderer. He's one of the most respected historians in all of England."

"He knew about the monstrance." Frederick's voice was as derisive as a prosecutor's.

Her eyes narrow, she put hands to her hips, elbows thrust out. "And so did I! Does that make me a murderer?"

"Patel might think so."

Her shoulders slumped. There was that. She'd almost forgotten about the detective chief inspector's suspicions. Her false sense of security came from being protected by her two champions, each of whom had become most dear to her.

Frederick must have been taken aback by the stricken look on her face. His hand went to her shoulder, and he gave it a gentle squeeze. "I'm frightfully sorry. I know you had nothing to do with this nasty business, and I believe the detective chief inspector believes you're innocent too."

He returned his attention to his soup, and when the bowl was empty he spoke. "I think you ought to go back to the States."

"I can't deny that I haven't given the prospect some thought. I *am* scared. But I love the work I've been doing, and it can't be done anywhere but England. I can't wait to go back and duplicate all the work that was stolen last night. I can't wait until the de Quincy sisters' letters are published, until my dissertation on the five Catholic families is complete.

"My work may sound dull to others, but it's the only thing I've ever done that's given me satisfaction. It's so completely fascinating to read letters from those who lived half a millennium ago and to see they loved in the same way we do today, that mothers worried about their offspring the same as mothers do today, and the things that gave pleasure to men then are much the same as they are today."

She tucked a swatch of her dark hair behind an ear. "Sometimes when I'm holding an old letter in my hand and reading their words in faded ink, I get chills."

He didn't speak for a moment, then he said, "I do understand. I get chills too." He gave a bitter laugh. "You've got the same passion for what you do as Ralph Ellerton had. That's why I engaged him in the first place."

At that very instant, it crossed her mind to toss her name in the ring to replace the slain man. It *was* her dream job. But the poor man hadn't even been buried yet. How crass would that look? "I'm trying to determine if you think that's a good thing or a bad thing."

"I am too."

She sighed. "I need to get some new notebooks and a laptop."

"I'll take you this afternoon. It'll do us both good to get away from this place."

He held the phone close to his mouth and spoke in a low voice. It wouldn't do for someone to overhear him. "I've had a chance to look at all the information on his computer, as well as her laptop."

"And?"

"And I haven't found a bloody thing."

"Damn. What about Ellerton's phone?"

He felt as if he'd been kicked in the gut. "The police got them."

"Bollocks!"

"Fortunately, there wasn't anything on them."

"Have you found out if the American girl knows where it is?"

"She doesn't. The good thing is, none of them know where it is, either."

"What's so bloody good about that? At least if one of them had it, we'd have the opportunity to nick it."

"I hadn't thought of it that way."

"That's why this operation needs both of our heads."

He bit at his lower lip. "I've got bad news."

There was silence on the other end. A long, frightening silence. Finally, the other man spoke impatiently. "What now?"

"Rockford knows about the monstrance."

"That is bad news."

"But…if anyone has the skills to find the monstrance, I believe it's the girl."

"Then know where she is at all times. Employ everything you've ever learned about surveillance. Let's hope she leads us to the monstrance."

"And when she does?"

"Kill her."

EPISODE 4

CHAPTER 9

He put her bags into the skinny boot of his car, walked around to the driver's side, and got in. Antonia wondered if she would ever adjust to the driver being on the wrong side.

Once he was on the busy thoroughfare, she said, "I'm not going back to my flat."

He showed no reaction. "Not ever?"

"Not ever. The only thing there I cared about has been stolen."

"What about your clothes?"

She shrugged. "I just can't go back there."

"I'm glad."

She'd liked it better when he said *I'm glad* about her not having a boyfriend. She was so pathetic. Any time he indicated he *cared* about her in any way made her feel like she'd chugged a gallon of champagne.

"If you'd like, I can send along one of my employees to fetch your clothing."

"That would be great."

"Now that I've contracted for nighttime security, I'll feel much better knowing you're at Siddley."

First, he'd made her feel like she'd imbibed champagne. Now, his concern made her feel as if she were in a free-falling elevator. The way her luck had been going, if he said one more sweet thing, she'd throw up in his expensive car.

She needed to divert her thoughts away from Frederick the Hunk. *Remember Range Rover Girl.* Blondie was bound to have first dibs on him. "I can't stay at Siddley."

He stiffened. His grip on the steering wheel tightened. "I think you'll be safer there than anywhere else in England."

"Be that as it may—and I'm still leery of Siddley because of all that's occurred there—I need to be where no one can find me."

"As long as you continue to do your research, that's impossible."

"But I have to continue my research."

"Then the murderer will be able to follow you home."

She let out an exasperated sigh. "Don't you see, Frederick, I can't just move in at Siddley Manor?" *What will Lady Caroline think?* She wanted to ask about her rival, but she didn't. There was hope in not knowing.

"Afraid we don't have enough room?" he quipped.

"I just want anonymity."

"That's not going to happen." Frederick made much better sense than she.

They came to a roundabout—another of those reasons she refused to drive in England—and he yielded without coming to a stop. These darn intersections made no sense to her, but Frederick didn't seem to have any problem navigating them.

"I can't continue to stay in Bagsy's rooms." She felt really silly calling a grown man whom she'd never met Bagsy.

Frederick turned off the main motorway, casting a quick glance at her. "Why can't you?"

"What if he comes? I can't chase the poor fellow from his own room."

"I assure you my brother thinks Siddley's an old pile not fit for a bachelor's lifestyle. He rarely leaves his flat in London to come here."

She could not understand how anyone could turn his back on the opportunity to live at the finest stately home in all of England. As the crow flies, it was less than fifteen miles from Siddley to central London.

She eyed Frederick's profile. He not only had straight white teeth, he also had a regular-sized, perfectly nice nose without any hook or bumps. Another anomaly for an Englishman. Which was somewhat surprising, given that half his ancestors looked to have had significant honkers. "Does Siddley cramp *your* bachelor lifestyle?"

He gave a mirthless chuckle. "I'm somewhat clueless about wild and swinging bachelors. Siddley's been the recipient of all my energies almost since the day I left university."

Without even meeting Bagsy, she knew which brother she would prefer. But, heck, she was becoming convinced that she preferred Frederick over any guy she'd ever known. "Then you must be infinitely better company than your brother—in my opinion." Had she been too forward? She didn't want to throw herself at him.

"You should reserve judgment until you meet Bagsy."

"But if he prefers London, it's not likely our paths will cross."

He turned onto the street that would take them to Siddley and shrugged his shoulders at the same time. "I have a feeling a murder might just beckon him home."

"All the more reason for me to get out of his bedroom."

In the distance she saw the chimneys of Siddley protruding from treetops and was amazed that such a historic property surrounded by modern-day suburban London still retained a country home aspect. How had the Percy family managed to preserve so many trees and so many unspoiled acres?

"I'll have the maids ready one of the ladies' rooms for you. Humor me. I'll feel better knowing I can keep an eye out for you."

There went that champagne feeling again. When it was just the two of them, she experienced a special connection to him. She felt as if Range Rover Girl did not exist.

How could she protest any more? Siddley *was* the place where she most wished to stay.

As he drove up to Siddley, they passed two different pairs of groundskeepers, their heads bent as they searched for metal beneath the carpet of grassy parkland in front of Siddley. One of each pair toted a metal detector, the other a shovel. She also saw clumps where they had evidently investigated metal bits.

At Siddley's main entrance, a group of about a dozen tourists gathered on the elevated portico. "It's good to see publicity about the murder hasn't kept paying guests away," he said.

Instead of parking at the front of Siddley as he usually did, he drove around its perimeter and parked at the very rear, next to a police vehicle. Then turned to her. "Can I interest you in a walk around the lake?"

"I'd love to."

Their walk began along a well-worn footpath on the side of the broad lawn. Were Siddley in the United States, the path would have been a concrete sidewalk, she thought. The Brits, apparently, eschewed concrete. Which she found rather charming.

"I've been thinking," he said as they came to the first thicket of mature trees, "that with your excellent memory you ought to be able to duplicate the e-mails you exchanged with Ellerton."

They began to walk through a shaded bower. It was dark and cool, almost clammy, and smelled of earth and a floral scent she couldn't identify.

She gave a little laugh. "I've been thinking the same thing." Why was it her thoughts so often meshed with his? "Now that I've got a computer, I'm going to attempt to reconstruct our e-mail exchanges."

"I don't suppose you want to return to your office in the basement?"

"It does give me the creeps to know *he* was there."

"It gives me the creeps to think he could be someone we know."

"I know." It was a horrifying prospect—one she could not get out of her mind.

They passed a little temple constructed in the Grecian mode with fluted columns supporting a domed roof. It seemed terribly romantic to her—likely because it was at a similar temple at Blenheim Palace where Winston Churchill proposed to Clementine.

"Oh, Frederick! Can we go sit in the temple for a moment?"

"If you'd like."

They sat on its cool marble bench. From there they could glimpse a sliver of Siddley's modest lake. "This is a lovely spot."

His shimmering amber eyes met hers. "I'm glad you like it."

"Of course, I'm just a Siddley Slut." *There I go again.* He was sure to find her unbelievably crass.

He had the decency to laugh at her attempt at humor.

She found herself wondering if Frederick, when he decided to marry, would make his proposal at a place like this temple. The very thought of receiving a marriage proposal from Frederick set her heartbeat skipping. Which was perfectly ridiculous since she had sworn she wasn't marrying until the waning days of her childbearing years.

The thought that he might ask Lady Shatteringly to marry him affected her stomach in the same way as a Porta-Potty. With that thought, she leaped to her feet.

They continued on their footpath. "Do you think Mr. Ellerton might have been gay?" she asked casually.

"Ellerton's sexuality never crossed my mind. Why do you ask?"

"I know he wasn't overtly effeminate, and we know he wasn't married…"

"So a man of a certain age who's never married must be gay?" His step slowed, and he eyed her, a mischievous flash in his amber eyes, his mouth twisted into an amused smile.

In the sun, his hair looked much lighter. It was the color of richly variegated wet sand. Against her will, she thought of what beautiful children he and Ice Princess would produce together, and the thought saddened her. Just as did the realization that she could never belong in their world. It was as if he were ordained at birth to end up with a woman like Range Rover Girl.

"I don't like to stereotype anyone," she said. "For all I know, Mr. Ellerton could have been completely asexual. But Hard Ass did say one of the neighbors thought he'd had a male roommate until about six months ago."

"I think I see where your line of reasoning is going. You're hoping the murderer is a crazed former lover of Ellerton's?"

She stopped. Swallowing over the lump in her throat, she peered into Frederick's face. "It's better than thinking the murderer is someone we know."

He turned her to face him squarely, gently gripping each of her shoulders. "I'm so sorry you're having to go through all of this."

"It's *your* house that's become an extension of Scotland Yard."

"There is that." He smiled. "I'm sorry *we're* having to go through this."

They started to walk again. "I plan to do whatever it takes to find the monstrance," he said. "It's the only way to rid our lives of this nightmare."

"An arrest and conviction would be even better."

"I assure you, that is my aim, also."

When the path began to enter a thickly wooded area, he turned back. Was he afraid the murderer was hiding in the woods? They covered the same route they had already walked. "For the time being, I'd just as soon you not return to the basement to work. The police are there now, but we can't count on them staying."

"Point me in the direction where you want me, and I'll bring along my trusty new laptop."

"For the present, I'd like you to work in my office. The desk is large enough to accommodate the two of us, and besides, this isn't the time of the month when I need to be at my desk very much."

His cell phone rang. "This is Rockford," he said.

She watched him. He listened, nodding, his eyes widening. After a moment, he said, "Thanks, Nigel. I appreciate your looking into this so quickly. Cheers."

He put the phone back into his pocket and faced her, shaking his head. "Five million pounds."

"Holy moly! That's like eight million dollars! For one gold artifact!" Her head askance, she eyed him. "So you sent him a photo of the Holbein?"

"Right after I escorted you to your room last night." He looked down at his phone and poked at the menu. "Here, I'll show it to you."

"That's not necessary. I've seen the real thing."

He flashed her a merry smile. "Right-o." He kept shaking his head as if in disbelief. "It's all about the provenance, and the Holbein with Cardinal Wolsey will definitely give the monstrance valuable provenance."

"But I don't understand how the murderer—if he got the monstrance—could own up to its provenance without being accused of Mr. Ellerton's murder."

"If the monstrance should end up at one of England's stately homes—in the possession of an old aristocratic family—its ownership would never be questioned."

"Then you're saying an aristocrat might be behind this awful scheme?"

"Good lord, I should hope not! I was just speculating."

"You're making my head spin."

"I don't mean to make that pretty head spin."

Pretty? She experienced that same sense of effervescence she had the previous night. As they returned to the basement, she felt almost as if she were stepping through clouds.

By the time they returned to the house, only two vehicles remained parked there at the rear, and one of them was Frederick's. They descended to the basement by way of the stairwell that led to Ellerton's office. Patel's men had all gone, and Patel was about to leave.

"I wanted to tell you," the detective chief inspector said to Antonia, "I talked with the Oxford police, and it turns out there aren't CC cameras on your street."

"Well, that sucks." She really ought to watch her language better around Frederick. She really ought to behave in a more ladylike fashion. No proper British peer would utter such a comment.

That very proper British peer approached the DCI. "I thought you might be interested in knowing the estimated value of the Percy Monstrance."

The chief inspector cocked a brow.

"My source at the Victoria & Albert puts the value at five million quid."

Patel whistled. "Definitely murder-worthy. To someone possessed of a criminal mind."

After Patel left, Frederick escorted her to his office and installed her there. "OK with you if I put you on this side of the desk?" he asked, referring to the seat directly opposite his.

"As long as there's a place to plug this in. My battery has to be charged."

He found a plug and helped her set up, which involved moving another chair. "If you'd rather, you can have my desk chair."

"No. This one's just fine." She plopped into the armless wooden chair.

"You sure?"

She nodded.

"Then I'll leave you. I need to speak with the groundskeepers about their metal-detecting assignment."

"Let me guess. You're not happy with the way they've torn up the grass."

He shot her a mock scowl. "How do you do it?"

"Do what?"

"Invade my thoughts?"

Their smoldering gazes locked, then he turned and left.

He was gone from Antonia longer than he would have liked. He'd come close to losing his patience with some members of the grounds crew who took to excavating the landscape with rather too much gusto. They had been busily excavating his heretofore velvety grass, leaving haphazardly filled-in holes at somewhat regular intervals. He gritted his teeth and kept telling himself *five million pounds*.

His directions to them earlier had been clear: minimal damage to the lawns upon positive metal detection. If the lawns needed to be disturbed, neat patches should be carefully lifted, and each attempt at excavation must be restored in the best manner possible.

He had known there would be bits of metal that would emit a signal that in no way compared to a large gold monstrance that would weigh several pounds, but apparently he had not conveyed said information in a readily understood manner.

While getting Antonia installed in his office, he'd run off a copy of the photo he'd taken of the monstrance so he could show them what they were searching for.

The head gardener, Hopkins, was a good man, and Frederick trusted him implicitly. He had been at Siddley since he was sixteen years of age, and in the ensuing thirty years he'd thoroughly educated himself about horticulture. Frederick would put Hopkins's knowledge up against the horticulturist at Kew Gardens.

When he returned to his office, Antonia whirled around and smiled at him, only barely able to contain her excitement. "I've had a productive few hours."

He came to stand behind her. As his head bent to peer at her monitor, he caught a whiff of her lavender scent. He was completely unprepared for his visceral reaction to her delectable femininity. Nevertheless, he forced himself to act aloof. "How's that?"

"I think I've remembered the subject of every e-mail exchange with Mr. Ellerton. First, I printed out a calendar so I could go back and trace which days we corresponded. If I concentrate—without any distractions—I'm fairly good at remembering what days I do things. You know, like, I made a birthday cake for Simon on April twenty-first, and while it was in the oven I scanned some pages to send Mr. Ellerton. That kind of stuff. By the same token, filling in the boxes for each day, I could eliminate the days it would have been impossible to have e-mailed him."

She held up the calendar. "See, I've accounted for every day." She pointed to highlighted boxes. "These with the yellow highlighter are the days I corresponded with Mr. Ellerton, and I've noted what subject we discussed."

"Very impressive. I can't believe you remember your movements every single day for the past four months." It was almost incomprehensible that such a remarkable mind came attached to such a beautiful woman.

"Actually, it's just the last three months. I wasn't confident enough in my archival skills to initiate contact with Mr. Ellerton until three months ago."

"It's rather good to know you've had your limitations." He sat on the corner of his solid desk, facing her.

"Though I remember what was discussed, I don't actually have the passages I shared with him. I'll have to duplicate that research."

"That shouldn't be too difficult."

She shrugged. "Not really. It's just that I'll have to physically return to those other homes in order to find my original sources."

"You're talking about homes of the five secret Catholic families?"

"Yes. Siddley, of course, is not one we discussed because Mr. Ellerton certainly didn't need my help with that."

"And I don't suppose Chumley is, either, since you've never been there."

"So that does narrow it down to three: Monlief Hall, Castle Paxton, and Blyn Court Castle."

"We should start with the closest one."

"We?"

"I feel responsible for you. If you'd never come to Siddley, you wouldn't have found Ellerton's body and all the grief that's come since. And Monlief Hall's less than ninety minutes away. I'll take you there this afternoon."

"Are you sure you don't mind?"

"I wouldn't offer if I did." He eyed her computer. "Bring your laptop. And flash drive. This time you need to be sure to back up every single piece of research."

"Aye, aye, my lord." Her lashes lifted as she met his gaze and offered him a provocative smile. What was there about her that was so seductive? He was quite sure she had no notion of how profoundly she affected men.

"Say!" he said as she was gathering up her things, "Chumley's on the way. Should you like to stop off and see it?"

"I've been dying to get there. Chumley's the only one of the five homes that's not close to a rail line, so it's been difficult for me to manage it."

"Then I'm happy to be of service." He picked up his phone and punched in a number. "Thought I'd ring my cousin to see if he can show us around."

While he waited for an answer, she asked, "Are you two close?"

He shrugged. "Not terribly, but we tend to keep turning up at the same places."

Richard answered. "Say, Bessington, it's Rockford." It was a good thing he remembered to use his cousin's fairly newly acquired title. "I've a friend who's keen to see Chumley. Do me a good turn and show her around this afternoon."

"Why do I sense that your friend is a beautiful woman?"

Frederick smiled. "You must have radar for that sort of thing, old boy."

"I shall look forward to meeting your friend. Will you be coming along, too?"

"I will. My friend doesn't drive."

After he hung up, his eyes locked with Antonia's. "I suggest you bring your bag. You'll want to spend the night at or near Monlief."

CHAPTER 10

Her first view of Chumley nearly transported her to another time, a time when her arrival would have been in a carriage—or on horseback; a time when women wore dresses with long, full skirts that cinched at the waist; a time when men wore...tights. Her eye traveled to the man sitting beside her in this very modern sports car. She most definitely preferred that jeans rather than tights hug his long, sinewy legs.

Maybe her aversion to tights on men was because she couldn't purge from her mind the vision of a corpulent Henry VIII. Why did Gordo the Serial Husband have to be the first man who came to mind when she thought of men in tights? Yuck.

As Frederick slowly approached the three-story redbrick manor house, she studied the pair of twin ogees that topped each side of the building's facade to give it a characteristically Elizabethan look. She wondered if the ogees were made of iron or tin.

Unlike Siddley, there didn't appear to be many tourists here. Just a few cars parked in the parking court, which did not have more than twenty or thirty spaces. Chumley suffered from being close to neither a motorway nor a rail line. Its lack of paying tourists translated to a bit of a neglected appearance. From the front, no formal gardens could be seen. The landscape was mostly a scattering of trees and vast expanses of grass where sheep grazed.

She had read that one of the earls of Bessington in the Regency period had spent vast sums landscaping the grounds as well as sprucing up the interiors in the chinoiserie mode. He would be rolling over in the family vault if he saw how neglected his property was now.

But he wouldn't be alone. All those Georgians who'd taken the Grand Tour and expanded their country estates while adorning them with statuary and paintings they'd brought back from the Continent would be dazed to see how severely reduced their lands had become in the twentieth and twenty-first centuries.

It made her sad—until she thought about the hard lives and extreme poverty of the other 99 percent of the eighteenth-century population who were not landowners. She laughed to herself.

"Why are you laughing?" Frederick drove toward the back of the house.

"I was just thinking about the days when this house was built. It was a time when monarchs thought they ruled by divine right and aristocrats thought God intended them to be superior to everyone who wasn't in their class." She certainly hoped Frederick wasn't possessed of such a mind-set.

He nodded. "Very shabby of my ancestors. Some of them actually wrote things like *No one of my class was there* or *She was very pleasant; a pity she's the daughter of a banker.*"

Antonia let out an exaggerated sigh. "I'm glad you think the way you do."

He parked and came to open her door. As they walked away from the car, a fortyish man carrying a racquet and dressed in tennis garb came up from behind. "Welcome to Chumley."

Antonia and Frederick turned to him, but he wasn't looking at Frederick. His lazy perusal of her only lacked drool to look like some pervert.

She did not like it when men stared at her like that. Putting on an exaggerated gawk, she stared right back at him. If it weren't for the man's arrogance, he could be attractive. A bit older than she liked. She'd guess he was over forty. The tennis apparently served him well. His skin was a healthy golden, and his waist was trim. He was only a couple of inches taller than her five-eight frame. His closely cropped, fashionably styled dark-brown hair was slightly threaded with gray. When he smiled, she noted his teeth were crooked and not Colgate white. Now, he looked like a typical Englishman.

"Hello there. I'm Lord Bessington, or Bessington to my acquaintances—of which I hope you will become."

"How nice of you." She felt like some performing puppet. "I'm Antonia Townley."

He turned to Frederick and extended his hand. "How are you, Rockford?"

"Good. Lovely day for a ride."

Bessington's gaze flicked to the Aston Martin. "Beautiful company. Beautiful car. You're a very fortunate man."

Frederick smiled like a lad trying to charm his teacher.

Bessington's attention returned to Antonia. "Rockford says I'm to have the good fortune to show you around Chumley."

"I've been dying to see it."

"You'll be fascinated to hear of Antonia's research," Frederick said. "It appears she knows more about our families than we do."

Bessington's brows quirked. "How is that?"

"I neglected to tell you she's a doctoral student at Oxford."

They entered into a broad hallway that had wooden floors and a wide wooden stairway that only went up, though Antonia knew the house had a basement. Obviously this staircase was originally intended for the family members since the basement was the domain of the domestic staff—in days gone by.

Bessington stopped dead in his stride and whirled around to face Antonia. "Don't tell me you're the bird mentioned in the newspaper! The one who found the body?"

Frederick frowned. "I wish you wouldn't rake up that unfortunate occurrence. This poor *bird's* been through an awful lot."

Unfortunate occurrence! She did love British understatement.

Bessington's eyes met hers. "So sorry, Miss Townley." He set his racquet on a bench, then returned his attention to her. "What historical period do you specialize in?"

"Tudor. Particularly the reign of Henry VIII and shortly thereafter."

"After you show us around, Antonia will have to tell you about her discovery."

"I'm eager to hear more." Their host met her gaze, then eyed the wood paneling that surrounded them and launched into his tour. "Obviously, this is not the main entrance to Chumley. It's the entrance that was closest to the former stables." He shrugged. "Unfortunately, the stables were pulled down in the early twentieth century to make way for a garage for motor cars as well as a swimming pool, which was filled in later in the century."

"Where I'm from—California—we don't see people filling in swimming pools very often."

"Ours was very large and very expensive to maintain—and repair. When my uncle—from whom I inherited—was told how much it would cost to repair, he had it filled in." Bessington then turned and waved at the nearby staircase, which was brightened from mullioned windows on the exterior wall. "This goes to the family wing, which is mostly bedchambers. Follow me along this corridor, and I'll show you our armory."

What was it about men and their armories? She almost laughed at herself. It wasn't like she'd known many men who had their own armories. Of all the rooms in these old homes and castles, armories were the least interesting to her. But then, she didn't enjoy the aspects of history that centered around battles and warfare. Give her a juicy love letter written from a lady-in-waiting any day.

"How thrilling," she said dryly.

As they ambled along the faded Persian runner that covered the corridor's well-used wooden floors, Bessington said, "So, Rockford, how's Lady Caroline these days?"

Antonia felt as if she'd fallen down the rabbit hole. And not in a good way, either. If Lord Bessington knew about Lady Range Rover, there must be an understanding between her and Frederick. Then why in heaven's name had Frederick gone and said *I'm glad*? The thing of it was, he didn't seem the philandering type. There was something so solid about him. Like Siddley Hall itself.

"Good enough, I suppose." Frederick did not sound overjoyed. Was that good? Or not? She was so out of her element in these aristocratic circles.

The next half hour was spent in the armory, where Frederick and Bessington attempted to one-up each other over their respective armaments. There was absolutely nothing interesting to Antonia about the antique weaponry.

Next, they went to the sparsely furnished great room. She supposed its vast size made it difficult to furnish in a usable manner or to be relevant in the modern day, although an effort had been made. Some half a dozen aging Persian rugs effectively divided the great room into smaller ones with groupings of sofas and armchairs.

The room's most remarkable feature was the enormous fireplace. A tall man like Frederick could comfortably stand up inside it. She found herself wondering how many oxen and lambs could have been roasted there at one time.

But the room was entirely too large and the acoustics too auditorium-like for any conversational intimacy. The only thing she could see it fit for was a ballroom, and how often did one need a private ballroom?

From the great room, they climbed stairs to an elegant drawing room that clashed with the medieval aspects of the house but was lovely with its rich Persian carpets and Oriental touches. If she wasn't mistaken, the twin mirrors on opposite side walls were crafted by Thomas Chippendale.

Two facing chintz sofas before a fireplace only slightly smaller than the one downstairs looked inviting. In fact, this room looked as if present-day members of the Bessington family spent time here. A round table skirted in tapestry featured an assortment of photographs in silver frames of varied sizes.

She moved closer to it. Some black-and-white photos dated to the 1920s and '30s. She recognized one of George V with a flapper-looking woman. One of the larger black-and-white photographs was of a brunette Queen Elizabeth with a man in a robe—definitely not the kind of robe they gave you in the luxury suite at Caesars Palace. Many of the photos looked more recent. Absent were any photographs of children or of the present Earl of Bessington. She looked up at him. "There's not a Lady Bessington, is there?"

He shook his head. "I am happily single."

Her gaze went from him to the portraits hanging on the wall. These were what she liked best. They might not be Holbeins or Gainsboroughs, but they were authentic looking and spanned all the centuries this fine old house had been in existence. The history of fashion and hairstyles for both men and women over the past five or six hundred years could be traced in these portraits.

Even though the Tudor period was her own specialty, she appreciated the Georgian portraits where men wore their powdered hair long and women looked and dressed like Marie Antoinette. Now that was elegant. And to think, all those silks worn by men and women alike had been produced by Chinese silkworms!

Next, they crossed the hallway to the dining room. While the huge room, which was original to the old brick manor house, retained its massive fireplace and creaky wooden floors, it also featured elegant, multitiered crystal chandeliers of a much later period. The long cherrywood table that could probably seat thirty dated to the nineteenth century. It displayed a king's ransom in silver. Candelabra, pitchers, and ornate tea services marched down the table one after another from its head to its foot. "I hope you've got good security," Antonia quipped.

"We do have some rather valuable pieces of silver at that." Bessington shrugged. "When I get the money from the university, one of my first duties will be to beef up security." He turned to Frederick. "I suppose you've given thought to beefing up your security at Siddley?"

"Actually, I have."

"Given thought to it or done something about it?"

Frederick glared at his cousin. "Both." He turned to the painting above the head of the table. "Who's that, Richard?"

That he'd slipped and called his cousin by his Christian name told Antonia that Frederick hadn't become accustomed to his cousin's title yet.

"That's the sixth earl—the one who fancied gardens and Chinese-looking interiors—and one of the few of my ancestors whose portrait I actually recognize." His gaze connected with Frederick's. "What I need is a curator like you had, someone to be an expert on the family history and all that."

"That would be difficult," Frederick said, "since you've sold all the family's papers."

"There is that," Bessington lamented. He looked genuinely sad. He might not be a walking encyclopedia about his ancestors, but she could tell by the way he so proudly showed her around that he held great affinity for Chumley.

"How long since you succeeded?" she asked.

"Just a year and a half."

Her brows elevated. "And you never lived here before?"

"No."

"I'm surprised, given your obvious interest in Chumley."

"It's not as if I hadn't known for the past couple of decades that Chumley would come to me."

"So you studied up about it?"

"As much as I could. I've learned a lot more since I came into the title."

"Yet you sold your archives to Portsmouth University?"

"That was the hardest decision I've made since succeeding. In the end, I realized the university had much better resources to protect our papers for posterity than do I. And they paid most handsomely. The funds will help with needed improvements to Chumley. I mean to make Chumley Manor a destination."

She almost had to bite her lip to keep from voicing her opinion. Opening one's home to the masses would be a last resort to her, even though she was grateful that she'd been able to tour those that were open to the masses.

"So, other than security, what other improvements are you considering?" she asked.

"I'm going to invest in a first-class website, nice leaflets, and good signage. As to Chumley itself, I plan to expand the car park, get new draperies and upholstery in the public rooms, and restore the gardens to what they were in the eighteenth century. Can you think of anything else?" he asked Frederick.

"Those all sound good to me. I'm assuming the roof and electrical and plumbing are in good order?"

Bessington sighed. "I wish I could say they were. There's little pleasure in spending for things that don't improve the aesthetics."

"But spending on maintenance is a necessary evil."

"Indeed, it is."

"I think one of Chumley's attractions—other than its remarkable history—is its lovely setting here," Frederick said. "It's wise of you to spend most of your efforts restoring the gardens."

"I'd like to make it a place where families would come to spend the day exploring the unspoiled land—at least the few hundred acres we've managed to hang on to. Come," Bessington said, "allow me to show you the library. It's quite my favorite room in all of Chumley."

"I wasn't aware of there being especially memorable libraries in Tudor homes," Antonia said, "at least in comparison with some of the grand ones that came later, like the Victorian library at Arundel."

"Please don't expect anything as grand as Arundel Castle's." Bessington turned down an altogether different corridor that led to Chumley's main staircase. This was obviously the oldest section of the house. Even the wall art here dated to Tudor times, and the paintings were dark. She wondered if they lacked color because they were covered with centuries of grime.

The stairs were rather narrow and gloomy. Compared to those at other stately homes she'd toured the past half a year, they were modest. The wood there, like everything else in the entry, had darkened with age. Darkness prevailed in the wood-floored entry hall, which was lit from a lone mullioned window.

The three of them began to mount the creaking stairway. "Our library was enlarged and expanded during the Restoration. The room was formerly one story. The original ceiling was removed, and along the upper story's perimeter, bookshelves were added on all four walls."

When they came to the library, her jaw dropped. "It's magnificent," she rasped, clearly impressed. It was one of the finest private libraries she had seen. And England was home to a plethora of fabulous private libraries. The long room opened to soaring ceilings and upper galleries of handsome leather-bound books.

The lower floor was pretty darned impressive, too. Huge Oriental carpets stretched between tall masonry fireplaces on each end of the room, and plump asparagus-green sofas paired up in front of the fireplaces. Heavy Jacobean tables on chunky wood legs were scattered throughout the room.

But the star of the massive room was the beauty of its bountiful leather books. "And I thought your silver valuable," she exclaimed. "These books must be worth a fortune!" As soon as the words were out of her mouth, she wanted to retract them. How crass they must think her to reduce everything to its monetary value. "I'm curious. What's your oldest book?"

"Our oldest is not actually on display. It's too valuable."

She faced him, a brow cocked.

"A Shakespeare folio."

"No way!"

The look of sheer pride that crossed his face made him look like the scrawny duck who'd just sired a brilliantly plumed peacock. "Yes way." He began to move across the room. "Allow me to show you some of our other prizes."

For the next twenty minutes, he gave her a most enlightening tour of the library's collections, most of them between two and three hundred years old. It was impossible for him to conceal his pride in either his ancestral home or this library.

Whatever amount of money he had received from the university for the family archives would have been but a fraction of what the books here could have fetched. They were worth a fortune. "I commend you for hanging on to this library," she said. "It's magnificent."

"Good choice," Frederick said, "selling the archives and preserving this. All those old household ledgers and personal correspondence take an expert—someone like Antonia—to decipher."

"I would never sell a single book here."

While Bessington was conducting the tour, something in the back of her mind kept niggling at her, then she realized what it was.

They were not going to make it to Monlief Hall that day. She was quite sure Monleif's closing time had come and gone by now.

Frederick must have been thinking the same thing because he finally said, "I say, Antonia, I'm afraid we may have missed Monlief."

Bessington's gaze swung from Frederick to her. "I believe my cousin's right, but I can't say I'm disappointed. Now I shall have the pair of you as my dinner guests."

"Oh, we couldn't," Frederick said.

Bessington ignored him and focused his complete attentions on Antonia. "Don't listen to him, Miss Townley. It's only fair, you know, that I get to find out about this exciting research of yours, especially since it pertains to *my* family."

She glanced at Frederick. "He's right, Frederick. He's given us his afternoon. Now the least I can do is tell him about the Catholic families."

"What Catholic families?" Bessington asked.

"I'll tell you about them all in good time. First, though, I must ask a question."

"Yes?"

"Does Chumley have a priest hole?"

"Yes, actually. I'm sorry I neglected to show it to you. It's in the dining room. Come, we'll go see it now."

The priest hole was the size of a small closet and was accessed from a wooden panel. The panel had been cleverly concealed by a row of choir-like chairs that had been built into the wall. The built-in chair on the end hinged open to reveal the hiding place for Catholic priests after the Dissolution.

"This is so exciting!" Antonia scooted into the windowless space, which was maybe three by six. "This is my first priest hole."

"Ah, a priest hole virgin," Bessington said.

Frederick wore an amused expression. "It's not every day you hear *priest* and *virgin* in the same sentence."

"And hole," Bessington said with a smirk.

Antonia's cheeks grew hot. "The Blessed Virgin Mary is sometimes paired with priest." She came back out and addressed her host. "So your family knows about the Catholicism?"

He shrugged. "Why is it I have a feeling you're going to further enlighten me?"

"Because she is, old fellow."

"Then let's discuss it over dinner. Come, let me show you my newly remodeled kitchen."

"Don't tell me you actually cook," she said.

"Remember, until eighteen months ago, I was just Richard Craine, a regular bloke getting by the best he could."

She wondered what an earl-in-waiting would do for a livelihood.

She followed him down a stone corridor that jutted off the rear of the house. "This wing's a rather new addition—new being within the past two hundred years."

Though the kitchen's pine cabinets and earthy tiled floor did not look modern, she recognized much of the design here was state-of-the-art twenty-first century. And then there was the cream-colored Aga. Much better than an open fire.

The kitchen was one big square room with everything useful lined up along one long wall. There was a large, casual pine table with mismatched chairs in the center of the room, directly below a suspended lantern. Four wooden ladder-back bar stools lined a granite-topped peninsula that was just steps from the kitchen's food preparation area.

Bessington went straight for the wine rack, grabbed a pinot noir, and began to uncork. "I hope red's OK?"

Antonia nodded as she seated herself at one of the bar stools. "It's what I prefer."

Frederick came to sit beside her, and once the three of them had glasses in hand, Bessington said, "I hope you've brought overnight bags."

"Actually, we did," Frederick said.

"I can't tell you how pleased I would be to have you stay here. It gets a bit lonely in this big, rambling house all by myself." He set down his glass and held out his hand, peering at Frederick. "If you'll just give me your keys, I'll have my butler get your things and put them in the guest rooms."

When he left the room, Frederick turned to her. "I hope you don't mind the overnight thing."

"To be completely honest, I'm thrilled. I never thought I'd ever get to spend one night in an English stately home, and in the span of twenty-four hours, I will have slept in two!"

"If our rooms aren't adjacent, I plan to ask that they be so. I need to be within hearing range."

His sweet words of concern—and the wine—made her insides feel like molten honey. So molten it bubbled. "I'll feel better knowing you're *in hearing range.*"

He moved close to her, draped an arm around her, and spoke in a low, husky voice. "If you'd like, I could allow Richard to think… that we have reason to share the same bedchamber. I promise not to take advantage of the situation."

The way she felt right now, she warmed to the idea of Frederick taking advantage of the situation, but she was also cognizant that she needed to retain his respect. She wanted to savor this moment, the way he made her feel, the smoky, fruity scent of the wine on his breath, the warmth of his body touching hers. Their eyes locked. "I trust you."

"Does that mean you want us to share a…bed?"

She couldn't answer for a moment. The very concept of sharing a bed with him made her breath grow short. "All I know is that the only time I feel safe is when you're with me."

A force too powerful to deny compelled her to lock sultry gazes with him. His head moved closer. She could feel the heat of him.

The closer he came, the surer she was that he was going to kiss her. Her heartbeat thundered. Then he straightened up like someone had shoved a two-by-four down his pants. "As long as I draw breath, I won't let anything happen to you, Antonia."

At that very moment she didn't think she'd ever care to draw breath again if something happened to Lord Wonderful. She felt as if she were bound to him by some mysterious force, though there was nothing mysterious about it. What wasn't to idolize about the guy? He was good looking, rich, titled, intelligent, owner of the best stately home in all of England, and most of all, he was considerate and caring. He should be the bloody love of her life!

Then she thought of Ice Princess, and it was like throwing freezing water on her endorphins.

He cleared his throat. "There's one matter with which I may need your help."

Up until now, she had been the needy one. "Anything. Anything at all."

"It may be difficult to behave as a gentleman with you so bloody close."

It was a moment before she could answer, a moment before she, in her breathless state, could rustle up some levity. "So ya want me to borrow one of Chumley's suits of armor to sleep in?"

CHAPTER 11

Bessington was gone for about ten minutes. "I had Williams put your things in adjacent rooms. Is that all right?" His gaze swung from Antonia to Frederick.

Frederick shrugged. "Close enough."

His eyes wide with amusement, Bessington smirked. Frederick wondered why he'd ever agreed to stay here. He'd never particularly liked this cousin, who was several times removed. He supposed Richard wasn't a bad chap. It was just that he had a propensity for doing things that annoyed. Like devouring Antonia with his hungry gaze the moment the poor girl got out of the car.

And throughout the tour of Chumley Manor, Bessington had actually boasted. Several times. One simply didn't boast about one's ancestral home. Didn't the braggart know an earl was supposed to say things like *It's a bit shabby, but it suits* or *We're doing our best to keep dry rot at bay* when visitors volleyed compliments about one's house?

But no, Bessington had done his bloody best to try to impress Antonia. *Chumley's Sheraton sideboard is likely the finest in England...I don't think there's a better Turner than ours...We've got more swords than Siddley.* It was bad enough the way he tried to hold up his home as so bloody grand, but it was even worse the way he ignored Frederick's presence to give his full attention to the beautiful American.

Even when Bessington began to cook their dinner—a talent Frederick admittedly lacked and was somewhat impressed over—the damned fellow was so full of himself, he talked down to them as if he were the world's most applauded chef. "I have no tolerance for anyone who doesn't use fresh garlic," he had told them as he demonstrated the way he put fresh cloves of garlic into a press.

Frederick was so out of his element in a kitchen that he, first, did not know garlic came in cloves or things that looked to Frederick's nondiscerning eye rather like small onions, and, second, he'd had never heard of a garlic press.

Bessington's butler-type person, who did not dress like a butler but wore khakis and a golf shirt with Chumley's logo, returned Frederick's keys shortly after Bessington started to cook.

From start to finish, it took the show-off a full two hours to prepare the dinner—and three bottles of pinot noir were consumed during the process.

Despite his cousin's didactic performance in front of the Aga, the Italian concoction he whipped up was truly scrumptious. Prawns in Alfredo sauce over pasta.

Frederick thought it really too utterly pretentious to light candles to take a meal on a scrubbed pine table in the kitchen, but that is exactly what Bessington did. He also made sure he sat next to Antonia.

Once they sat down to eat and Bessington no longer had cause to perform, he addressed Antonia. "Now, Miss Townley, I wish to hear all about your research."

"I've made a rather interesting discovery. While you might not be surprised that your ancestors secretly practiced Catholicism—because of the evidence of the priest hole—I have uncovered evidence that points to there having been five related upper-class families of the era who continued to secretly observe their Catholic faith. My dissertation is actually titled 'The Five Secret Catholic Families.'"

Bessington smiled. "And we're one of them?"

"Yes, and Frederick's family is another."

"Frederick?" He smirked at Frederick. "This is the first time I've ever heard anyone except Bagsy call you that."

"It was my idea," Antonia said. "I know that calling male peers by their titles is the thing to do, but I just can't. To me, it sounds like locker room jargon, and I don't happen to wear a jock strap."

Frederick and Bessington exchanged amused glances and broke out laughing.

Antonia looked at his cousin, a pleading expression on her lovely face. "I hope you'll allow me to call you Richard."

How could he or any man refuse her anything when she looked up at him like that?

"If you like, Antonia." That was the first time Bessington had not addressed her as Miss Townley. "So other than the Godwins, who built Chumley, and the Rockfords, which other families?" Bessington asked.

Frederick found himself glaring over the rim of his wineglass at his host. "They weren't Rockfords then."

"Oh, yes. The Percys."

Bessington gave Antonia a querying gaze. "Let me try to think how everyone was related back then. I've been boning up on the family history ever since I succeeded. I know that Lord Godwin's wife was the daughter of the Duke de Quincy. Were the de Quincys one of the families?"

She nodded. "Very good."

"Let me see…Lady Godwin's sister married…oh," he said, disappointed, "Percy." He thought for a moment, then said. "I don't have a clue who the other two families could have been."

"The Percys' daughter, Katherine, married John Parr."

"Parr of Castle Paxton!" Bessington exclaimed.

"Right-o," Frederick said. "The last one is Sir Percy's sister, Elizabeth, who married Sir Thomas Montague of Monlief Hall."

"So that's why you were going to Monlief today."

Frederick had decided he wasn't going to bring up the monstrance. Nothing about it had been mentioned in the newspapers. As far as he was concerned, the fewer who knew about it, the better.

"By getting a fresh start in the morning, I'll have all day to pore over the archives," Antonia said.

"Sorry I sold ours, but Chumley needed the seven-figures-plus they fetched."

Frederick had to stop himself from wincing at the mention of seven figures. Bad form. One didn't discuss what things cost—or fetched.

"I understand your reasons for doing so," Antonia said. "Subsequent generations of your family will be happy to have the family history preserved in a fine library. As soon as the university has them cataloged, I can sweep in and do my research."

"You can't now?" Bessington asked.

She shook her head. "I asked Simon how long I could expect it to take for the university's library to catalog them, and he said it could be years. I really hate that. Maybe you could use your influence. Did you retain any proprietorial access?"

"I did, actually, and I'll be happy to help." He refilled wineglasses. "Have you been to Monlief before?"

"Yes," she said, "but all my research was stolen."

Frederick was sorry she had brought up the theft. He didn't like others knowing about the chaos going on at Siddley right now.

"Theft of intellectual property?"

She frowned. "I guess you could say that."

"As soon as your competitor publishes your findings, you can have charges brought against him."

Her eyes narrowed. "I'd rather put a bullet in him." Then she flashed Bessington a smile. "Just kidding, thought that *is* what the thieving, no-good, low-life scumbag deserves."

Bessington gave her a sympathetic nod. "Let's hope the scumbag is apprehended." Seconds later, his eyes widened, and he spun to face Antonia square on. "What an extraordinary coincidence that your research was stolen at the same time as that poor librarian was killed!" Then his gaze swung to Frederick. "Nasty business."

"Yes, it is." Frederick was surprised that Antonia had let the topic die without elaborating and telling him about the connection between the two crimes, about the monstrance, and generally running off at the mouth as would most any other young woman he'd ever known.

He had meant to speak to her and ask that she stay mum on the subject, but somehow he just hadn't found the right time. Amazingly, he hadn't needed to. It was as if she were reading his mind. And vice versa. This connection between them was really uncanny.

He was in uncharted waters. No other woman's thoughts had ever before fused with his in such a way; no other woman had ever affected him quite like Antonia did.

Bessington lifted the wine bottle and addressed Antonia. "Can I refill your glass?"

"If I have another glass, I'm afraid Frederick will have to carry me to our room."

Our room. Why did Frederick so thoroughly like the sound of that? He had pledged to be on his best, most respectful behavior.

Bessington arched a single brow. "I wasn't aware that you two…"

"I don't think you should go there, Bessington." Frederick glowered at their host as he refilled Frederick's glass as well as his own.

"You're not driving, Antonia," Bessington said. "How about just half a glass?"

"It *is* awfully good." Her voice was different. Squeakier. Could it be the wine? She held out her glass.

"I get it from one of my favorite vineyards in Italy."

Did he think that would impress Antonia?

"Italian grub, Italian wine," she said, "so if we stayed tomorrow night would we have sushi with sake?"

Bessington laughed. "No. I'm afraid I just have a great affinity for Italy."

"He lived in Milan for a while."

"So do you speak Italian?"

"Lamentably, no." He passed around the basket holding the hot loaf of bread.

"I couldn't live in a foreign country unless I made the effort to learn their language," Antonia said. "That must have been difficult for you, not being able to fluently converse with the natives."

"Most of my associates spoke excellent English."

Did the twit not realize Antonia had just put him down?

Frederick wondered why Bessington didn't ask about Alistair. After all, he was the one who had put the fellow up for the job as librarian's helper.

When their plates were emptied, Antonia brought up the subject. "I understand you're related to Alistair."

"Alistair?" His brows lowered. "Oh! Penworth! The lad's some kind of cousin, but I couldn't tell you much more." His glance darted to Frederick. "You wouldn't have known his family because he's related on my mother's side. How's he working out?"

"I can't answer that," Frederick said. "The man he reported to is dead."

"I think he's still learning," Antonia said. "He's young yet—but he's awfully nice. Very prompt, too. Most dependable."

"I do hope you'll keep him on even though the librarian's been...the newspapers said he was murdered."

Antonia gave him a you-poor-moron look. "It's not a common occurrence for someone to drive a dagger into his own chest."

Bessington winced. "Have they found out yet who did it?"

Frederick shook his head.

"One wonders why a librarian would be murdered. Do you suppose he was in some kind of love triangle?" Bessington asked.

"I know nothing about his personal life," Frederick said. "Shall we change the subject, please?"

"Can I interest you in dessert? I have to apologize that it's not homemade."

The notion of an earl puttering around a kitchen preparing dessert almost summoned a laugh from Frederick.

Antonia held up her hands. "No dessert for me. The dinner was fabulous, and I'm full."

"As am I, old chap." Frederick peered at his watch. "I can't believe it's so late."

Antonia jumped up and began to clear the table. "I'll just help you wash up."

Frederick could not imagine Caro ever offering to help wash dishes. He wondered if she'd ever washed a dish in her privileged life. He moved to the end of the bar and stationed himself on a stool to talk to them as they cleaned the kitchen.

He was actually surprised Antonia wasn't more wobbly on her feet. He could tell she'd had more wine than she was used to. Her fuzzy words and the luminescent looks she kept sending his way betrayed her attempts to appear sober.

Once they'd rinsed the last plate and closed up the dishwasher, he said, "It's been a great evening, Bessington, but I'm going to have to call it quits. I didn't sleep well last night."

"That's perfectly understandable, considering what happened at Siddley yesterday." His cousin offered him a sympathetic look. *Damned fellow.*

Antonia set down the tea towel and shot him another of those scorching gazes of hers. "I'm awfully tired, too. It has been a very long, trying day." As she spoke, she sauntered up to him and casually dropped a crooked arm at his shoulder while he remained seated on the bar stool.

Heaven help me.

EPISODE 5

CHAPTER 12

"I'll show you to your rooms—or room." Bessington blew out the candles, then turned off the lights before they entered the dimly lit corridor.

Antonia slipped her arm through Frederick's. He felt like an adolescent with his first girl at the cinema. Her every touch had a profound effect upon him—mentally as well as physically. Like the callow youth he'd once been, he kept pondering his next move. Or nonmove, in this case.

As they followed their host, Frederick kept berating himself. He'd almost kissed her. Not that there was anything wrong with that—under normal circumstances. But these past two days hardly constituted normal circumstances.

Because of his worries for her, it was expedient that he keep her under his watchful eye at all times. That was—or should have been—his chief aim in sharing a…bed with Antonia. The very thought of sleeping with her played havoc with his libido. He mustn't have her thinking the suggestion to share a room was a ploy to have sex with her. He wouldn't like it all if she thought he was some selfish bloke only interested in his own gratification.

Another reason he couldn't allow himself to get carried away kissing her was that she had consumed considerably more wine than she was used to, and because of that, she was perhaps a little more…affectionate than normal. What kind of prick took advantage of a young lady under such circumstances?

Chumley's corridors, at least the three they'd traversed since leaving the kitchen, were not nearly as well lit as those at Siddley. They were narrower, too. A bit menacing, actually. He was sure without Bessington's guidance, he might never find his way to or from his bedroom, wherever in the hell it was.

They proceeded to mount a steep wooden staircase. At its top, an electrified wall sconce provided a small sphere of light. "This is the family wing."

"Frederick *is* family," Antonia said, a little giggle hitching into her voice as she lifted her smiling face to his. When she looked at him like that she looked incredibly young. Like about seventeen. Which should make it easier for him to be strong. Fatherly.

Though what he felt for Antonia was far from paternal.

With every step they took down the hallway, the floorboards creaked. *Good.* At least no one could sneak up on them. It seemed almost incomprehensible there was a murderer on the loose, a stinking murderer who'd wormed his way inside of Siddley Hall. Damn but he was glad Antonia wasn't going to be alone tonight. He worried like the devil about her.

"The room to our right is my bedchamber," Bessington said as they passed the first of several closed doors. Almost at the opposite end of the corridor Bessington stopped, swung open a door, and flicked on the light. "I think you'll find that Williams put the lady's bag in this, the most feminine room."

Nodding, Antonia strolled into the room. "Oh, Richard, it's lovely."

Why did she have to call him Richard? It sounded entirely too familiar. She'd only met him today. And he was an earl. Everyone called earls by their last names. Everyone except Antonia.

Frederick had to admit he liked it when Antonia called him Frederick. There was something intimate about it. *Don't go there, old boy.*

Though it could use some sprucing up, the room was lovely. It was done up in cream and pale blue. The faded wall-to-wall carpet was also sky blue. The curtains at the pair of windows were of blue-and-white floral with pink roses thrown in. A smallish canopied bed of faded light-blue silks was the focal point of the room.

She turned back to Bessington. "Thank you for everything, Richard. It's been a most pleasant night."

He smiled at Antonia, then addressed Frederick. "Well, old fellow, yours is the next one. I don't suppose you'll need me to escort you." He winked.

Frederick offered a handshake. "Awfully good of you to put us up. And the food was excellent."

Bessington closed the door behind himself.

"Now how do you suppose they knew which bag was yours?" Frederick asked, a devilish grin on his face.

She gazed up at him with sparkling eyes. "Do you suppose the hot pink could have tipped them off?"

His gaze lasered to the bag, which had been set upon a chair. "Right-o."

She followed his line of vision. "I'm glad Williams didn't attempt to unpack my stuff." She sighed. "If we were at Windsor Castle, a servant would have—"

"Unpacked all your things and hung them up."

"So you saw the same documentary I saw."

He cleared his throat. "No, actually I've spent the night at—"

"Oh, my God! I don't believe this!" She glared at him, her lower lip working itself into a pout. "I suppose Ice Princess has been a guest of the queen, too."

He gave her a puzzled look. "What are you talking about?"

She shook her head vigorously. "Nothing. Forget I opened my mouth."

He strode across the room, picked up her hot-pink bag, and started for the exterior door. "Shall we move next door?" Williams might not be the only one who thought a lone female was staying in this room. If Frederick had learned anything from this nightmare of the past two days, he'd learned one couldn't be too careful.

The pout vanished as she flashed him a sweet smile. "A very good plan."

The bedchamber he'd been assigned had probably been grand a very long time ago, but that was no longer the case. Because Frederick did not know much about decorating, he couldn't really diagnose the room's problems, but for starters, the room's limp curtains needed to be tossed. They had faded so dramatically that identifying the former colors in the grayish striped silk pattern was purely conjecture.

The walls, too, needed painting. At some point, a smoker had obviously resided here. The formerly cream-colored walls were now beige. He knew the original color because a painting had fairly recently been removed from the corridor-side wall, leaving a tidy little cream rectangle—and a hole the size of a twopence where the nail had been.

"En suite, do you think?" he asked, moving to a doorway and turning on the light to the adjacent room. It *was* a bathroom. Very retro with smallish tiles and sinks with legs.

She came to look over his shoulder, which necessitated standing upon her toes—and which meant she was really, really close. Her lavender scent wafted up to him. *God, give me strength.*

"This bathroom looks very much like the one in Bagsy's room," she said.

"I expect there was a time in the early nineteen hundreds when it became fashionable to modernize by creating these little loos. They must all have used the same builder."

"Then he must have been building in California, too, because my grandmother's bathroom looks just like that—and her parents built their house in 1933. *The only thing we have to fear is fear itself*—my favorite line from Franklin D. Roosevelt's inaugural address. Can you guess when?"

"Ah, I knew there must be some connection. One doesn't normally launch into the topic of fear while commenting on the bathroom." His brows arched. "Would it have also been in 1933?"

"You're so shatteringly smart."

Her words were blurring. "Why don't you use the loo first?" he suggested.

She shook her head. "No. You. Once I've taken off the mascara, I'll make a beeline to the bed in the dark. I'm just shallow enough to not want you to see me without makeup."

"I saw you without makeup last night."

"You did not!"

"I did, too. You cried so bloody much, all your mascara rubbed off onto your handkerchief—or whatever it was you used to sop up the tears."

"That's right. You *have* already seen me at my ugliest."

His voice softened. "It would be impossible for you to ever look ugly."

Her cell phone rang. She rolled her eyes. "I bet it's Surly Simon." She started for her purse, which she'd set upon the secretary desk. "Guess I'll have to come up with a new nickname for him since he's being so nice. Sensitive and Simon, though, somehow do not seem to go together."

If she was going for alliteration, why not call him Salacious Simon?

She picked up the phone. "Hello, Simon...I'm not going to speak to you if you're going to shout at me like that. And cuss!... *Hell* is too a cuss word!...It's none of your business..."

Frederick knew that good manners dictated that he move into the bathroom and start brushing his teeth. He made a great show of going through his bag, making it look as if he were having diffi-culty finding his toiletries while listening to every word she uttered to that interfering don who was smothering her with his unwanted attentions.

Frederick tensed. They *were* unwanted, weren't they?

"I know," she continued, "you're just concerned over my wel-fare, and I do appreciate that, especially because of all that's hap-pened...All right, I'll tell you. I'm spending the night at Chumley Manor...Of course I'm not alone...That's really not your business, Simon...All right, he's here with me...How did your panel go? Was Dr. Wimberly there?"

Frederick could not spend half an hour combing through that small bag. He snatched up the leather shaving kit and headed for the loo.

When he returned to the bedroom a moment later, she was get-ting close to terminating the call. "Tomorrow we'll be at Monlief Hall...I plan to work all day duplicating the research I've already conducted there...Of course I could use your help...All right. See you there."

There was another thing that hadn't changed in the last twenty-four hours. Last night Frederick had wanted to punch Simon in the face even though he'd never met him. Now he *had* met him, and he still wanted to slug the man's bespectacled face.

She went to put the phone back in her purse, then stopped. "I better charge it." She went to her suitcase and got the charger.

"So Simon's to help you tomorrow?"

"He'll be a tremendous help, and I'd best enjoy it while I can. He'll be back in class the day after tomorrow."

"It's so nice that he's shown such a fatherly interest in you."

She stopped what she was doing and gave Frederick an icy glare. "I wish you wouldn't say stuff like that—and most especially *not* in front of him. Simon likes to think he's hip."

"The man's a lecher." Frederick bloody well hoped that term did not apply to himself. Would Antonia think him fatherly, too?

"That is simply not true."

Was there something between her and her professor? Simon certainly acted as if there were. Frederick wanted to ask if Simon was more to her than an instructor, but it wasn't his business.

She plopped on the room's only bed. "I wonder if Richard has Wi-Fi?"

"My guess would be no."

"I don't actually have to have the Internet. Would it bother you if I type up notes about Chumley that I gleaned from today's tour?"

"Not at all. I've got a Scandinavian thriller to read." He went to his bag for the paperback novel.

"Oh, darn," she exclaimed. "That butler of Richard's didn't bring in my laptop."

"I can go get it for you."

There was a soft rap at his door. What the hell? He and Antonia exchanged querying expressions, then he strode to the door and opened it.

His cousin stood there, holding up Antonia's new laptop.

"Sorry to disturb you, old boy, but Williams found this on the drive as he was leaving. Is it yours?"

"It's Antonia's. How in the hell did it get on the driveway?"

Bessington shrugged. "I suppose that means you didn't leave it there?" His gaze went to Antonia.

In one way, Frederick was glad she was fully clothed. He wouldn't want his cousin to get the wrong idea about her. Yet, another part of Frederick was disappointed he couldn't let Bessington—as well as that bloody Simon—think he had a claim on her. "Of course we didn't leave it there!"

"I asked Williams about it, but he assures me that when he removed the bags from your car, it wasn't there. He said he looked in the interior as well as the boot."

"Was the car still locked when he got out the bags?"

"I asked him that, but he wasn't sure. He had automatically depressed the *open* button as he walked to the vehicle."

Antonia came and took the laptop and set about trying to boot it up. She hadn't said a single word. Which wasn't a good thing. Antonia was proficient at chattering. Her silence meant she was upset. And for some peculiar reason, he was upset whenever she was.

"Good lord," Bessington said, "this means some thief trespassed on my property! I'm going to ring the police."

"I don't think whoever it was is interested in stealing from you," Frederick said, his voice as grave as his thoughts.

Bessington's brows lowered. "What do you mean?"

Frederick didn't want to further alarm Antonia. He moved into the corridor and lowered his voice. "Someone's stalking Antonia, and we believe it's the same person who murdered Ralph Ellerton."

"Your librarian?"

Frederick nodded.

"All the more reason to ring the police!"

"We had the Oxford police out last night when her flat was burglarized, and then Scotland Yard again this morning when her laptop was stolen."

"But her laptop's right here."

"That was a different one. This one's new." He moved back into the bedchamber.

"I bloody well don't understand why anyone would be stalking Antonia." Their host's eyes narrowed. "My God, all these breakins—as well as a murder—it's all frightfully alarming!"

Frederick felt obligated to alleviate Bessington's fears. "Whoever murdered Ellerton may have reason to believe Antonia knows how to locate something the killer wants."

Frederick's gaze shifted to her. His concern about Antonia was rapidly mounting. "Thanks for bringing it to us." Frederick went to close the door on Bessington, who straddled the threshold.

"Sure you don't want me to ring the police?"

Frederick addressed Antonia. "Would you like Bessington to have the police come out?"

Her eyes filled with tears, and she shook her head.

"Thanks again, old chap." Frederick closed the door on his cousin and rushed to Antonia.

She had gone ashen, her limbs shook, and she was almost hyperventilating. "He's stalking me."

Frederick hauled her into his arms. "I know. I know. But you're safe. I give you my word I won't let anything happen to you."

CHAPTER 13

He understood her need to be held. The poor girl was just short of hysteria, and with good cause: a murderer was stalking her.

Frederick had thought holding Antonia would give her comfort, a sense of security. He hadn't been prepared for how powerfully he was affected when her slender body pressed against his. He felt like a man drugged. It was astonishing, really, how an act so devoid of lust could unleash such a sense of incredible well-being.

Even more than that, he'd never before felt more manly. His vow to protect her had not been mere cocky bravado. For this woman he could slay dragons with his bare hands. He could be something different, something akin to a fearless warrior with porridge-soft insides.

"I want you to *kold* me," she whispered.

He peered down at her. Those long, dark lashes of hers rested lightly on her cheeks, her perfect front teeth nipping at her quivering lower lip. "*Kold* you?" he asked. Her act of slowly nodding was almost erotic in its sensuousness. Then she looked up at him, all soulful and innocent and seductive at the same time. "It's a combination of kiss and hold. I just made it up."

It wasn't she talking; it was the wine. But the very notion of kissing her awakened him even more fully to this lovely creature's vast appeal. But, of course, he could not let her know she affected him like that. He needed Antonia to believe that he was indifferent to her, that he was merely her protector. "Kiss and hold sounds like a poker game."

Her lips puckered into a pout. "That's not romantic."

The last thing he needed right now was to be romantic. A gentleman should not attempt to utter words of affection under such circumstances, and a gentleman certainly should never seduce a lady who'd had too much to drink.

He tried to fortify himself against her overwhelming appeal. "I'm not going to kiss you, Antonia." His voice came off more harsh than he'd intended.

She stiffened. "You don't have to worry that I'm trying to snare a husband. Matrimony's as abhorrent to me as it is to you. I merely thought a kiss would be nice."

"It's the wine talking. I don't want you to do anything that you'd regret tomorrow."

She flung back her head and regarded him through narrowed eyes. "Wine doesn't talk, silly."

He chuckled and hauled her more tightly into his chest, his arms encircling her tightly.

And then they heard a man's voice—Bessington's?—screaming out from the next room.

He bolted for the door. Antonia was at his heels. When he opened the door, he whirled to her. "Stay here with the door locked. I'll be right back."

She shook her head in defiance. "I'm too scared. That noise was right next to here."

At that instant, the door to Antonia's original room whipped open, and Bessington hurried into the corridor. "Sorry to alarm you."

He looked perfectly fine, and Frederick felt like driving a fist through his face for scaring them like that. Good lord, what was coming over Frederick? An excessively peaceful chap, he'd suddenly turned into a Mike Tyson wannabe—but only in Antonia's presence.

Frederick glared at his distant cousin. "What's happened?"

"I hate to alarm you, old boy, but we've got a prowler."

Frederick felt like he'd been hit by a double-decker bus. A prowler didn't just happen to be at Chumley at the same time as Antonia. It was the murderer, more likely. "Where?"

"I went to close the curtains in this chamber—I was told doing so would protect the fabrics and furnishings from the sun's damage—and I saw a dark-haired man striding across the lawn, heading toward this wing. As I was unarmed, my first thought was that I just wanted to scare him off, so I opened the casement and yelled like bloody hell for him to get off my property."

Good lord, the fiend had been heading toward Antonia's room! Did he know which room was hers?

"Do you think it scared him off?" she asked as she rushed toward the window.

"It appeared to. He ran into the wood, but I have no way of knowing if he actually left Chumley or not."

"No night security at all?" Frederick asked, moving to stand behind Antonia as she peered out into the black night. He wasn't pleased at what he saw—or what he didn't see. Chumley had no outdoor lighting. The night's feeble moon glow only dimly illuminated the fountain in the center of the lawn.

Bessington shrugged. "I thought a sophisticated alarm system would serve my purposes and be a lot cheaper."

Frederick did not begrudge a single cent he spent on security at Siddley. He just hoped to God none of the guards ever were needed. "I wonder if he's armed." As he spoke, Frederick felt Antonia's heat as she moved closer to him and slipped her arm along his waist.

"Good question. Shall I ring the police now? Not that in this sparsely populated area we've anything more official than a mild-mannered constable."

By the time said mild-mannered constable arrived on the scene, Antonia could be dead.

"I think you and I had better investigate," Frederick said. "I suspect since he realizes you're on to him, he'll flee."

Bessington smiled. "Which wouldn't be a bad thing,"

Frederick would prefer to catch the bastard. He turned to face Antonia, taking both her hands in his and speaking gently. "I want you to stay in our room and not open the door to anyone."

"I want to come with you."

"You can help your boyfriend better by staying here," Bessington said. "In the event we need assistance from the constabulary, you'll be able to ring them for us."

She solemnly eyed Frederick. In those few seconds while their gazes were locked, he actually felt as if he *were* her boyfriend.

She finally nodded.

He moved to the corridor, then turned back to her. "You've got my mobile number?"

She nodded again.

"You hear or see anything suspicious, ring me immediately."

"Frederick?" She sounded morose.

"Yes?"

"Take care."

He was not unaffected by her concern. Nodding, he turned back into the corridor and closed the door.

When he and Bessington reached the stairway, he asked, "Do you have a weapon?"

"Good lord, no!"

"That's not entirely accurate. You've got a bloody arsenal in the armory."

"So I do—not that any of them are in working order."

"Our intruder needn't know that."

"Right-o." Bessington led the way through darkened corridors to the armory, where he turned on the light. "Fancy a sword?"

Only the gravity of the situation kept Frederick from laughing at the image of Bessington prancing around Chumley's gardens with sword in hand. "Let's get something close to a rifle, preferably one with gleaming metal that might reflect moonlight." It was then that he saw some ornamental daggers. "Perhaps we could each take a knife, too." He immediately thought of poor Ellerton with an antique dagger plunged into his chest.

"Good idea—on both accounts, old boy."

"Make it fast. I don't like leaving Antonia." He couldn't shake the feeling that the intruder was only interested in her.

Bessington extracted a huge ring of keys from his pocket and opened a case. He grabbed a musket and tossed it to Frederick. "This is the closest thing I've got to a rifle, old boy."

"Then it will have to do."

His cousin took out another, then grabbed a pair of knives that were sheathed in brittle leather cases. Frederick took his and shoved it in his trouser pocket. Now armed, the two men hurried from the room.

"Let's return to the lawn where you saw him," Frederick suggested. "You said he had dark hair. What of his age? Build?"

"It's bloody difficult to see in the darkness. I didn't really observe. I merely reacted. My impression is that he's of medium build and height and possibly about your age."

"What was he wearing?"

Bessington did not answer right away. "Trousers and jacket, both dark in color."

The better to blend into the night. It was a wonder Bessington had seen him at all.

"You truly believe Antonia's being stalked or something?"

"It's possible."

"And this didn't start until after that bloody bad business at Siddley? You know, she *is* a lovely young woman—"

"It didn't start until *after* my librarian was murdered." He hated to even say the word *murder* in context with Antonia.

"I'd better get a torch."

"Every time I go for mine, the damn batteries have run down."

"I've got rather a lot—because of the especially dark corridors we've got at Chumley." Bessington drew up at a sideboard and opened its drawer. There was a click, and then there was light.

Now the two men walked with purpose, quickly and almost with swaggers.

They were on the ground floor, striding toward a bank of windows that opened to Chumley's rear gardens. Such as they were.

One of those windows was a door. Bessington opened it, stepped out, and began to fan his torch slowly over the lawn, starting nearest to the house and working outward. Here, at the rear of the house, the lawn stretched for a couple of hundred yards before petering out into a copse of aged trees that looked milky in the faint moonlight. In the center of the lawn there was a raised rectangular fountain that apparently was not in working order.

"I say," Bessington called out, his voice loud enough to be heard in the next village, "I've rung the police; so, I'd advise you to get the hell off my property." He continued to direct the torch's light over the darkened landscape.

Uncharitably, Frederick thought of how badly his cousin's gardens needed to be restored. That was one thing on which Frederick and Bessington were in perfect agreement. "I suggest we examine the fountain," Frederick said. "It could hide a lurker."

"So it could." His cousin began to stride toward it.

Frederick whipped out his mobile and called Antonia. After three rings, she answered. Relief rushed over him. "Just checking to make sure you're all right."

"I'm fine. I'm standing at the window, watching you right now."

"Good. Stay there so I can see that you're OK." He terminated the call.

"You have a night watchman at Siddley?" Bessington asked.

"As of today, I have a whole crew of night watchmen."

"I'm utterly clueless, old boy. How many constitute a crew?"

"In our case, four."

"I'll be glad when Chumley's bringing in the kind of crowds you get at Siddley."

Frederick hated to tell Bessington that because of its lack of accessibility, Chumley would never attract as many tourists as Siddley. "We do have the advantage of being twenty miles from central London."

"There is that." Bessington drew up to the fountain and began to shine his light from left to right as both men stood in the eerie silence, prepared to defend themselves if the need should arise.

The water's surface was green from lack of circulation. How expensive could it be to get the damned thing fixed? This scum pond would surely repel visitors. If the now-headless nymph in the center hadn't already. Apparently, the nymph formerly spouted water from some orifice on its head—when the fountain had been in working order, that is.

While his cousin kept his torch directed at the fountain, Frederick began to circle its thirty-foot length.

Though he'd felt invincible when he'd held Antonia in his arms, he now was aware of his own mortality. What good would a useless musket be against a Glock? That is, if the perpetrator had a Glock. Which, of course, he had no way of knowing. Frederick kept one hand on the hilt of his knife.

When nothing dodgy was found, he didn't know whether to experience relief or anger. He really wanted this guy.

"Are you careful about locking all your exterior doors each night?" Frederick asked when he returned to Bessington.

"It's Williams's job to make sure all the doors are locked before he leaves for the night, and I do have an alarm system that makes a big ruckus if one of those doors is opened before the system's been disarmed."

"Good lord, how many exterior doors have you?" That had to be an awfully expensive system if each outside door was wired. These sprawling old homes could have dozens of doors.

Bessington began to stroll back toward the house, his gait casual. "I have no idea, actually. Not as many as Siddley Hall, I should suspect."

"Be glad Chumley's not as large as Siddley. The bigger the place, the higher the cost to maintain."

When they reached the old brick house, Frederick said, "Shall we take just one spin around the perimeter? Make sure everything's OK?"

"Yes, that will put our minds at ease."

Not really. The murderer was still out there. Maybe no longer at Chumley, but he was loose nonetheless. And he might be at Chumley. Thank God Frederick was keeping Antonia close. He could not shake the feeling that her life was in danger.

The side of the house was so dark it was menacing. The tall, gabled roof was situated so it obstructed what little moonlight there was, throwing this whole patch of neglected grass into near total darkness. Frederick was grateful when Bessington took out his torch to light their way.

He would discount nothing from potentially hiding the prowler. He checked behind every shrub, looked behind a single, well-weathered bench, and even walked some thirty yards to examine behind a huge, spreading oak whose trunk was the size of a small car.

Because there was no sign of the intruder, Frederick was dissatisfied. Yet he was thankful that Antonia was unharmed. Or was she?

His heart hammering with fear, he hurried around the home's perimeter. He needed to get back to her.

As he and Bessington reentered the house, he watched as the other man locked the entry door. "I'm worried about Antonia," Frederick said. "Can you show me the way? I'm hopeless at finding our room through your labyrinth of corridors."

"Just follow me and my trusty torch."

In a few minutes Frederick found himself opening the door to their now-darkened room. She had turned off the overhead lights, and a soft glow from the beside lamp provided the room's only illumination. Antonia was slumped on a chaise that had been pulled up against the tall casement.

She was deadly still.

CHAPTER 14

His heartbeat roaring, he stood frozen with fear for several seconds. She was so incredibly still. Was she dead? He couldn't see if her chest was rising and falling without getting closer.

But he was paralyzed by fear.

He tried to assure himself that nothing was wrong with her. His worried gaze studied Antonia's profile as half her face flattened against the chaise's upholstered top. He drew in his breath as he watched her. She was just as beautiful in repose. The thick fringe of her lashes brushed the skin beneath her eyes.

What lovely skin it was, the creamy caramel of those with Mediterranean ancestry. Even her straight nose was perfection. Not too small, nor too large.

As if an alarm bleat had gone off, he rushed to her, suddenly cognizant that she might need him. What if she needed medical attention? Every second could count. He came to settle a hand on her slender arm, gently grasping it. Thank God it was warm. Her lids fluttered ever so slightly.

She was in a deep, alcohol-induced sleep. His normal heart rhythm was restored.

He couldn't let her sleep there all night. Already it was getting chilly by the window. "Antonia?" He squeezed her arm, but she didn't move. Dropping to his knees, he began to remove her boots. Then he went to the bed and pulled back the faded silk spread before returning to scoop her into his arms. She wasn't as heavy as he'd expected someone of her height to be. In fact, she felt almost delicately frail, almost as delicate as her light lavender scent.

There wasn't even the slightest flutter of lash when he placed her on the crispy white sheets. She merely rolled to her side and continued in a deep sleep. He stood there for several moments, drinking in her remarkable beauty and rather marveling that she was just as smart as she was pretty.

His glance moved to the other side of the bed. Where he would sleep. He crossed the room to get his bag, took it to the loo, and changed into his pajamas before heading to bed. This would be a first for him: the first time he'd chastely shared a bed with a woman. He closed the draperies, turned off the bedside lamp, and climbed up on the bed.

In total darkness, he lay there beside her lavender-scented body and was oddly reassured by the steady rhythm of her breathing.

The following morning Antonia awakened first. She was mortified to discover that she was lying beside Lord Hunkness wearing her jeans from the day before and a very wrinkled blouse. *Oh my God! I passed out.*

Incredibly humiliated, she took one long, longing look at Frederick slumbering in his plaid pajamas before she stole away from the too-soft bed. She snatched her suitcase and went to the bathroom. For the next half hour she showered, shampooed, did a blow-dry job on her hair, applied makeup, and dressed in fresh clothing that consisted of another pair of jeans and a clingy, long-sleeved tee.

When she emerged from the bathroom, she watched as Frederick bent over, restoring his neatly folded pajamas to his bag. He must have changed into his jeans and a fresh button-down shirt when her shower was running. He turned around and smiled at her.

Even with a day's growth of beard—which she normally did not like on a man—he was really, really good-looking. The stubble was darker than the tousled blondish hair on his head. "Good morning," he said, a kind of familiar affection in his cultured, veddy, veddy upper-class voice.

"I. Am. So. Embarrassed. Tell me you didn't have to remove my boots."

His deep grin pinched at his lean cheeks. "I didn't *have* to remove them, but I thought you'd be more comfortable."

She rolled her eyes. "As if I'd know anything. I was plastered."

"No harm done. You weren't driving or anything."

"You can't accuse me of not exercising full disclosure. I did inform you and Richard that I didn't handle wine very well." She suddenly thought of something. Her head tilted toward him, she warily eyed him for a moment. She clearly remembered being smoochy kootchy with him, and him telling her the wine was "talking." How humiliating! No way was she going to bring up that. She'd humiliated herself enough already.

Regarding him somberly, she lowered her voice and said, "Thanks for being a gentleman."

He shrugged, then glanced at the clock on the mantel. "Bessington will no doubt have outdone himself to prepare us a dazzling breakfast. Give me a few minutes to shave and brush my teeth, then we'll go to kitchen."

"Monlief opens in forty-five minutes. I'd hoped to make the opening. Simon's supposed to be there."

"We may be able to make it."

During the reign of Charles II, Monlief's Tudor edifice had been pulled down, and an impressive baroque structure replaced it. As they approached it via a long, winding gravel drive, the morning sun cast a glow, making the building's Portland stone golden. As at Chumley, sheep grazed in the sweeping meadows that fronted the magnificent building.

Its chief feature was a central rotunda from which the house's wings fanned out. Back in March she had spent a couple of weeks researching there and had found the librarian, a Mr. Bly, most helpful. But she'd never met the present marquess. She turned to Frederick, whose gaze was locked on the road ahead. "I suppose you're acquainted with the Marquess of Granworth."

"Actually, I've never met him. I believe he's a great deal older than my parents."

"He may be dotty."

"He must be in his eighties."

"I won't tell you the year of his birth so I won't be accused of having that photographic memory you incorrectly attribute to me."

"Is his wife still alive?"

"The marquess is a bachelor."

"Has he ever been married?"

"According to *Debrett's*, no."

A moment later, she said, "I am afraid that when Simon and I are busy doing research, it will be as interesting to you as going to a fabric store—which my daddy says is the most boring thing on the planet."

Frederick pulled into a space in the car park. There were already more than twenty cars there. "I can't say that I've ever been in a fabric store, but I think your father must be a very wise man."

"I can never think of *wise man* without thinking of Stephen Hawking. Did you see that *Vicar of Dibley* Christmas episode where the elderly gent was talking sort of spastic, and the vicar asked him why?"

Frederick started chuckling as he nodded. "Because he was supposed to be one of the three wise men in the Christmas play, and Hawking was the wisest man he could think of."

"Cool. You and I watch the same programming."

"That's just one show."

"You like Ken Burns, too, don't you?"

"OK. Two."

"That makes two for two."

He turned off the engine and faced her, his eyes narrow. "I see your professor's already here." His glance went to Simon's red-and-white Mini Cooper. She could not understand why Frederick seemed to dislike Simon so. This week especially, Simon had been such a considerate dear.

There wasn't a curator at any stately home in England who wasn't acquainted with Simon, and Monlief was no exception. In fact, Mr. Bly had studied history with Simon when they were undergraduates. She expected the two were visiting with one another right now.

She and Frederick got out of the car, and she collected her laptop. "It will please you to know I've also brought along my flash drive."

"Good." They walked toward the front of Monlief. "So are the archives in the basement here, too?" he asked.

"Yes. Now that you mention it, all the ones I've been in are located in basements. Is that some kind of rule?"

"Not that I know of. I expect it's because the upstairs rooms are more coveted by residents and tourists, and boxes of old papers can be put anywhere."

"It's probably best that those irreplaceable old papers not be exposed to sunlight."

"Which reminds me of Bessington last night. Didn't you think it a bit odd that at midnight he was closing the curtains in the room next to us?"

"I did. It wasn't like the sun was doing any damage then, and it was a weird thing for an earl to be doing. It just didn't seem like a guy thing."

"I assure you," Frederick said, "Bessington is not gay."

"Oh, I didn't mean it that way. I just thought it…odd."

There was a queue of about a dozen tourists in front of the home's main entrance.

"Do you know what time the next tour starts?" he asked.

"Yeah, I was just checking the website on my phone. Monlief has tours beginning every thirty minutes."

He looked at his watch. "So the next is at ten?"

"Yep."

They circled around to the back of the house. It was then that she realized how similar the stairwell to the basement here was to the one that led to Mr. Ellerton's office. As they began to descend, she once again experienced that foggy sensation she'd had the day of the murder. Something then had struck her as significant, but her memory was incapable of retrieving it.

The shock of seeing poor Mr. Ellerton's dead body had prevented her from processing anything intelligently. When the thought first crossed her mind, it had left her confused. She couldn't shake the feeling there was something in the exterior stairwell that was vital to unraveling the murder, some clue she was overlooking.

If only she could remember.

She and Frederick descended the stairwell and soon came to Mr. Bly's office. The door was open, and he and Simon were talking. They looked up and smiled at her. Simon barely nodded at Frederick and mumbled something that sounded vaguely like *Rockford* before rushing to her. "How are you this morning? Any more break-ins?"

She shrugged. "No break-ins, but a prowler."

Simon's brows lowered, and he glared at Frederick. "Did you do anything about it?"

"Bessington and I searched the grounds, but we didn't find anything. Under the circumstances," Frederick said, a devilish glint in his eyes as he flashed Simon a wicked smile, "I couldn't possibly leave Antonia alone the rest of the night."

Simon glared back. "No, of course you couldn't." Simon's voice lacked its usual stridency.

"Before you get the wrong idea, Simon," Antonia said, "I have to confess that I was no company for anyone. I crashed after drinking too much wine, so even if I did spend the night in the same room with this guy, nothing whatsoever happened."

Simon looked relieved.

"If my cousin had lived close to a proper municipality, I'd have called the police, but he assured us the local constable was neither particularly close nor was he particularly efficient." Frederick pulled his cell phone from his pocket. "I'm going to ring Detective Chief Inspector Patel right now and let him know about it."

"Did you see the prowler?" Simon asked Antonia.

She looked at Frederick. "No. Did Richard tell you what the fellow looked like?"

Frederick looked up from his cell phone and nodded. "He said his hair was dark, and he was of medium height and build and probably close in age to me."

"Does that sound like anyone you know?" Simon asked her.

"I know very few people in the UK, but that description's pretty generic." She noticed Mr. Bly eyeing Frederick quizzically. "I'd like to introduce you to the Earl of Rockford."

Frederick and the curator shook hands and exchanged greetings, then Frederick stepped away and began scrolling on his cell phone screen.

"You're in luck, Antonia," Simon said. "Alfred has kept a record of every box you looked at when you were here in March."

She smiled at Alfred Bly and at Simon. "That is good news. It should save us a lot of unnecessary work."

"How long do you expect to be here this time?" Mr. Bly asked her.

"Not as long as before. I'm hoping to finish in a couple of days."

"I shall be happy to help in any way possible." The curator lowered his voice to a respectful level. "I was sorry to read in the newspaper that you were the one to discover poor Ellerton's body. What a horrible shock it must have been."

"It was awful."

"Do they have a motive? Or a suspect?" Bly asked.

She shrugged. "All I know for sure is that as of last night, they had no suspect." For some reason, she didn't like discussing the monstrance with anyone else.

She and Simon got the keys from Mr. Bly, and they went to start looking through boxes.

"Are you still with Antonia Townley?" Patel asked Frederick.

Frederick held the phone close, even though he wasn't in the same room with Antonia now that she'd headed to her work area. "Yes, I am."

"I may have to bring her in for further questioning. Has it occurred to you she could have ransacked her own flat?"

Frederick felt as if his blood were boiling. "I was with her the night she discovered it. The girl was almost hysterical. She shook with fear."

"It seems quite a coincidence. Her office and Ellerton's office ransacked the same night she's sleeping at Siddley Hall. She wouldn't have even needed a key. All she had to do was stroll down a few corridors."

"That's ridiculous!"

"You saw the dead man's blood on her hands. She *was* the last person to see him alive. She *claims* to have discovered his body, but the fact remains that I have an eyewitness who saw her standing over Ellerton's body, holding the dagger—which has now been determined to be the murder weapon."

"That's bullshit." Frederick was quite certain he hadn't used that word since he'd been a twelve-year-old lad at Eton. From the day of his father's death, Frederick—as head of the family and its main representative—had striven to always comport himself as a gentleman. He'd certainly blown his image with that damned DCI.

"She's a real lightweight," Frederick said. "No way could she overpower Ralph Ellerton—or even have the strength to drive that dagger into a man's chest. It wasn't a particularly sharp instrument. It would have required brute strength."

"I'm just telling you, if there's no break in this monstrance theory by Wednesday, I'm going to bring her in."

That gave them just three days. No way could they even get to the other two houses and reproduce her research in so short a time. "Come on, Patel. Give us a chance to duplicate her research, see if we can attempt to track the monstrance. Antonia Townley's the only person who can do that."

"Assuming there is a monstrance."

"I'm inclined to believe in its existence."

"A word of advice, Rockford. Don't put too much trust in a pretty face."

So the DCI *had* noticed Antonia's beauty. The guy really was a Hard Ass. "It will take her a few weeks at least to attempt to duplicate her research."

"I'll give her a week." Patel disconnected.

Damned pain in the ass.

A moment later Frederick joined Antonia and Simon, each of them standing over separate desks, their heads bent, as they examined the boxes of opaque envelopes stuffed with museum-worthy papers. "I'm yours to direct," Frederick said.

"Why don't you trot along and visit with the lord of the manor and leave this to us experts?" Simon said.

"Simon!" Antonia admonished. "Frederick is perfectly capable of assisting us, and I for one welcome his help." She scooted her box over and pointed to a row of boxes on some industrial-looking shelves lined against the wall. "Why don't you go get that box, number seven one three, and come here. I'll tell you what we're looking for."

Frederick's hands were balled into fists, fists he'd enjoy crashing into that damned Simon's bespectacled face. For Antonia's sake, though, Frederick ignored Simon's obnoxiousness.

Their search was narrowed to correspondence that had occurred among members of the five Catholic families in the years between 1530 and 1550. Fortunately, dates had previously been assigned to each box as well as to each of the acid-free envelopes within the boxes. Whenever he found a letter that fit her parameters, he gave it to her—as did Simon. Within twenty minutes, she had enough to start copying the contents of the letters onto her laptop as Frederick and Simon continued to search for additional correspondence.

Frederick was glad when noon came and they could break for lunch. Stooping over those boxes was hard on the back.

Unfortunately, he'd have to suffer Simon's company at lunch.

"The tea shop here at Monlief's pretty good," she told them. "Shall we ask Mr. Bly?"

"I asked him to lunch with us this morning," Simon said, "but he's meeting with Lord Granworth."

As they neared Bly's office, Bly called out, "I say, Lord Granworth has extended an invitation for you all to join him for lunch in his private dining chamber."

"How nice," Antonia said. She smiled up at Frederick. "Three lords and three stately homes in three days. How cool is that?"

As they followed Mr. Bly up the stairs to the ground floor, Simon came close to her and said, "I've heard Lord Granworth is… eccentric."

"In what way?"

Simon shrugged. "Not sure. I've just heard he's not what one expects."

"The main house at Monlief," Mr. Bly said, "is public rooms. These are left in pristine condition for tours and for special events like weddings."

"Does Monlief have a family wing?" Frederick asked.

"Yes, it's a separate wing that was added in the early nineteenth century."

As soon as Bly opened the door into the family wing, Frederick was taken aback. The stench! He'd be damned if it wasn't a combination of cigarettes and dog urine, neither of which he fancied under any circumstances.

The curator led them into what would have been a very impressive drawing room. Because of his own collections and because of his degree in art history, Frederick readily identified some genuine Chippendale pieces and a Romney portrait. Any Persian carpets that might once have covered the marble floors had been removed.

And Frederick readily understood why.

"Hello," their host greeted them as they walked into the room. A corgi wearing a bow tie napping on his lap, the elderly peer sat on a Louis XVI settee, one of a pair placed near the elegant chimneypiece. A blanket had been flung over the sofa's damaged silk. "Won't you all sit across from me? Except Bly can sit by me. I apologize for the blankets, but in my private chambers, my puppies have free rein."

Frederick's gaze swept around the room, and he counted no less than six ornate doggie beds in which velvets and gilt had not been spared. Like the dogs themselves, some of the beds were large, some small.

"Which of you is the researcher?" Lord Granworth asked. The aging peer looked every day of eighty with his cotton-ball hair, frail frame, and heavily wrinkled face. He wore a brown pullover V-neck sweater paired with tweed trousers. The index finger yellowed from years of cigarette use made Frederick question every word he'd ever heard about the health risks of smoking.

"I am," Antonia said. "Thank you for opening up your family archives to me."

"I'm very proud of the Montague family's history. Before I die, I want to do a book on my illustrious ancestors. I'll need someone like you to help."

"It sounds interesting," Antonia said. "I shall have to get back with you after I finish my dissertation. Whenever that may be. You might be interested to know that your family is one of the five I'm writing about."

"I'll wager you're writing about the first marquess! Now that was an interesting man—"

"Actually, my research is limited to a much earlier period: around the reign of Henry VIII."

"Yes, the first marquess was a colorful man. He had thirty-eight illegitimate children and ten legitimate ones—including my great-great-great-great-grandfather." He paused and lit a cigarette. "I hope my smoking doesn't bother you, but my doctor assures me that because the ceilings are so high, the smoke quickly dissipates without hurting anyone's lungs. Except for mine," he said with a laugh.

All the visitors' heads tilted back as they peered at painted ceilings that were twenty feet above them. Too bad the smell didn't dissipate, too.

Behind them, one of the larger dogs—a Lab—growled as it came close to Simon. Frederick smiled. He always had favored larger dogs. This one must be quite clever.

"No, no, Mr. Cuddles," Lord Granworth admonished, his voice as if he were talking to a baby, "that's no way to treat a guest. Come to Daddy."

It was as if the creature understood Granworth. Mr. Cuddles directed one last growl at Simon, then pranced over to his "daddy" and jumped into his lap, sharing space with the corgi he'd just awakened.

"Your lordship," Mr. Bly said, "I'd like to introduce you to our other visitors. We've got the Earl of Rockford," he indicated Frederick, who nodded, "and Dr. Steele from Oxford." Simon nodded.

"Rockford? Is that the Percy family?"

"Yes," Frederick said.

"Of Siddley Hall?"

Frederick nodded again. "Yes."

Granworth stubbed out his cigarette in an already overcrowded ashtray and turned to Bly. "Wasn't there something on the news about Siddley recently?"

Bly shook his head morosely. "Terrible business. Very shocking. The librarian was murdered."

Granworth whirled to Frederick. "You didn't kill him, did you?"

Frederick could see Simon smirk, and he'd like nothing better than to wipe that smirk off his face. "Of course not! I was excessively fond of him."

"Who else would have reason to kill that kind of fellow?" Granworth asked, shrugging in dismay. "Have they caught the murderer?" Mr. Cuddles began to lick the marquess's face, and his "daddy" kissed him in return.

Frederick was quickly losing his appetite. "No arrests yet. I just spoke to the DCI on the case." He was not about to repeat that Patel's number-one suspect was Antonia. Damned fool inspector.

"I hope I don't bore you, but I'd like to show you visitors a few of my personal treasures." Granworth kissed Mr. Cuddles and put him on the floor, then rose, holding the corgi.

The others stood and followed their host. Just as Frederick was getting accustomed to a dog wearing a bow tie, he spied a sleeping poodle wearing a hot-pink sweater. Perhaps Granworth *was* in his dotage.

Lord Granworth led them into the family dining room, where beef sandwiches and pots of tea awaited at five place settings. He came to stand in front of an elegant sideboard draped in tapestry and holding a single object: a large gold tankard. "This is Charles II's personal tankard. I daresay it's nearly as valuable as the Percy family's lost monstrance."

Frederick was astonished. How was it that Frederick's own family—the family that had owned the monstrance—hadn't known it was lost, and this man did? "When, may I ask," Frederick said, rather icily, "did you hear of the Percys' monstrance?" Frederick's first instinct was that the murderer had spoken with him. Recently.

"I can answer that," Bly said. "Lord Granworth likes to be apprised of bits of family history I discover among the family's papers. I recently came across a reference to the monstrance and told him of it."

Antonia whirled on the curator. "Why didn't you tell me about it? You knew I was particularly studying those five families and especially interested in any Catholic references." She sounded mad. Restrained, but mad, nonetheless.

Bly's brows lowered. "I must not have discovered it until after you'd gone."

"I wished you'd have at least e-mailed me about it. How could you have not known I'd be interested in anything relating to their Catholicism?"

"So you were," Bly said, shrugging. "I did speak with Ralph Ellerton about it."

Frederick and Antonia eyed each other. As far as Frederick was concerned, they had another suspect. Or pair of suspects.

"First thing after lunch," Antonia said, "I'd like to see the reference to the monstrance."

"I'll see if I can't find it," Bly said.

Just as they were to sit at the table to partake of lunch, a tinkling sound, like soft running water, was heard. Frederick turned his head just in time to see a Yorkshire terrier, leg lifted, wet the floor less than a foot away from Simon. Uncharitably, Frederick wished the dog had lifted his leg next to Simon's trousers.

Frederick's punishment for such mean thoughts was that not a thing was done to clean the floor, and Frederick had to attempt to eat lunch just feet away from the dog's puddle.

"You are eating on one of the greatest prides of the Montague family," Lord Granworth said. "This china, which you can see is in excellent condition, was especially made for the Montagues by Josiah Wedgwood. It was said the Montagues helped make him the most famous potter in the kingdom."

Frederick looked down at the rich, apple-green plate. It was quite remarkable that the gilt edges were still in such outstanding condition. He pushed aside his sandwich to see the hand-painted bouquet in the center. The pinks and purples were still vivid. "Lovely."

"It's beautiful," Antonia said, smiling at their host. "Look, Frederick's flowers are different than mine."

"Yes," Lord Granworth said, smiling. "Each one is different."

"Since your family was so supportive of Josiah Wedgwood," Antonia said, "I'm surprised to see so many Sèvres pieces in your family chambers."

Frederick gawked at her. "How could you possibly know so much about French and English potters?"

She shrugged. "My father indulged my interest in European porcelain and allowed me to study at Sotheby's for a bit."

Frederick addressed the marquess. "Miss Townley's a veritable fount of knowledge on nearly every subject."

Antonia went to protest, but their host silenced her. "Back to your original question, Miss Townley, it's my impression that the Sèvres pieces were acquired at a later period," Lord Granworth said. "In fact, one of the Granworth brides brought several pieces with her when she married. She was French." He said that with distaste.

Midway through lunch, Granworth faced Frederick. "I believe our families are soon to be joined."

Frederick set down the small pot from which he'd been pouring tea. "Is that so? Enlighten me, please."

"Why, you're to marry my grandniece's daughter, Lady Caroline."

Frederick's brows lowered. "Who could have told you such a thing?"

"Lady Caroline herself, when she visited here yesterday."

What in the hell was Caro doing? She must have come here directly from Siddley. It couldn't have been a planned visit, because she had first wanted to spend the day at Siddley.

His stomach plummeted. He had known that his activities and possibly even his conversations had been under surveillance. Dear God, Caro couldn't be the one!

Could she?

EPISODE 6

CHAPTER 15

Antonia was as anxious as Frederick was to finish lunch. Though they had known each other but a short time, he was learning how to read her body language, to gauge the little nuances in her voice. Not only those things, he had come to know how her mind worked, and right now he was certain she was impatient to see that letter that mentioned the monstrance.

As curious as he was to see the letter, he had a more pressing need. He had to speak to Caroline. And that could not be handled over the phone.

Between the dog puddle practically at his feet and the smell of cigarette smoke clinging to him, Frederick had lost his appetite, but he did not want to appear rude by not eating his sandwich. Every time the marquess was engaged in conversation with someone else, Frederick would break off a chunk of his sandwich and dangle it below the table. Each bite was promptly snapped up by a well-fed canine member of Lord Granworth's household.

At the conclusion of the meal, he excused himself. "I thank you very much, Lord Granworth, for your hospitality. It's been a pleasure meeting you, but I have pressing business which calls me away." Then he eyed Antonia. "May I have a word, Antonia?"

She whipped the napkin off her lap, set it on the table, and rose, facing their host. "It truly has been a pleasure, your lordship."

"The pleasure was mine." Granworth looked down to the corgi in his lap. "Wasn't it our pleasure, Missie Sweet Pea?"

The dog answered with a succession of polite-sounding barks. Crazy the marquess might be, but he just might have the ability to communicate with his four-legged family.

Frederick and Antonia quickly found the door that led out into Monlief's neat parterre garden. She went to the end of the pavement and stopped dead, whirling around to face him. This time he could tell from her body language that she was not happy with him. Had he misread her expressions? Had she actually wished to stay in that glorified dog kennel?

"I wanted to let you know I'm going to have to leave you here at Monlief for a few hours," he said. "I have an important meeting I'd forgotten."

"You don't need to concern yourself with me." Her voice was icy, and if possible, she stiffened even more. "Simon's here with me."

"I *am* concerned. I feel responsible for all that's happened to you."

She glared. "Don't." She spun around and started for the west end of the house.

He reached out and snagged her arm. "You're not to go off by yourself. For God's sake, Antonia, someone may be trying to kill you!"

That got her attention. Her haughtiness collapsed.

His voice softened. "I plan to register at the hotel in Winton so we'll be close to Monlief to continue your research. I shall collect you at five."

She wrenched herself away from his grasp. "That won't be necessary. I can take care of myself."

"No, you can't. If it weren't for me, Patel would have arrested you by now."

She froze, her eyes widened.

"And if you're not more careful about that pretty neck, I just might let him. Better jail than to end up like Ellerton."

She swallowed.

"I'll be back by closing," he said. "Then I won't be letting you out of my sight."

Simon and Bly exited the family wing and began to stroll toward Frederick and Antonia. She turned her back on Frederick and went to the two other men.

Once he reached his car, he took out his phone and scrolled to *Brat*, his longtime moniker for Caroline. The trick was not to let her know how mad he was. What woman would agree to an assignation with a furious man?

"Hello, Rockford." Her voice was light and honeyed. "How are you?"

"I need to see you this afternoon."

"I don't see how I can manage that. It's my hair day."

"Manage it, Brat."

"You sound so ominous."

"Where are you?"

"At Carstairs."

He mentally calculated how long it would take him to reach her family home and knew he wouldn't be able to drive so long a distance and be back before Monlief closed, forcing Antonia to leave with Simon.

And Frederick couldn't have that. "I'll need you to meet me in Wetting." That seemed about halfway between their two locations.

"Where in Wetting?"

Hell if he knew. As a huge commuter feeder to London, Wetting possessed one of the larger train stations. "What about the rail station?" They could grab a cup of tea or coffee before he verbally attacked her.

"When?" Her voice had turned icy.

"Leave as soon as possible."

"Very well, but I still think you sound ominous."

"Hopefully we can put all our cards on the table when we meet. Cheers." He terminated the call.

Before he started the car, he rang Antonia. She answered on the third ring. "Quick question," he said. "In your study of the suspected Catholic families, did you come across any research that the Hinckley family had any Catholic sympathizers?"

"Hinckley?" she muttered as if she were thinking aloud. "Possibly...I uncovered no correspondence about Catholicism, but one of the early Hinckley wives was a younger daughter of Sir Percy."

He had forgotten about the distant relationship between his family and Caro's. "Right-o. I knew I could count on your photographic memory. Cheers." He cut off her protests by ending the call.

How could she feel so much like her heart was breaking when he'd never even kissed her? She'd been an idiot to allow herself to mistake his gentlemanly concern for romantic affection. He had never given Antonia any reason to suspect his feelings for her were anything but platonic. Sure, he'd said she was pretty. But that didn't count. Everyone said she was pretty.

And he had said he was *glad* that once. The two-timing hunk of irresistibility.

She hadn't known him long, but she was pretty sure Frederick wasn't the kind of guy who'd be fooling around with another woman if he were engaged.

That pretty much explained why he hadn't taken Antonia up on her smoochy kootchy offers. He *was* a gentleman.

Of course he belonged with Range Rover Girl. Antonia from Silicon Valley had no place in the life of an English earl. But why in the heck did that English earl have to be so darned appealing?

Her aching heart swelled with memories of how tender he'd been to her the two previous nights and with memories of how good it had felt to be held in his arms.

Now she totally understood that Frederick and Lady Caroline Hinckley were pledged to one another. Even if Frederick had acted a bit miffed at the luncheon table when Lord Granworth revealed his betrothal.

Frederick's irritated response was downright puzzling. She just couldn't get a read on him where Lady Caroline was concerned.

As she descended the stairs to Monlief's basement archives, she realized she was incapable of getting a read on her own emotions. She was torn between never wanting to see Frederick again and wanting to travel back in time to the past few nights to relive each tender moment together.

Thank God Simon and Mr. Bly were deep in conversation, because she couldn't have contributed a single syllable to it, not when all she could think of was Frederick and Range Rover Girl.

But once she was back in the basement, her thoughts flew to the source of the reference to the monstrance. She waited for a break in the men's conversation and tapped Mr. Bly on the shoulder.

He faced her, a brow raised in query.

"I am most anxious, Mr. Bly, to read that reference to the Percy Monstrance."

"I wish I'd written down exactly where I found it." Brows lowered, he shuffled to his desk and started poking around in the mounds of papers stacked there. "Wish I could remember what day it was that I found it."

"Surely you remember who wrote it!" It was impossible to keep the outrage she felt from creeping into her voice. She had always been forthright with Mr. Bly about the topic of her research. How could he not have shared that particular correspondence with her?

He drew in a breath. Clearly, he was not happy with her.

Simon came up to the curator's desk. "I have to say, Harold, I'm disappointed you didn't share it with me, either."

"I never thought it was significant."

Antonia's eyes narrowed, and that same anger edged into her voice. "You thought it significant enough to share with Lord Granworth."

"I apologize to both of you," Mr. Bly said impatiently. "I'd completely forgotten about Miss Townley's interest in the Catholic connections." An embarrassed look on his face, he shook his head and added, "I must admit that I had to look monstrance up. I wasn't sure what one was."

Simon shrugged. "That's perfectly understandable. It's not that commonly used a word in England these past five hundred years."

Mr. Bly continued to search on his desk.

Antonia was convinced Mr. Bly was lying. Though it was difficult to understand that everyone was not possessed of a memory as keen as her own, she could not believe that he had forgotten who wrote the reference to the monstrance.

Maybe if he'd read it last year, his memory lapse would be understandable, but he'd read it sometime in the past eight weeks. A man did not get in the position he was in if his memory capacity was that skimpy. At the minimum, he had to have earned a master's degree, but most of these librarians held doctorates.

What possible motive could he have for lying? Fear strummed through her entire body. The only reason she could think of was that he was in cahoots with the murderer. Her limbs began to tremble.

She suddenly wished Frederick hadn't gone.

Why was it he was the only person she really trusted? She watched Simon as he thumbed through the papers on Mr. Bly's desk. "I hope you don't mind, old chap, if I help you look?"

"I welcome your help."

As did she. She was awfully glad Simon was here. But she'd rather have Frederick. Even if he did belong to Range Rover Girl. Uncharitably, Antonia wished an incurable case of rosacea on Lady Caroline's china-doll complexion.

"I'll be back in my little office." She headed down the corridor. During her two weeks there in March, she'd thought the place pleasant enough. But not now. This dimly lit hallway was menacing. She kept remembering the horror of finding Mr. Ellerton's body, kept imagining the murderer was lurking here.

Or was she imagining?

He didn't see her Range Rover in the car park at the rail station. Knowing Caro, she hadn't left right away. She would never leave the house unless she looked runway ready.

At the rail station's eatery, he got each of them tea and went to stake out a table. Sitting there awaiting her, he tried to make sense of everything. Caroline *had* been at his desk just before Antonia's flash drive was erased. She must have done it. But why?

What could she possibly hope to gain? She couldn't need money. The Hinckleys were seriously rich. Of course, they'd all lost pots of money on the exchange in the past few years.

And why in the hell had she gone to Monlief yesterday? It was too much of a coincidence that she visited just ahead of his and Antonia's visit.

If she *were* guilty of electronically spying on their Siddley goings-on, she might have tried to get there first in the hopes of finding the information the killer was so hell-bent on obtaining. But Frederick knew for a fact Caro did not possess Antonia's skill at archival research.

Nor did she possess skill in electronic surveillance. If she were involved in any of these nefarious goings-on, she had to be working with someone else. Someone like the killer.

But, hell, he'd known her all his life. He thought he knew just about everyone she knew. He tried to think of anyone she was especially close to. Caroline had never had a lot of girlfriends. She preferred male company, and for the past several years she had not tried to conceal that the male she most wanted was Frederick.

She wasn't particularly close to either of her siblings—from whom Frederick had stolen their pet name for their sister: *Brat.* Her two elder brothers were many, many years her senior. She had always been a huge daddy's girl. He spoiled her enormously. And there was nothing she wouldn't do for him.

Could that be it? Had her father put her up to these activities?

No way, though, could Frederick believe Caro guilty of any of this crap. Just running through these scenarios in his mind made him feel guilty.

None of it made any sense. What possible motivation could she have?

It didn't make sense, either, that she'd tell Lord Granworth she and Frederick were going to marry. What could she possibly hope to gain by that?

From the window he could see her elegant gait as she approached the rail station's lobby. Her silvery-blonde hair was down today, and she looked much more feminine than she had the day before. A thin periwinkle-blue scarf the color of her eyes swathed her neck. In fact, from her jeans to her oxford cloth shirt, she was all in blue.

Her long legs reminded him of Antonia. Which caused him to examine his watch. He was determined to return to Monlief before closing. He couldn't entrust Antonia's safety to anyone else.

When Caroline saw him, she smiled and walked straight to the table. "You've gotten me tea. How lovely of you." She sat down and faced him. "Now you simply must tell me why you're sounding so ominous."

"After you tell me why you told the Marquess of Granworth that we were getting married."

Her pretty face flushed. "How humiliating for me that you found out. I thought my poor great-great-uncle just toshy enough that he'd neither remember what I said nor repeat it. Grants—that's what we call the marquess—is from an era that believes any single woman past the age of consent is to be pitied as a hopeless spinster. I merely made up our betrothal to keep him from treating me like I had leprosy."

"And so you honored me?"

She shrugged. "I thought because you're an earl, it would make him proud. I've always been one of his favorites, likely because I adore dogs, too. I honestly didn't think he'd remember. He's ancient, you know."

"Yes, I know." He could understand why she thought Granworth might not remember things. The old marquess did appear to be in his dotage. "You know, Caro, I hold you in great affection, but at this time I hold a greater aversion to marriage."

She laughed. It sounded hollow and as sincere as a mortician. "I assure you, I'm not ready to give up my freedom, either. But if I *were* interested in marrying, which I truly am not, you would be at the top of my list of prospective husbands."

He settled his hand over hers. "I feel the same."

Their eyes locked, but it made him feel uncomfortable. Especially because of what he had to say next.

"Is my silly little prevarication the reason you wanted us to meet here?" she asked, looking up at him with those remarkable pale-blue eyes.

"No, Brat, there's something else." He cleared his throat. "Why did you erase the flash drive on the computer in my office?"

Her mouth gaped open, and she was speechless for a moment as his words sank in. "I most certainly did *not* erase your flash drive!" Her voice shook with fury. "I wouldn't even know how to go about it. You know I'm hopeless with electronics." Her eyes became watery. "Why would you accuse me of doing such a thing?"

"Because you were at my desk close to the time the deed was done. And a couple of other things you did seemed suspicious."

She dabbed at a fallen tear with her bare hand. "I can't believe you're abusing me like this."

Not the tears! He couldn't stand to see a woman cry. Especially when he was responsible. He covered her hand again. "I'm sorry, Caro. Truly I am. It's just that things at Siddley have been beastly since the murder. I'm not myself."

"You're being beastly."

"And I'm not finished being beastly. I've got to ask you one more question."

She raised a single, perfectly shaped brow.

"Why did you go to Monlief yesterday?"

Her eyes rounded, and it was a moment before she answered. "Because you asked me to meet you there!"

CHAPTER 16

"What in the hell are you talking about?"

"I'm talking about that e-mail you sent me, telling me to meet you at Monlief!"

"I didn't send you an e-mail!"

Hands shaking, she began to fumble in her purse, which was another of those big leather bags like Antonia carried. She yanked out her phone and began to scroll. "Right here."

"Come on, Caro. When have I ever e-mailed you?" He took the phone.

"I know you usually text, but I thought if you were at your desk, it made perfect sense that you'd rather send an e-mail."

He looked at the screen on her mobile. Good lord, there *was* an e-mail to her, sent from his server, his e-mail address.

Sorry you had to leave Siddley so abruptly. Can you meet me at Monlief later this afternoon? I'll make up for your aborted visit. Rockford.

Then it occurred to him she could have sent it to herself when she was sitting at his desk, so he checked the time it was sent. Two hours *after* she left Siddley.

"I did *not* send this to you." Now the murderer was boldly using Frederick's computer. Was he playing a cat-and-mouse game with Frederick? Everyone knew Frederick and Caro were close. Many expected they would marry. Was this the killer's way of trying to scare him off? By putting Caroline at risk?

Wonderful. Now he had to worry about two women whose lives were in jeopardy.

"So why didn't you just ring me?" he asked.

"I was about to when you didn't show up at Monlief, but then I got the second e-mail from you."

He shook his head, his eyes flashing with anger. "I did *not* send any e-mails to you."

He scrolled down to the next message.

Sorry to stand you up. Pressing business. I'm on my knees begging your forgiveness. Rockford.

"You really didn't e-mail me?" Her voice sounded almost childlike.

"I did not."

"I should have realized it wasn't from you when you—in the e-mail—didn't refer to me as *Brat*. Why would someone play so cruel a prank on us?"

"I have a pretty good idea, but I'm not at liberty to share it at this time." No sense scaring the poor girl. He thought of his mother's words the previous morning when she said she wanted him to have a bodyguard. That's the way he felt right now about Caro.

And Antonia. He'd like to have both of them protected around the clock.

He drew in a deep breath and met her gaze. "Listen, Caroline, I'm frightfully sorry about all this beastly business."

"I think I deserve an explanation. Who did send me the e-mail?"

"I wish I knew."

Her pretty blue eyes rounded. "You don't think it's the murderer?"

Caroline was much too intelligent, too perceptive. "Possibly."

She gave a mock shiver. "I can't believe he knows about me. About us."

"He knows entirely too much about Siddley and everyone associated with it." His lips folded into a grim line.

"It really is frightful."

"I'm sorry you're involved." He trailed a hand down her perfect porcelain cheek. "I want you to go to Antibes. Just until I know you're out of danger."

She nodded solemnly. "But I shall worry about *you*. If I do go, will you promise to keep me informed?"

"By e-mail?" He cracked a smile.

"Frederick Percy! This is nothing to joke about."

"Sorry."

She rose. "I'm going home and packing."

He walked her to her vehicle.

"Please take care," she said, her voice soft.

"Right-o."

With every step he took toward his car he thought of Antonia being without his protection, and his worry mounted. Could this whole business with Caro have been designed to draw him away from Antonia? Once again, he felt as if a bus had slammed into him.

By the time he reached the road to Monlief, he accelerated. His grip on the steering wheel tightened; his pulse pounded.

It was just late enough in the afternoon that the traffic had started to snarl. The sun had begun its journey to tuck itself beneath the horizon. He had to get to her before dark. Why did he feel so certain she was in jeopardy? He hoped to God he was wrong.

As he drove, he called his secretary. "I've got a job for you."

"That's what you pay me for," Emerson responded.

"This may take a bit of poking around, but I need you to engage for me the services of electronics surveillance experts. I need to search my office and Ellerton's for bugs, hidden cameras, anything. Also my bedchamber and those close to it.

"And I want to have them install hidden surveillance cameras in the offices. But—and this is important—no one except you and me are to know what they're doing at Siddley."

"Are you saying that these workers need to go *undercover*?"

"That's exactly what I'm saying. Have them pose as fire inspectors or electricians or something."

"Anything else?" she asked.

"Yes. See if I can pay additional for someone to monitor those cameras around the clock and alert me when something suspicious is observed."

"Our own CCTV."

"Yes."

Antonia hated that basements didn't have windows. She hated that the hallways in this basement were so darned dark. And she hated that Frederick had left.

Antonia was careful to keep the door to her office open. She didn't want anyone sneaking up on her. Keying in the research was enough to keep her busy until Mr. Bly was ready to lock up for the evening. She was pleased that Simon and Frederick had not given her any documents that weren't relevant to her research.

If only she could keep both men to assist her. She could complete her work in a couple of days instead of the two weeks it had previously taken.

Fifteen minutes later, Simon joined her. "Did Mr. Bly find that letter I'm so keen to see?" she asked.

He shook his head morosely. "Sorry, Antonia. I did my best to find it for you."

"I have the feeling he's hiding something. I think he's lying."

Simon sat on a corner of the metal desk, facing her. "Why do you say that?"

"I just don't buy that he can't remember who wrote it. Think about it. He's probably more well acquainted with the early

Montagues than anyone on the planet, yet he's suddenly confused and can't remember who wrote the letter. The letter he thought significant enough to tell the marquess about."

"That does seem a bit improbable."

"Does he have a doctorate?"

"Yes, he does."

"Therefore, he's bound to be in possession of pretty good memory faculties."

"I know for a fact that he is."

"So why would he be so evasive?"

"For a very good reason."

Her brows lifted. "Which is?"

"Financial gain."

"You think he's trying to get the monstrance and try to sell it?"

He shook his head. "I'd stake my life on the fact Harold Bly would never do anything that was against the law."

"But he had to be lying!"

"I think he may be trying to get the monstrance, but not to sell it. He wants his employer to gain ownership. It's a good bet that Lord Granworth has some type of bonus system in place. If Bly helps him find things of value—even if it's just a manuscript by a famed personage—Bly gets rewarded nicely."

"Oh, we forgot to tell you! Frederick has a friend—actually a former professor—who's at the V&A. Frederick got him to investigate the value of the monstrance. What would be your guess?"

Simon shrugged. "I suppose it could fetch one or two million pounds."

She shook her head. "He estimates its worth at five million."

"Why so much?"

"Provenance. The Percys possess a Holbein that shows none other than Cardinal Wolsey holding the Percy Monstrance."

"Wolsey himself, eh? Yes, I should think that would most definitely boost the value."

"But I doubt if Mr. Bly or Lord Granworth know about the Holbein."

He nodded. "Since it *is* in a private collection."

"It's never left Siddley since it was painted." She noticed a corner of one of the irreplaceable letters was ruffled, so she put back on one of the cotton gloves and smoothed it out. "If Mr. Bly found a reference to the monstrance in some correspondence from the era I'm studying, would he not put it back?"

"That's a question I cannot answer. Naturally, a librarian's job is to catalog resources and to track them by means that others can follow."

"It does seem as if he would have put it back where he found it and make note of its location—"

"Or he could have kept it."

"But you looked at everything on his desk, didn't you?"

"There are other places. Like the drawers, briefcases, even safes."

Her brows lowered. "I feel like going in there and shaking the man."

He got off the desk and returned to his perusal of documents. "Instead I suggest you channel your energies into the job that brought you here in the first place."

"Aye, aye, Dr. Steele."

They worked in relative silence for the next hour before Antonia straightened up from her typing and sighed. "I'd dearly love to break the cardinal rule of a researcher."

"And what's that?"

"I'd like to take my documents home. I'm not that fast a typist. It'll take me days to catch up here."

"You, young lady, are excessively fortunate that you're even allowed in here with these irreplaceable documents."

"I did have to provide a gazillion letters of recommendation—one of which came from the highly respected Dr. Simon Steele."

"Perhaps that same highly respected historian can persuade Harold Bly to allow said historian's star pupil to stay here after hours—under my supervision, of course."

"Oh, Simon, would you? That would be awesome. Are you sure you don't mind?" Their eyes met and held. The look he gave her was so terribly tender it made her uncomfortable. She looked away and began to shuffle the papers in front of her.

"I shall go ask Harold right now." He got up and started for the door.

She spun around. "Dare you make one more inquiry about the monstrance document?"

"I shan't wish to anger him. I'll request the after-hours privileges first."

"Maybe he'll have softened up enough to volunteer the monstrance document?"

"My, but Antonia is quite the optimist," he muttered as he started down the hallway.

Five minutes later, he was back, grinning in that sly manner that had previously so annoyed her. "So he's consented?"

Simon held up a key. "He even entrusted me with his spare key."

"I could just kiss you." As soon as the words were out of her mouth, she regretted them.

His bespectacled gaze scorched. "Then why don't you?"

She felt awfully uncomfortable. "Don't be silly, Simon. That's just an expression."

"How silly of me." He sounded mildly disappointed.

God, but she didn't want to go there or anywhere near there. She had enough on her plate right now. She didn't need to start worrying about rebuking advances from a man *almost* old enough to be her father.

He was her dissertation supervisor, too. She couldn't risk anything that would jeopardize that relationship. She coached herself to be cognizant of not saying anything that could in any way be construed as flirty.

So she returned to her typing, and Simon returned to searching for pertinent documents.

"Oh, my God," Simon said. "I've found the shit document."

Her fingers froze on the keyboard, and she turned to him. "shit document?"

He was reading the fragile piece of paper and laughing to himself. He nodded. "That's what Ralph Ellerton called it."

"Why?"

"Allow me to read it to you."

"First, I gotta know who wrote it."

"Oh, it was written by Sir Percy to his sister's husband, Sir Thomas Montague of Monlief."

"Go on."

"Well, it starts off about his grief over his daughter's death…"

"Which daughter?"

Simon's gaze returned to the page. "Katherine."

Antonia nodded. "At Castle Paxton."

"Yes, but allow me to read the funny part." He carefully unfolded the letter and scanned until he got to the pertinent section. "He's referring to Martin Luther—this was obviously before the Dissolution—and writes *throw back into his paternity's shitty mouth, truly the shit-pool of all shit, all the muck and shit which his damnable rottenness has vomited up.*"

Antonia started giggling. God, it felt good to lighten up. "I take it Sir Percy didn't like Martin Luther."

"What good Catholic would?"

"Good point."

When it was time for him to leave for the day, Mr. Bly came to her tiny office to say good-bye. Once he was gone, she began to feel uneasy. Had Frederick forgotten about her? She had told him she could leave with Simon. She had acted snippy. She deserved it if Frederick gave her what she asked for.

Even more than missing Frederick, she felt uneasy. It had to be getting dark outside. She and Simon were alone in this basement labyrinth of corridors. And, of course, there was a murderer on the loose.

She suddenly remembered Frederick's suspicions that Simon was the killer. Which was perfectly ridiculous. Or was it? Her heartbeat began to accelerate. Why did Simon have this sudden interest in being with her every minute?

Her cell phone rang, and she couldn't help it, she smiled. It had to be Frederick. It was. It was as if some mystical force connected them.

"Where are you?" Frederick snapped.

"Simon and I will be working late at Monlief."

"I'll be there whenever I get out of this blasted traffic." He hung up.

Just hearing his voice settled her nerves.

She and Simon silently worked alongside each other for another hour before his cell phone rang.

"Simon Steele." He listened a few seconds. "Certainly. I'll be right there."

Antonia watched him, a brow lifted in query.

"There's a chief inspector at the door. I think Rockford must have told him we were here." He rose. "I said I'd let him in."

"I wonder why Frederick didn't give him my cell number?"

"Patel has my number. Perhaps he'd already given that to his chief inspector."

As Simon walked away, she nodded and returned to her typing.

She didn't hear him return until a single footfall sounded in the doorway. Why would Simon be alone? When she went to face him, the room went black at the same instant she heard the light switch click. Before she had time to react, she felt strong, masculine hands savagely clamp on her mouth.

Then she heard another pair of footsteps. The first man's hands parted, only to place those same brutally strong hands on either side of her face to immobilize her.

So that the second man could affix duct tape to her mouth. She tried to scream, but the sound was completely muffled. She was terrified. Were they going to kill her?

The next thing she knew, duct tape was wrapped around her eyes, encircling the back of her head. She thought of how painful it would be when the tape was pulled from the hair.

If she was still alive then.

One of the men's arms came around her like a vise. Then he lifted her into his arms and began to carry her off.

In the opposite direction from where Simon had gone.

CHAPTER 17

Every possible impediment hindered him getting to Monlief before closing time. After sitting in snarled traffic for forty minutes, he'd rung Antonia back to make sure she would still be there.

"As it happens," she'd said icily, "Simon and I are planning to work well into the night. You really don't have to come."

"I'm coming," he barked, ending the call.

Since he was so much later getting to Monlief than he'd wanted and since he couldn't shake the feeling that Antonia was in danger, Frederick decided to come in the back way. As the crow flew, it was a much shorter route. It was also a far less traveled road. Which meant it had poor lighting and the possible delay for a cow crossing the lane.

With every mile he traveled, his worry over Antonia mounted. Was Simon trustworthy? Could Frederick count on him to watch over her, to help keep her safe? *If she's unharmed when I get there, I vow not to leave her again until that damned killer is caught.* Or until the Percy Monstrance was located.

His headlights shone on a tasteful sign pointing the way to Monlief. He made the turn to the west. If it weren't for the tall hedgerows on either side of the single lane, he would have been concerned he'd run his car off the road. It was too dark to see the pavement—if one could refer to the bumpy lane as pavement—but the towering hedgerows displayed in his headlights on either side kept him on the straight and narrow very well.

When the hedgerows stopped, he came to the gates that clearly marked Monlief's rear entrance. He brought his car to a stop, got out, and walked up to the gates. There did not appear to be a lock, just a U-shaped catch, which he easily lifted. He swung open one of the gates, and the opening was just wide enough for his car.

Once inside the grounds, he could only barely see Monlief's domed roof reflecting the pale moonlight. Some fifty yards behind the house he passed a Dumpster. Just as he cleared the big, square mass of steel, he saw the silhouettes of two men. They'd been moving toward the Dumpster. Night watchmen?

It was a good thing he wasn't speeding. He might have hit them. He certainly hadn't expected anyone to be poking about the grounds at night.

When his headlights shone on them, the two men began to speed away like they were racing ahead of a raging fire. Then he saw something that damned near stopped his heart.

The men were wearing ski masks!

And one of them was carrying Antonia. To the Dumpster.

She's dead. They were going to dump her body with the daily waste. He could tear those bastards apart with his bare hands.

He stomped on the brake. As his car skidded to a stop, his head just missed colliding with the windshield. Slamming the car into park, he leaped from the vehicle and shouted, "What in the hell are you doing?"

Only then did he notice her kicking. *Thank God she's alive!* He bolted for her. It never crossed his mind that one of them might have a gun. All that mattered to him at that moment was that he rescue her from those fiends.

The realization that she wasn't dead emboldened him. "Put her down, or I'll shoot." The only gun he'd ever possessed was a rifle for shooting grouse. And it was locked up at their hunting lodge in Yorkshire. But those men needn't know that. He was a lord. He always sounded authoritative.

To his utter amazement, they did precisely what he asked, then vanished behind the Dumpster.

As much as he wanted to apprehend the despicable pair, his first duty was to check on Antonia. As he raced to her, he heard a car start. The sons of bitches had hidden their vehicle behind the Dumpster! He looked up in time to see a dark sedan speed toward the rear gate.

It was far too dark for him to read the number on the plates, especially since they hadn't turned on the car's lights.

"Antonia?" he called, his voice panicked. "Are you all right?"

Then he saw that damned duct tape on her lovely face. "Here, let me get that off you." He moved closer. "I'm awfully afraid this may hurt. Is that going to be all right with you?"

She nodded.

Then he yanked. It sounded like stripping off Velcro. Poor girl. He'd done the mouth first. "I'm afraid you might lose some of your lashes." Fortunately, she was blessed with luxuriously plentiful long, dark lashes.

"Go for it," she said, her voice trembling.

He removed the tape from her eyes, then he carefully pulled it from her hair as she winced. Next, he untied her bound wrists.

The second her hands were free, she launched herself into his arms.

He stood there for several moments, holding her trembling body, stroking her back and her hair, and dropping soft kisses into her lavender-scented locks.

She finally looked up at him as if he were some deity. "I knew you'd save me."

He felt rather like James Bond at that moment. And God help him, he couldn't help himself. He hauled her into his arms and hungrily kissed her.

This was the perfect ending to a horrible ordeal.

If anything could be better than kissing Lord Hunkness, it was the knowledge that he was *not* engaged to Range Rover Girl.

He didn't have to tell Antonia; he'd shown her. A man in love with Ice Princess could never kiss Antonia from the States with anything close to the intensity Frederick had put into his searing kiss.

Even though she was still breathless and trembling, she started to giggle.

His hands moved to her shoulders, and he put space between them while he searched her face, a puzzled look on his. "How can you laugh at a time like this?"

She reached up to brush his forehead with the soft pads of her fingers, sweeping away a stray lock of hair. "I was just wondering if you've been drinking wine."

Brows lowered, he was silent for a moment, then he understood. "You are terrible. I should have let those killers carry you off."

She moved closer to him, encircled his waist, and pressed her cheek against his sternum, a smile warming her all the way to her toes. "So it wasn't the wine talking. It was really Frederick." She looked up at him. "I like the language you speak."

He stiffened.

She had known the stuffy earl was going to get all formal on her. Next came his big, audible sigh. "As pleasant as this has been, I want to get you the hell out of here."

"We've got to find Simon first. I hope they didn't kill him."

"Why isn't he with you?"

She started heading back to the main house. "That's what we need to find out. He'd gotten permission from Mr. Bly for us to work late. It was just the two of us. Then he got a call on his cell from a policeman, some kind of chief inspector who said he needed Simon to let him in, that he needed to question us."

They came to the door the thugs had just taken her through. Frederick tried it, and the door swept open. This auxiliary entry was lighted only by a small wall sconce that gave off about the same amount of light as a single taper. She could only barely see the broad stairwell that descended to the basement, and she wasn't about to go down there until it was better lit.

"You weren't suspicious?" Frederick asked, then under his breath muttered, "Where in the hell is the damned light switch?"

As he continued trying to find the switch, he asked, "How would a chief inspector just happen to know Simon was working in the basement of Monlief after dark?"

"That really sucks that I didn't think of that."

Frederick finally found the light switch and turned it on.

As soon as the light snapped on, Simon called out in a very loud voice, "Antonia?"

"I'm here, Simon!"

"Thank God." His voice sounded wrenching.

"At least he's not in the sedan that sped away," Frederick mumbled as they started downstairs.

"Frederick!" Anger stung Antonia's voice. "Shame of you for suspecting Simon."

Footsteps raced up the stairs, and Simon met them at the landing. The three of them stood there beneath a large oil painting of a formidable-looking Montague ancestor dressed in a naval uniform from the Horatio Nelson era.

"My God, Antonia!" Simon looked mildly deranged. "What in the hell happened?" Then he glared at Frederick. "Surely you weren't playing some vile prank on me?"

"Of course not, Simon!" she scolded. "Frederick saved me from two masked abductors."

"You were abducted?" Surprise and shock both registered in his voice. "Dear God, what happened?"

"I'll tell you everything in time," she said. "The important thing is that I'm OK, and you're OK."

Simon turned to Frederick and spoke with contrition in his voice. "It appears I am much in your debt, Rockford. I can't tell you two how furious I am with myself for being duped." He shuddered. "Duped like an idiot—and obviously by the murderer—or murderers."

"Let's get the hell out of this place," Frederick said. "We can discuss everything once we get to the hotel."

She thought that sounded pretty good.

Frederick looked down at her. "You'd best get your laptop."

"Aye, aye, my lord. I takes me orders, and milord orders that I'm to take my laptop everywhere I go from now on." She began to walk downstairs, Frederick beside her and Simon just in front of them.

"I'm surprised they didn't want your computer," Frederick said.

"Methinks they wanted my mind."

"Pity she's not more dull," Simon quipped.

"On this, I'm in perfect agreement with you, Dr. Steele," Frederick said.

After she got the laptop, Frederick insisted on carrying it. Then he faced Simon. "We're going to spend the night at the Staines hotel in Winton. It's less than fifteen minutes away. We can eat there—unless you've already eaten?"

"No," Simon answered. "I'm sure we're both hungry."

She was pleased that Frederick and Simon seemed to have come to some sort of truce.

A few minutes after they arrived at the hotel's quiet, wood-paneled restaurant, Simon joined them. They crossed a tartan-patterned carpet and sat at an antique table of dark wood that nearly matched the blocked walls. The room resembled a library in a stately English home. At the opposite corner, there was a comforting fireplace. It was just chilly enough outside that she welcomed the fire. On either side of their table were floor-to-ceiling bookshelves featuring red-bound books and a scattering of decorative plates on stands, most of which were coats of arms. Or hunting dogs.

They quickly ordered, and soon the waiter was decanting a bottle of expensive red wine that Frederick had selected.

"I want to hear about this abduction," Simon said. Her former Surly Simon had morphed into something totally different. Tonight he was contrite. She would never have guessed he was capable of such a nonauthoritative demeanor.

"First," she said to Simon, "tell us what happened after you got the call and left me."

"I simply went down the corridor past Harold's office, then climbed the stairs to the door he comes in and out of. No one was at the door that leads outside. I stepped out and looked for a vehicle, but there wasn't one. I came back in and locked the door." His gaze locked with Antonia's. "I wasn't comfortable leaving you alone. Then it occurred to me that someone who'd never been in the archives before—which I was assuming the chief inspector hadn't— would likely be standing at the portico in front of the building. So then I had to traipse throughout the public rooms of Monlief. I hoped to God I wasn't going to set off an alarm. There are a lot of practically priceless items there."

Frederick nodded. "And I'm guessing that when you got to the main entrance, no one was there, either?"

Simon nodded ruefully. "It then occurred to me that I'd been tricked, and I raced back to the basement. Only to find Antonia gone." He reached across and softly touched her arm. "It is outside of my capabilities to convey to you how upset that made me. I am so thankful you're unharmed. They didn't hurt you, did they?"

"I'm not sure." She fluttered her lashes at Frederick. "Do I still have eyelashes?"

"You still have eyelashes." He glanced at Simon. "They put duct tape across her mouth and eyes."

Simon winced, then peered at her face closely. "Yes, I can see the red marks where the tape was, now that I'm looking."

She frowned. "Just what every girl wants to hear."

"Now tell us everything, Antonia." Frederick's voice was... well, it was like Simon's *used* to be when he was being dogmatic with his students.

"They came up behind me when I was typing. I didn't hear a thing. Then they shut off the light."

"That's rather bizarre," Frederick said.

She loved to hear him say *roth-ah*.

"Why would they do that when they were already wearing ski masks?" he asked.

She shrugged.

"Surely they turned the light on in order to put that damned tape on your mouth and eyes," Simon said.

"No." She shook her head. "They did that in the dark. One held my head stable while the other did the dirty deed. I had the impression the strips of tape were precut."

"Did you recognize their voices?" Frederick asked.

"They didn't say a single word."

Simon and Frederick both said the same profanity at once: "Shit!"

She knew why they had both cursed. Her somber gaze moved from Simon's to Frederick's. "The two men didn't speak so I wouldn't recognize their voices." The chilling realization that she knew the men—the murderers—set her heartbeat racing, her stomach plummeting.

Frederick nodded. "That also explains cutting off the lights and covering your eyes."

"They didn't want me to recognize their body size or build."

"That's not all bad," Frederick said. "That means they didn't want to be recognized because they planned to set you free."

"So," Simon said, "they didn't plan to kill you."

"How gratifying," she said dryly.

Frederick glanced at his watch. "While we're waiting for the food, I think I'll go check us into the hotel." He eyed Antonia. "I'm going to request one room with two beds for me and my sister."

She felt awkward in front of Simon, advertising the fact she and Frederick were sharing a room. Even more so after that searing kiss less than an hour previously.

Simon watched Frederick leave the room, then he lowered his voice. "I wish you wouldn't put too much trust in Rockford."

She rolled her eyes. These two guys really did *not* like one another. "I wish you wouldn't try to malign him. He's been awfully considerate of me."

"Just remember he's used to getting his way. He could easily have employed a couple of thugs to stage a mock abduction. Don't you find it a bit too much of a coincidence that just at the precise moment you were being toted from the building, Lord Rescuer comes racing to your aid?"

"I'll admit that looks coincidental, but coincidences do occur in real life," she said.

"Understand that I have known Harold Bly for twenty years, and I can vouch for his moral compass." He gazed solemnly at the doorway, then lowered his voice even more. "Has it not occurred to you how odd it is that the supposed chief inspector knew to call me away from you?"

Her stomach did an odd flip as she nodded solemnly. She wasn't going to like what Simon was going to say next.

"Only two people knew I was in that basement with you: Harold Bly and Rockford."

EPISODE 7

CHAPTER 18

Antonia didn't want to believe Simon's accusations. Not Frederick! Frederick couldn't have, wouldn't have staged that abduction just to earn her complete trust. There were so many other ways he had already ingratiated himself with her, so many ways he'd already shown he genuinely cared about her.

There were so many ways, too, in which he was as much a victim as she.

But as she peered at Simon across the table from her, she kept coming back to Frederick's prolonged absence that afternoon. What *had* he been doing? Why had he left so abruptly? Why had he so evasively avoided mentioning his whereabouts?

And what about the corrupted flash drive the other day? She'd never been certain of his whereabouts at the time it had been wiped clean.

There was the fact that he certainly had the resources to hire slimeballs to ransack her flat and to kidnap her, but she couldn't believe he would do either of those things.

She held a deep-seated conviction that Frederick was a true gentleman. Just the night before, he had refused to take advantage of her blatant availability when she'd asked him to kiss her.

The very memory of tonight's kiss nearly stole away her breath. He couldn't have been acting! That kiss had been one of those bursting-the-floodgates kinds of kisses. She had never before experienced a kiss of such intensity. On both their parts.

No, despite all her troubling suspicions, she would stake her life on Frederick's inculpability in Mr. Ellerton's murder.

Her gaze connected with Simon's. She hated to show her anger when he was merely concerned about her welfare. "I understand why you might think that about Frederick," she said, "but I assure you he's incapable of doing any of those things."

Fury flashed in Simon's mossy green eyes. "One man's already been murdered. I'm terrified for you. You can't stay with him tonight."

"I'm staying here," she said, her voice firm. "It's close to Monlief, and I was hoping we could get an early start tomorrow." She paused, oddly aware that there were no rims on Simon's glasses. What a ridiculous thing to be thinking of in a situation like this. "Besides, it's much better than being alone. I'm a scaredy-cat."

"I refuse to leave you here with him. My lectures aren't until afternoon tomorrow. I'm going to get a room here so I'll be close— if you should need me."

She knew she should protest, but having Simon staying at the hotel gave her a double level of protection.

She was one trembling, teary-eyed wuss if ever there was one. Right now she was tearing up big-time. "Oh, Simon, you're such a treasure."

He peered toward the doorway, and his demeanor instantly went frigid. She turned and saw Frederick entering the dining room. She couldn't help it. Her heart swelled at the sight of him— and the memory of how hungrily he'd kissed her. Because of that kiss, the connection she'd felt toward him these past several days had only strengthened.

When Frederick reached the table, she looked up at him, a quizzing look on her face.

He nodded as he sat. "We've got a room with two beds."

"It's so late," Simon said, "I'm going to go ahead and take a room here, too."

"You don't have to work tomorrow?" Frederick asked.

Simon glared at Frederick. "Not until afternoon, old chap."

Before these two refined men resorted to fisticuffs, she thought it best to change the subject. She eyed the dog plates on the nearby built-in bookcases. "OK. Multiple choice question. Which of the following potteries does that dog plate come from? Royal Doulton, Wedgwood, or Royal Crown Derby? Let me clarify, first. The plate dates to the early nineteen hundreds, before the big potteries all merged under the Wedgwood/ Waterford group."

Frederick and Simon exchanged amused glances with one another. "You first, old boy," Simon said. "My knowledge of English history does not extend to the Staffordshire potteries."

Frederick shrugged. "Right-o. While I was exposed to the study of some porcelains in my art history coursework, I shall have to plead ignorance."

Antonia smiled. Her ploy had worked. "I really didn't expect either of you to know it was Royal Crown Derby. I have to resort to an Elaine Benes phrase: *He's a guy!*" she said with an Elaine Benes exaggerated shrug.

His eyes flashing with mirth, Frederick said, "But she was referring to a baseball player—whose name escapes me."

"I wouldn't expect a Brit to know the name Keith Hernandez."

"It was a great *Seinfeld* episode."

"So we're three for three now." And somehow, that made her feel better.

Their hotel room conveyed much the same impression as the dining room. Tartan fabrics in deep reds and greens and dark wood furniture continued the theme of a cozy retreat for an English or Scottish huntsman.

She strolled into the bathroom and was pleased to find a deep soaking tub, heated towel racks, and a long vanity with a black marble top.

Frederick came to stand behind her. "You still insist on me showering first?"

"Absolutely. My makeup comes off only at lights-out time."

Because of their shattering kiss, she felt a proprietary claim on his body, too. So at the mention of him showering, enticing images of his lithe, lean body beneath the cleansing spray surged into her mind.

She needed to direct her attentions elsewhere. She took her laptop to her bed, sat on top of the spread, and bolstered herself with pillows against the headboard. "I'll just be typing in more notes from yesterday's tour of Chumley while everything's still fresh in my mind."

Nodding, he whipped out his cell phone and set it on the nightstand between their beds. Then he picked out his plaid pajamas and shaving kit from his bag and took them into the bathroom.

A moment later, she heard his shower running, and just seconds after that, his phone beeped. Her gaze unconsciously flicked to it. She could easily read the text on the screen.

I'm not leaving the country until you get rid of the American.

Her breath stilled. Her stomach plummeted. Her entire body began to tremble.

Antonia was the only American currently associated with Frederick. It was obvious this "Brat" signing the message wanted to get Antonia out of the way. Did that mean…murder? Was she to be the next victim?

Brows lowered, she moved closer to see who'd sent the text. The message was not only signed Brat, but it was also apparently put in Frederick's address book as Brat's number.

Could that be a familiar form of Bradley? Or could it refer to a male whose last name was something like Bradstreet? Heck, it could even be a semi-affectionate endearment for a female. Her stomach clinched. Could it be Range Rover Girl?

Antonia really didn't want to give any credence to Simon's allegations about Frederick, but she couldn't help wondering if Brat was one of the men who'd tried to abduct her.

From the tone of the text, though, Brat wasn't a hired hand. Brat was at least an equal partner, if not the one calling the shots.

Not that Antonia could believe for a moment that Frederick was behind Mr. Ellerton's murder, or that he would kill to get a monstrance he hadn't even known about.

Or had he?

Once she'd revealed to Frederick the possible existence of the monstrance, he immediately knew what a monstrance was—unlike just about everyone else they'd spoken to about the Catholic icon. Not only had he immediately acknowledged the Percy Monstrance, but he instantly connected it to the Holbein painting.

She couldn't take her eyes from the menacing text message. No way could she believe Frederick would ever harm her.

But Antonia Townley was not completely a wide-eyed Pollyanna. She was a pragmatist. Forewarned was forearmed. She would not blatantly put all her trust in Frederick.

Or in Simon.

She was an intelligent woman who could darn well take care of herself. If she hadn't been so capable, her parents would never have let her go off so many thousands of miles away from home.

Just the thought of home made her feel painfully lonely. She needed to reach out to her family. She could never confide in her parents about what had been going on the past several days without them demanding she immediately return to California.

Heck, her daddy would be so livid, he would hop on the next plane to England. And she couldn't have that.

Her heart still thundering in her chest, she returned to her laptop, opened up her e-mail program, and typed in her sister's address. If she could just write to Sophia, it would make her feel like...like she'd felt when she was wrapped in Frederick's arms.

When she had felt safe with him.

Profound loss reverberating through every cell in her body, she mourned him. For until the Percy Monstrance was found or Mr. Ellerton's murderer caught, she could no longer allow herself to feel safe with Frederick.

She started typing.

You've apparently drawn the black bean, which means you're to be regaled with my latest saga. Thought I'd give you a heads-up so you won't be broadsided if Scotland Yard should arrest me for the murder of none other than the curator/librarian of Siddley Hall. Because I coveted the man's job, I'm apparently Suspect Numero Uno. (Oh, and I did just happen to have the murder weapon in my hand!) You can read all about it on the Guardian *website, I expect.*

The handsome Lord of the Manor at Siddley Hall rescued me tonight from abductors who put duct tape over my mouth and eyes. As I write this, I'm spending the night with said lord, whom I've been warned may be trying to kill me.

Please don't tell Mom or Daddy any of this, or I'll tell them about your month with the "girls" in Portofino. There's nothing the folks could do to make me leave England when I'm so close to completing this dissertation—which I'm really enjoying. I'm only confiding to you in case.

Please don't worry about me. Our daddy didn't raise any Fainting Fillies. I'm not an idiot, and I'm reasonably sure I can take care of myself.

I wish my arms were long enough to reach across the ocean (and another continent) and hug you tonight. I miss you. — Antonia

After she hit *send*, she was still miserable, but somehow felt as if her load had been lightened.

Not two minutes later, her cell phone rang. Even before she looked at the caller ID, she cringed. She'd gotten mixed up over the time difference between England and California and reversed them. They were going to bed as she was getting up. Not the other way around. Obviously, as she was going to bed here in England, it was midday in San Francisco, and a panicked Sophia had just gotten her sister's alarming message.

Antonia snatched up the phone before it rang a second time.

"I'm telling Daddy," were the first words out of Sophia's mouth.

"Then you better be ready to explain to him about Portofino."

"Fine! If it's my reputation or my only sister's life, I'll happily drag my name through the gutter."

Antonia rolled her eyes. Sophia was the dramatic sister. She stilled, listening to the steady running of Frederick's shower. "I'm fine, really I am."

"Is he there with you? The Lord of the Manor?"

"No. He's in the shower."

"I want you to get out of there right now!"

"You know I can't drive in England, and we're in some small town that closes everything at dark. Besides, he's a perfect gentleman."

"So was the Marquis de Sade!"

"Now how would you know that?"

"I'm just sayin'. He *was* an aristocrat. I'm sure he had polished manners."

"That's enough talk about that French dude."

"It certainly is! Oh, Antonia, I wish I were there with you. What about that Oxford prof who's been so helpful?"

"He's here, too."

"There's three in your room?"

"Actually he's in an adjacent room." Antonia sighed. "I can't encourage the poor man. I think he's got a thing for me."

"And he knows you're sleeping with the lord?"

"I'm not sleeping with the lord! We're platonically sharing a room. He's supposedly protecting me."

"So if Lord So and So tries anything, you can call the prof, and he'll run to your rescue?"

While some things Frederick might try would be welcome—or would have been welcome before Simon made her mistrust him—Antonia knew she had to repel him. "That's the idea."

"You can't hide anything from me, Antonia. What aren't you telling me? Other than the fact you're sweet on his lordship."

Antonia's mouth thinned. How did Sophia always manage to read her mind so accurately? "I'm not hiding anything." Sophia needn't know about the monstrance. If Antonia attempted to tell her, she'd have to go into the recitation of what a monstrance was, and she didn't want to do that right now.

"As you say, our daddy didn't raise any idiots," Sophia said. "The librarian-slash-curator must have known something he was murdered for. Am I hot?"

"You're hot."

"Do you know how to find what it is he was looking for?"

"I know how to find it. I think. But it will take time." It suddenly occurred to her that she no longer heard the shower running.

Her gaze flicked to the bathroom door. Frederick stood there in his pajama bottoms. Bare chested, he was incredibly stare-worthy. He had one of those lean, masculine torsos like models in Calvin Klein underwear ads. Flat abs and narrow waist but no bulging pecs or massive shoulders, just taut, supple muscle beneath glistening golden skin. Every inch of him oozed masculinity.

"I thought I heard you talking," he said. His hair looked darker—more like a warm brown—when it was wet like that.

Antonia returned to her call. "Talk to you later." She ended the call and glared at him. "You'll take a cold." The last thing she needed to look at was that body. It would remind her of their scorching kiss, and she just couldn't go there.

He went back to get his top. "I thought I ought to check on you when I heard voices. Who were you talking to?"

"My sister."

"In the States?"

She nodded. "She's in San Francisco."

Shaving tote in hand, he left the bathroom. "The lavatory's all yours."

From beneath hooded eyes, he watched her as she went to her suitcase and took out an all-white nightgown, along with a cosmetics bag, and headed to the loo. Thank God the nightgown wasn't made of something transparent like lace. It looked like that thin cotton exported from India.

It would be better for him if she covered herself in a thick toweling robe. He needed to purge himself of his desire for her.

Especially now that he'd heard the end of her phone conversation. Had she been lying to him from day one? His pulse thudded. She'd insisted she had no romantic interest, yet she'd just told whoever in the hell it was on the other end of the line, "You're hot."

He seriously doubted Antonia was talking to her sister.

Right now, he was especially vulnerable to her betrayal. The way she had responded to his kiss earlier in the evening had made him believe there was no other man for her. Ever. The very memory of the way she had clung to him like a soft, breathless mold now caused him to struggle to breathe normally.

The overheard phone conversation disgusted him. Since he'd first laid eyes on Antonia being grilled by the detective chief inspector, Frederick had believed in her innocence. But if she were truly innocent, why would she be telling her contact, "I know how to find it. I think. It will just take time"?

His thoughts flashed to that first day, the first time he'd ever seen her. She'd sat there looking distraught under Patel's cold interrogation. And all the while, the blood of the dead man stained her hands. The very idea that she could have brutally murdered Ellerton sickened him.

If he had learned anything about Antonia, though, it was that she was highly intelligent. If she murdered someone, she would have had a better plan than to stand at the murder scene screaming while she grasped the murder weapon in her bloody hands.

Her actions at the scene of the crime were completely consistent with the symptoms of someone in shock.

He still believed she wasn't strong enough to have driven that dull knife into Ellerton's chest. And what motive could she have had to want him dead? With her knowledge of the Catholic families, she could have trumped up some reason to beg that Ellerton's wait before apprising him of the monstrance.

Five million pounds was good enough motive for anyone to commit murder. Anyone complete devoid of morality, that is. Hell, now that Frederick knew the damned thing was worth five million pounds, he himself might consider selling it. Even if it was the Percy family's famed monstrance.

If only he'd had a couple of million quid at the ready last year, he wouldn't have had to sell Tinserton. Parting with the old cottage was one of the hardest decisions he'd made since succeeding.

In the lavatory, the bathwater was still running. By now she would have stripped off her clothing and settled into the tub. In spite of his suspicions, he would like to be in that room with her, trickling water over her bare flesh, tracing lazy, soapy circles over her smooth back, caressing her sweetly rounded breasts.

The very idea aroused him. Damned American.

He stormed to his overnight bag, got his paperback novel, and placed it on the nightstand. As he did so, he saw his text message from Caro the Brat. He stiffened. He'd a good mind to ring her right now. Women! He wouldn't ring her, though, because he did not want Antonia to overhear any part of the conversation, didn't want Antonia to know her presence was so resented.

Just this afternoon Caro had said she wasn't about to give up her freedom. And now she was trying to dictate to him.

He yanked up the mobile and angrily punched in his response: *Go to Antibes, damn it!*

Brat was an accurate moniker for the arrogant, annoying, beautiful young woman.

Her text exemplified precisely why he remained single. He didn't want any woman giving him orders.

In bed, he tried to read his Scandinavian thriller from the last chapter he remembered, but he merely read words to which no meaning was attached. He couldn't rid his mind of the image of Antonia lying in the tub of soapy water, stretching out a bare, bronzed, shapely leg. With that vision emblazoned on his brain, he heard the splashing noises that indicated she was getting out of the tub. More agony.

A couple of minutes later the door to the loo opened, and she stepped out, barefoot and unbelievably virginal looking in her soft white gown as she gracefully crossed the room's carpet and scooted into the bed.

"You look lovely with no makeup." Why in the hell had he said that? Five minutes earlier he'd been mad as a hornet at her. Why did she have to affect him so profoundly? Why did she have to look so damned innocent?

"That's very kind of you to say; however, it's a well-known fact that while men truly believe they prefer women in their natural state, in reality they find women with subtle makeup more attractive than women without makeup."

"How would you know that?"

She pointed to her temple. "Useless trivia I've cataloged."

What happened to the anger that had consumed him a short while ago? The vision of a barefoot Antonia with flowing brunette locks and fluttering white gown impressed her innocence upon him.

"Are you ready for lights out?" he asked, his voice gruff.

"I've been ready."

He shut off the lamp. Lying in the dark, he was acutely aware of her closeness. Even the air was filled with her lavender scent. With every breath he drew, he throbbed with need of her.

Too bloody bad what he felt for her was *not* paternal.

As she lay in the darkness, she wished her daddy were there. Or Sophia. Or someone who loved her, someone she could trust with her life. The previous night she'd felt Frederick's support as solid as Siddley itself.

But now she just didn't know. *Oh please, God, don't let him be another Justin Manzanolli.* A slimeball wrapped in a great package.

Then she thought of Frederick's whopper of a kiss. It had made her feel sort of cherished, like when she was a child and her daddy carried her upstairs after she'd fallen asleep in front of the TV. Not that Daddy had ever even kissed her on the mouth. But the way Daddy made her feel so safe and secure and loved is exactly how she'd felt earlier that night when she was wrapped in Frederick's protective embrace.

What made that sizzler of a kiss even more special was the realization that Frederick—for that one minute—acted as if he needed her as badly as she needed him.

She could go to her grave without ever being kissed like that again.

She only hoped that such an interment was w-a-a-a-y off in the future.

CHAPTER 19

"Have you enough to keep those fingers busy typing?" Frederick asked Antonia at eight o'clock sharp the following morning. The three of them had arrived at Monlief's basement a few minutes earlier, and Antonia had begun transcribing the centuries-old correspondence onto her laptop.

She absently nodded as she squinted at the faded script in a letter on her desk. Then, as if she had suddenly remembered something vital, she spun around and smiled at Frederick. Every time she smiled at him like that, he felt like that gawky youth he'd been at the cinema with his first crush. "Simon must show you the shit document," she said.

This wasn't the first time he'd heard her say that word, but for some reason he found it as incongruous as picturing Ralph Ellerton saying *shit*. He raised a single brow. "I beg your pardon?"

She and Simon exchanged amused gazes.

"Here, old boy," Simon said, "I'll show you the letter in which your outraged ancestor lambasted Martin Luther." The don began to carefully shuffle through papers until he found it and shared it with Frederick.

Frederick chuckled as he read it. He hadn't realized old Percy was so religious. It was a shame this irreplaceable document wasn't in the Percy archives. It humanized Sir Percy. Still smiling, Frederick returned it to Simon. "Thanks for sharing. Have you typed that up, Antonia? I'd like a copy."

She nodded. "In fact, I think Siddley Hall should have the letter framed."

He thought about it for a moment. "Possibly." He had pulled his phone from his pocket.

Amusement flashed in her dark-brown eyes. "I bet you're going to call that poker-faced DCI."

He was relieved that Antonia wasn't as cold and distant as she'd been the night before. Of course, he too had been stiff with her after overhearing the disturbing phone conversation.

"A most intelligent woman, to be sure," he said.

"I suppose he does need to be informed about the abduction attempt," she said.

"Perhaps they can get prints from the duct tape. I saved it."

She shook her head. "Nope. They wore gloves."

Frederick frowned. "Then we might have to put our hopes in tire tracks."

"Too bad it wasn't raining like it was the night before the murder," she said.

"How do you remember things like that?" Frederick asked.

"Easy peasy. That afternoon we met you insisted we go to the garden—away from poor Mr. Ellerton's blood—but the bench was too damp to sit on."

"So it was." Why didn't he recall things with the clarity she did? Was it the eleven-year age gap? Was he losing it at thirty-four? "I'll just step down the corridor and ring the DCI."

Every time Frederick had tried to contact the detective chief inspector, he'd gotten to him promptly. This was no exception.

After Patel answered, Frederick began, "I'm afraid I've more bad news to report on our situation. Two men wearing ski masks tried to abduct Antonia Townley last night."

"What do you mean *tried*? The attempt failed?"

"Fortunately, I drove up as they were carrying her off, and I managed to convince them I had a gun. They put her down and fled the scene."

"In a car?"

"Yes, but it was too dark for me to get the numbers on the plates."

"Too bad. Where did this occur?"

"At the Marquess of Granworth's Monlief Hall in Hampstead. As you know, Miss Townley's attempting to reproduce the research which was stolen from her flat and her laptop. We came to Monlief yesterday, and Dr. Steele got permission for Antonia and him to work after hours."

"It certainly appears as if someone is keeping close tabs on her every movement."

"And mine, too. Someone's been sending e-mails from my computer at Siddley to a very close female friend of mine."

"What kind of e-mails?"

"That's what's so puzzling. They weren't threatening. They merely purported to be from me, asking my friend to meet me somewhere. What's so frightful is that the person sending them knew exactly where I was headed—and the person also knew that I care for this woman. I've wondered if they were sent to frighten me, to make me give up my quest to find the monstrance."

"I need the name of this female."

"Right-o. It's Lady Caroline Hinckley."

"Do I have your permission to examine your computer?"

"Of course."

"I may need to talk to this woman."

"You had better make it quick. I'm doing my best to get her to leave the country until things are…safe again."

"What's her phone number?"

Frederick scrolled to Brat and gave Caro's mobile number to the DCI.

"I'll send a chief inspector to take a report about last night's abduction and examine the premises. Is Miss Townley still at Monlief?"

"Yes."

"And Dr. Steele as well?"

"He leaves at noon."

"That shouldn't be a problem. I'll dispatch an investigator right away."

"I don't suppose you've anything new to report?" Frederick asked hopefully.

"There are lines of inquiry we're following but nothing significant at this time. I wish the bloody press would let go of the case. They've been like a dog with a meaty bone."

Things had been so hectic the past day Frederick had not watched the news or even read the newspaper that morning because they had rather raced over to Monlief to continue her research. Even though he hadn't told Antonia about Patel's deadline, it was as if she understood that the information had to be replicated as soon as possible.

After Frederick hung up with Patel, he rang Caroline.

"Rockford darling, please don't be angry with me."

She knew him too well. He was mad. "I was deadly serious when I asked you to go to Antibes. Your life could be in danger. And what in the hell did you mean about the American?"

"I don't like her. I could tell by the way she glared at me and the way she spoke to me, she doesn't like me, either. And even though neither of us is ready to settle down, when I do decide to settle down, I want it to be with you. We would suit. We're from the same backgrounds. I don't like the idea that the American will try to poison your mind against me, that she'll try to usurp me."

"That is the most bizarre, nonsensical thing you've ever said. Now listen to me, Brat. If you're not out of the country tomorrow,

I will never again be in the same room with you. Do you understand?" He was angry enough to wring her graceful neck.

"Yes," she finally said in a whimpering voice.

"By the way, Detective Chief Inspector Patel will likely be contacting you about those e-mails supposedly sent from me. As soon as you speak with him, you need to get the hell out of the United Kingdom. Do you understand, or do I have to speak to your father?"

"Don't tell Daddy. I'll go."

When Frederick returned to Antonia's small office, she turned and met his gaze. "What did Hard Ass say?"

"Antonia!" Simon chided. "It's not becoming for such a lovely creature to speak so crudely."

She met Frederick's gaze, her lips in a pout, and when she spoke, he found it incredibly seductive. "Do you think I'm crude?"

He was almost speechless. He kept thinking of the passion that had been in her kiss the previous evening. It was a moment before he could gather his thoughts. "Never that. You're a lady." He looked at Simon. "You really ought to apologize to the lady, Dr. Steele. After all, she is your pet pupil, isn't she?"

Simon glared at him. "Sorry, Antonia. I shouldn't chastise you. You are *one* of my best students."

Harrumph! Frederick thought. The man was bonkers over her.

"You know," Antonia said, her hands slowing over the keyboard, "with both of you helping me like this, I hope to finish up at Monlief tonight." She turned to Simon. "Will you come back tonight?"

"Of course I will."

No way was the cad going to allow Frederick to be alone with her if he could help it.

Frederick had avoided telling her about Patel's threats. He'd actually thought about telling her today, but now he knew he couldn't throw in one more thing to upset her. Not after the horror of the abduction.

He just had to hope she could race through this research and the three of their heads put together could figure out from her findings the whereabouts of the monstrance.

Before Patel tried to arrest her.

They worked in silence for more than an hour. He was actually enjoying looking at these ancient letters, many of which had been written by his ancestors. The trick was not to get sidetracked from the mission at hand. He needed to stick to the agenda. He had his narrow parameters of what kinds of correspondence she was looking for. He needn't look at anything else, no matter how interesting.

Since she was typing, she wasn't wearing gloves, but he and Simon wore cotton gloves to protect the delicate paper from the natural oils on their hands. When Antonia would pause to turn a page of a letter, she would pull on gloves, too—if she didn't ask Simon to flip the page for her in order to save time.

Frederick didn't like that she worked so well with that damned don.

When Chief Inspector Graves came, they all stopped what they were doing and gave statements. He was older than Patel, just as noncommittal and hard-nosed as Patel, but unlike Patel, he was damned near bowled over by Antonia. With her, his demeanor changed to something a good bit softer.

Frederick found it amusing to observe how other men reacted to Antonia. Simon was the most disgusting of all. The lecher was taking advantage of his position as her supervisor. Damned don.

While Antonia and Simon continued their work, Frederick showed the inspector the route the would-be abductors had taken. After they left the building, he went to the Dumpster. "Their car was parked right here," Frederick said. He looked for tire impressions but saw nothing of interest.

Graves nodded. "What kind of car was it?"

Frederick shrugged. "I was so concerned about Antonia—I was afraid she was mortally wounded or something equally as terrifying—I was focusing on her. To be perfectly honest, I was shocked when I heard the car start. I hadn't seen it before that. The Dumpster shielded it from view."

"You know the car's model? Or make?"

Frederick shook his head. "All I know is that it was a dark-colored sedan."

"And you didn't get the number?"

"It was dark."

The inspector continued writing. "I understand, my lord."

The chief inspector took his leave, and Frederick decided he'd ring Brat before returning. He felt beastly about the way he'd talked to her earlier.

There was surprise in her voice when she answered. "Rockford?"

"I don't want you leaving England mad at me. I'm just worried about you, Brat."

"I'm ever so sorry to have given you a moment's grief, darling man."

"You're going to Antibes?"

"Yes. In fact, I was just about to leave Carstairs."

"Did you talk to the DCI?"

"I did. He asked me to forward those e-mails to him, which I promptly did. That man certainly lacks amiability."

Frederick grinned when he thought of Antonia's nickname for Patel. "It's good to see he's consistent."

"Rockford?" Her voice softened.

"Yes?"

"Please be careful. What's happened at Siddley is so shatteringly upsetting."

"Right-o and cheerio." After he hung up, he felt a sense of relief. But still there were the problems with Antonia. In spite of those nagging suspicions after last night's phone call, he still feared for her.

She couldn't have faked her trembling response to the abduction, even if she could have faked the abduction. Which he did not believe she had done.

Why did all of this have to be so damned confusing?

Just as Frederick was about to reenter Monlief's basement, Simon came climbing up the stairs. "So you're off to deliver a lecture?" Frederick asked.

Simon nodded. "Two, actually. One's on medieval weaponry, and the other's on new finds in archeological explorations in the home counties."

"They sound interesting, but exhausting for you." Frederick broke his stride, planted his feet on the stone floors, and outstretched his hand. "See you around, Professor."

Simon did not extend his hand. "I shall be back in time to take Antonia to supper."

Frederick stiffened. "No need, old fellow. I'll be here to look out for her."

From behind his glasses, Simon's eyes narrowed with displeasure. "That's what I'm afraid of."

"Just what are you implying, Steele?" Frederick's voice had gone guttural, his hands balled into fists. He seriously did *not* like this damned don.

"After all that's happened to that poor girl, I don't trust anyone."

Frederick drew so close to Simon he could smell the kippers he'd wolfed down at the hotel's restaurant that morning. "It seems to me you have an unnatural obsession with your student, Doctor. I wonder if your superiors need to know about this?"

"Now see here, Rockford," Simon shouted. "What I feel for Antonia is pure."

"You're a lecher!"

The next thing Frederick knew, Simon's fist came plowing into his face. Not since he and Bagsy had horsed around as lads had Frederick been punched in the nose. Until now. That punch unleashed in Frederick a rage like nothing he'd ever experienced.

He began to pummel the other man with maniacal repetitions. Simon's body whipped into the stone wall, and the force gashed the back of his head, where a trickle of bright-red blood began to stream as he slumped to the floor.

Seeing the blood scared Frederick. He went as still as the rock wall. *I could have killed him!* Thank God Steele hadn't lost consciousness. "Terribly sorry, old chap." Frederick offered him a hand to help him up. He wouldn't have blamed Simon if he'd ignored it, but to Frederick's surprise, Simon placed his hand in Frederick's, and Frederick hauled him to his feet. Extracting a handkerchief from his pocket, he handed it to Simon so he could blot the blood.

Simon pressed the handkerchief to the back of his head. "Sorry I started it."

"Do you think you'll need stitches?"

Simon shook his head but winced. "It'll clot. Just takes time." He met Frederick's gaze. "I'm afraid, old boy, you've rather hit the nail on the head. I'll be thirty-nine next month. Never been married. Never even close. I thought I'd never find the perfect woman. Until Antonia Townley walked into my office.

"I know I'm acting the old fool, but I feel like the old prospector who unsuccessfully mined for twenty years. Never hit anything but worthless stone. Then one day he finds the most exquisite, perfect diamond. A man would be a fool not to try..."

Frederick's throat went dry. Steele's observations perfectly captured a lot of the same feelings Antonia had unleashed in him. *Damn it.* All Frederick could do was nod. He so completely understood where Steele was coming from. "I'm afraid you won't be able to lecture wearing that shirt. If you need a spare…"

"No problem. My flat's just around the corner from Kings." Still pressing the handkerchief to the back of his head with one hand, Simon held out his other hand.

The two men shook, and Simon left. Frederick watched him stroll away. "See you at dinner."

CHAPTER 20

Even though she was working in the basement, she knew it was dark outside. Simon still hadn't returned. Poor man. It was a lot to ask that he drive all the way from Oxford down to Hampstead—and fight rush hour traffic, to boot. But then, she thought, she had never asked him to do so.

She now wished she had called him and told him not to return to Monlief. She was almost finished and wouldn't need him. That long drive would all be for naught. If she hadn't been so immersed in her work, she would have remembered to call him.

But now it was too late. His classes had ended hours ago.

Had she not called him because she didn't want to be alone with Frederick tonight? Ever since she'd seen that text message, *Get rid of the American*, she'd been terrified. She had lain wide awake in her bed for hours the previous night, fearing for her life, afraid that were she to go to sleep, Frederick would slay her. All of these thoughts were at complete odds with her intrinsic admiration of the man, but one fearing her demise couldn't be too careful.

Not that she could let down her guard, not with Sophia calling her every ninety minutes to make sure she was still alive.

Frederick's cell rang, and she took that as an opportunity to look up from her keyboard. Her body was aching from nearly twelve straight hours of typing. It was astonishing, really, that she hadn't fallen asleep at the computer. She wished now she'd gotten her eight hours the previous night. Not once while she pretended to be asleep had Frederick tried to kill her.

She could tell from his conversation Frederick was not talking to Patel. Nor was he talking with Range Rover Girl. Which made her glad, but it made her mad that it made her glad.

He finally said, "Thanks, Emerson. I appreciate that you stayed late to stay on top of this."

Emerson? Wasn't that the name of Frederick's secretary? Antonia hadn't met Emerson, so she didn't know if Emerson was a he or a she. The actress Terri Hatcher had a daughter named Emerson, but then it could be a male's last name, like Ralph Waldo. It did seem like an English earl might have a male secretary.

Once he terminated the call, their gazes met.

Then she heard footsteps coming down the stone hallway. Because it was night and because of the nab-and-grab the previous night, she was terrified. Her hands gripped the arms of her chair, her gaze locked with Frederick's.

He obviously sensed her distress and rushed to the doorway. "Hello, Simon."

Simon entered the office. "Sorry I'm so late. Have you eaten already?" The poor guy looked beat. He also looked considerably older than thirty-nine. His receding, gray-streaked hair was a bit disheveled, and his face had a craggy look, especially around his eyes.

"We were waiting for you," Antonia said. "Also, I really wanted to be able to finish Monlief tonight so we could start at Blyn Court Castle tomorrow."

Simon lifted a brow. "Then you're finished here?"

She effected a contrite expression. "I suppose I didn't need you after all tonight. I'm on my last letter. Sorry you've come so far for nothing."

"That's all right. I didn't have anything else to do tonight."

"Give me a minute to type the last paragraph," she said.

"If you can tell where one paragraph ends and another begins, I'd like to know your secret," Frederick said. "All the letters I've read look to be one long paragraph."

"Of course, you're right, old fellow," Simon said. "It was expedient in those days to fill every centimeter of writing space. Leaving white space for indentations was unthinkable."

Now Simon sounded like his old, didactic self. Which she had sort of missed during this clingy, hovering phase he'd adopted recently.

As he spoke, she noticed a terrible-looking gash on his head. It was a couple of inches long and slightly scabby and slightly oozing. "My goodness, Simon! What happened to you? You look like you ran into a rhinoceros."

Simon's gaze flicked to Frederick, then back to her. "I really don't care to talk about it. I did something very stupid, and I reaped the appropriate consequences."

Her brows lowered. "Did your injury interfere with your lectures?"

"Not in the least."

She finished typing the letter and asked Simon to restore it to the appropriate box and lock up while she saved all the files to her laptop and flash drive.

After she restored her laptop to the case, she faced her assistants. "You two have both been tremendously helpful. I feel guilty for monopolizing so much of your time."

Frederick shrugged. "No one's holding a gun to our heads."

"Thank God," she said breathlessly.

"OK with you two if we eat at the hotel again?" Frederick asked. "I don't know about you, but I'm starving."

"It probably is the closest place," Antonia said.

When they arrived at the hotel's restaurant, they sat at a table closer to the fire, and she was glad. It had turned chilly.

"I have something to report," Frederick said.

Antonia gave him a sly, knowing look. "I bet it has to do with something you learned from Emerson."

"You're entirely too nosy." He nodded, but there was an expression of disapproval on his face. "Emerson informed me that the electronics surveillance experts I hired found extremely sophisticated listening devices in my office and in my bedchamber at Siddley."

Her heartbeat roared. "So that's how they seem to know our every move." The very idea was as upsetting as anything that had happened to her all week. Well, anything except finding Mr. Ellerton's body. Or witnessing her ransacked flat. Or having duct tape slapped around her eyes and mouth and being carried off by masked kidnapers.

"If the equipment is that sophisticated," Simon said, "I should think it could easily be traced to the purchaser."

Frederick shook his head. "Emerson asked that same question and was told that the devices come out of China and would probably be impossible to trace."

"I hope they were removed." Antonia gave a mock shiver.

"Actually, no. Now that I know they're there, I just won't reveal anything important when I'm in those rooms. It's best that the person or persons responsible for installing them doesn't know I'm on to them."

"How could someone put those there without being seen?" she asked.

"Emerson said she's going to personally question all the staff tomorrow to see if anyone saw anything suspicious."

Simon spoke as if he were thinking aloud. "I don't suppose there's any way to determine when they were installed?"

Frederick gave a disgusted head shake.

"Can the experts you hired trace the devices to the person listening in?" she asked.

"Unfortunately, no—one of the hazards of being wireless, I'm afraid," Frederick said.

Simon sighed. "What a pity."

Frederick was reading the wine list. "I'd like you to select the wine tonight, Antonia. You've got to be more knowledgeable than I."

"Since you're paying"—she smiled at him—"I'll order another really expensive bottle." She had almost choked the previous night over how expensive the wine he ordered was. She could get a very nice bottle of wine for half the amount.

"I suppose, old fellow," Simon said to Frederick, "you've a lot of cash at the ready now that you've sold off one of your historical properties."

Antonia's shocked gaze met Frederick's. "What property did you sell?"

He winced almost as if he were in pain. "Tinserton."

She groaned. "The cottage in the Midlands?"

He gave a solemn nod.

She wondered if this sale had just occurred. "When did you sell it?"

"The sale was finalized six months ago."

She was stunned. "But it had been in your family for...hundreds of years."

Frederick's eyes shut tightly. "Don't remind me."

Obviously, selling the property distressed him. As attached as he was to his family's history and holdings, she realized he wouldn't have sold Tinserton had it not been absolutely necessary.

"How did you know about the sale of Tinserton?" she asked Simon.

He directed a haughty gaze at her. "You forget my extensive expertise on England's Tudor architecture. I know every significant Tudor structure in the kingdom."

Simon was back to being his old pain-in-the-ass, didactic self. "How stupid of me," she said.

Now that she knew Frederick had been desperate for money, she felt terrible for thinking about ordering an expensive wine. "We don't have to have wine."

Frederick laughed. "Don't worry. Steele's right. I've now got plenty of cash at the ready."

When the waitress came, they ordered their food, and Antonia asked for a bottle of Bordeaux.

"So, are we going back to Siddley tonight?" she asked Frederick.

"I really wish we could go straight to Yorkshire now, but you'll need fresh clothes," Frederick told her. "By the way, Emerson said Kenneth put your clothes in one of the spare bedchambers. He's the one who fetched them from your flat."

"How lovely."

Frederick turned to Simon. "Sorry you won't be able to come up to Yorkshire."

What the heck was going on between those two? Before tonight, they had only barely tolerated one another. And now? Something had changed. The hostility was gone. Frederick sounded almost as if he would miss Simon.

"If you're still at Blyn Court come the weekend, I'll come on up," Simon said.

Frederick met his gaze. "I'll be a poor substitute for you."

Hallelujah! Her two favorite guys had buried the hatchet.

"I thought you did smashingly well. For a novice," Simon said.

Smashingly? Maybe she should fix Simon up with Lady Shatteringly. If only...

Once their food was delivered to the table, the conversation lagged while they ate. Antonia had said, "Screw the saturated fat," and ordered a completely decadent shepherd's pie after Frederick placed his order for one.

Saturated fat notwithstanding, it was delicious.

If only everything else could be as good as the meal. She couldn't purge from her thoughts the realization that during this past year Frederick had been desperate for money. How could she have been so stupid? She'd thought because he was an earl running a huge estate and because he drove a very expensive sports car, he was rich.

Were he rich, though, he would never have sold Tinserton. A place like that in its lovely rural setting could fetch a few million pounds. Compared to that, a couple of hundred thousand for an Aston Martin was pretty piddly.

Because Siddley was such a popular destination, she knew it was solvent. So why would he need a large amount of money?

That he had been in financial straits put a whole new light on the quest for the monstrance. Could Frederick be hoping to get his hands on the five million pounds the monstrance was worth?

Even if that were the case—which she could never believe— what possible reason could Frederick have for wanting to kill poor Mr. Ellerton? Not that Frederick could ever be responsible for so reprehensible an act. But she kept remembering Simon's suspicions.

Simon's mistrust of Frederick certainly explained why he had made the long trek to Monlief tonight. Dear, sweet man.

No matter what kinds of coincidences pointed to Frederick's culpability, she would never believe he would harm Mr. Ellerton. His grief over the man's death could not have been faked.

But what about his concern for her? That might not be genuine. His so-called worry over her well-being could be a ploy to track the Percy Monstrance.

What about how passionately he'd kissed her after he'd foiled her abduction? Surely no one could fake so searing a passion.

Could he?

As they sped along the dark roads toward Siddley, Frederick was reminded of their first night together, the night he and Antonia had traveled to Oxford. It was hard to believe that was just four days earlier. In some ways it seemed another lifetime ago.

How could he have grown so comfortable with her in so short a time? Why was it he experienced such an innate connection with her?

He thought of how she had affected Steele. When he'd confessed to Frederick that morning how he felt about Antonia, his words had sliced into Frederick's own subconscious as if he were pulling the same confession from the furthermost cells in Frederick's body.

Steele's admission had left the poor man so vulnerable, Frederick no longer loathed him. As he had witnessed Steele's wrenching display, Frederick was touched with something akin to pity. That arrogant, authoritative, assertive bastard had turned into a pathetic kitten because of Antonia.

Since that first night, Frederick had taken pains to get a read on what Antonia felt for Steele. He had now come to suspect that what she felt for the poor fellow was filial, but her romantic interests were the one area in which Frederick couldn't peg her.

"What happened between you and Simon?" Antonia asked when they were about ten minutes away from Siddley Hall.

"How do you keep doing that?" He hadn't meant to say it aloud.

"Doing what?"

"Reading my mind."

"Were you just thinking about Simon and how you two seem to have come to some sort of truce?"

"As a matter of fact, I was."

"You really shouldn't question how I was thinking the same thing. It's easily explained. Togetherness breeds familiarity, which breeds similarity. Give us another week together, and I might just start reading Scandinavian thrillers. Even though I don't like dark books."

He chuckled. "You read fiction? I took you for a nonfiction kind of girl."

"You're evading answering my question."

"So I am."

"So? What's up with you and Simon?"

"I'm not really sure."

"Did you two fight this morning? Is that how Simon got that nasty head wound?"

"I didn't start it."

"I sort of figured that out from what Simon said. I'm just glad you guys kissed and made up."

"We didn't kiss."

"It's just an expression."

He turned onto the long driveway that would take them to Siddley's front door. As he came closer, his headlights shone on the front of Siddley, and he saw what looked like a police car. What the hell? It was almost midnight.

Confirmation that it was a police car gave him that now-familiar feeling that he'd been knocked down by a swiftly moving bus.

"Look, Frederick!" She sounded as scared as he was sickened.

What now? Had something happened to Bagsy? Had there been another break-in? "I see." He screeched up parallel to the police car and got out.

A uniformed officer emerged from the darkened car, and on the other side, Patel stood.

Neither officer was looking at him. They closed in on Antonia, who had opened her own door.

"Miss Townley," Patel said, completely without expression, "I'm bringing you in for questioning in connection with the death of Ralph Ellerton."

EPISODE 8

CHAPTER 21

As Frederick sat there in the artificially brightened reception area of the police station, he looked at his watch. It was five in the morning, and they still hadn't released Antonia. During the hours he'd sat there with a motley assortment heavy on tattoos and tobacco odor, he'd wondered what in God's name he was doing there.

Even though he'd been angry with Antonia when he'd overheard the phone conversation with her purported sister, somehow he couldn't be mad at her now. He kept remembering how pitiable she had looked when she'd gone off with the pair of policemen. She'd given Frederick the most forlorn look as he'd stood on the pavement in front of Siddley, helplessly watching her being carried away in the police car. Hard Ass had rejected Frederick's request to accompany her.

"I'll be there when you're released," he'd told her, attempting to offer reassurance. To himself, he'd thought, *I'll get her an attorney and post bail, if need be.*

How right she'd been to slap the name Hard Ass on the stone-faced, by-the-book detective who was obviously caving to pressure.

As Frederick had shifted his position on the chrome-legged, armless chair, he'd spotted a crumpled newspaper whose headline "No Arrest Yet in Stately Home Murder" rather screamed out at him.

He had greedily read it—as well as several other similar stories in other newspapers—and found that nothing new had been reported. No wonder Patel was so anxious to make an arrest and get the press off his back.

As the hours ticked by, Frederick wondered what it would be like to be in Antonia's shoes. Away from family in a country where you were an alien. Scared and helpless and probably not understanding how the legal system worked.

No matter how long it took, he would be there when she was released.

His memories kept straying to the previous night in their cozy little hotel room. How incredibly innocent she'd looked as she moved from the lavatory and crossed the carpet in bare feet, her long dark hair falling against the soft white gown.

The image still had the power to arouse him.

No way could he allow himself to dwell on the way she had kissed him with such passion. A woman who could kiss him like that wouldn't be telling another man *You're hot*. Would she?

He hated to dwell on his own discomfort when she was in a much worse situation, but he was bloody tired of sitting in that damned chair. He got up and crossed the room to the reception desk. "Any news on Antonia Townley?" he asked.

The uniformed policeman punched her name into the computer. "That last name ends in l-e-y?"

"Yes."

The officer looked at his screen. "Nothing yet."

Frederick frowned and returned to his seat.

"Your wife?" the young man next to him asked. The fellow looked to be the same age as Antonia and smelled like whiskey.

"No, no. I'm not married."

The guy nodded. "Oh, she's a prostitute."

"No! Not that, either." If the guy got even the slightest glimpse of her, he'd know there was no way she could be a prostitute.

"So, mate, why are they 'olding your lady friend?"

Frederick drew a deep breath. "I'm afraid they suspect her of murder."

The young man's eyes widened.

A minute later, the guy turned to the fellow on the other side of him. "Fancy a fag?"

The pair of young men got up, and they moved to the glass exit doors, one of them fishing in his pocket for paper to roll his cigarettes. Both of them were oblivious to the fact their trousers were in danger of falling off their slender hips.

Why hadn't Antonia been released? Had they decided to charge her? Frederick had impressed upon that damned DCI that he wanted to be apprised of any actions concerning Antonia.

Just before dawn, she came strolling into the reception area, her big leather handbag slung over a shoulder, a dejected look on her face.

Until she looked up and saw him.

She couldn't have looked happier had her horse just won the Royal Ascot.

"You came."

He stood. "Of course I came. I've been here the whole time. In case you needed me."

His arm came around her, and they moved to the thick glass doors, through the vestibule and another set of glass doors, then to the lighted car park.

Once they were in the car and on the road, he said, "I'm glad they didn't arrest you."

"Me too. They would have if they actually had any real evidence."

Besides her e-mail to her sister, he thought. "I don't know why they couldn't have waited until morning before hauling you in."

"I suspect DCI Patel was hoping to make an arrest and get the press off his back."

"And there's probably a supervisor breathing heavily down his neck."

"I did learn something," she said.

"About Ellerton's murder?"

"Sort of. They were able to trace Mr. Ellerton's former room-mate, who was more than a roommate, if you know what I mean."

Early-morning lorries were the only vehicles on the road at this hour, he noticed, trying to purge his mind of what he'd just heard. What he wished he hadn't heard. It wasn't right that Ellerton's personal life was being raked up because as a murder victim he'd lost the right to privacy. "I suppose I should say that sounds promising."

"We shall have to see. He claims to have an alibi for the time of the murder. The police are investigating that."

"That is unfortunate."

She sighed. "I have pinned my hopes on that being the murderer."

"Because you don't want to admit the murderer is someone we know."

"No kidding, Sherlock."

As they drove along, the sun peeked over the distant horizon.

"Frederick?"

"Yes?"

"I don't want to hurt your feelings for the world, and I want you to know I will always admire Siddley Hall more than any other stately home in England, but—"

"But you don't want to sleep there."

She nodded. "I just can't, after all that's happened. I've been thinking about the person placing listening devices in your bed-room. That truly is shiver-worthy."

Should he tell her of his own recently installed listening devices? And of the monitoring that would ensure her safety? If he hadn't heard that damned phone conversation with the *hot* guy the last night they were at the hotel, he would have told her. He *had* trusted her.

But now, he just didn't know.

"Agreed," he finally said.

"Is my overnight bag still in your car?"

"Yes, I followed you straight to the police station."

"Then can we start for Yorkshire and Blyn Court Castle?"

"It's what I had originally wanted."

"That was when you weren't going to be sleep deprived. I promise to keep talking to you to make sure you don't fall asleep at the wheel."

"Very kind of you."

Her phone rang. He would guess it was Simon. Even if the two men had rather patched things up, Frederick still didn't like the way the man fawned over his student.

"Good morning, Simon. How did you know I wouldn't still be sleeping? I'm not that early of a riser—under normal circumstances…Why are you calling me at so ungodly an hour?…I'm not going to listen to those accusations."

Frederick was convinced Simon was warning her against him.

"Aren't you interested in knowing why I'm up so early?…I've spent the night at the police station…I wasn't allowed to call anyone…No, I've left…Of course they didn't arrest me…We're on the way to Yorkshire…Yes, I am with *Lord* Rockford."

Frederick could tell Simon must have emphasized his title in a deprecating manor. And whether Simon was pitiable or not, Frederick was once again seized with the desire to punch the don right between his bespectacled eyes.

"Don't you dare!" she said.

For a second, Frederick thought she'd invaded his thoughts.

Then she continued, "You could jeopardize your position at the university if you abandon your lectures and come gallivanting after me…I'm not listening to this. I'm going to hang up on you." And with that, she terminated the call.

When her phone rang again a few seconds later, she picked it up. "Listen Simon, neither Frederick nor I have slept all night. I suspect as we near Yorkshire, we'll find a hotel to crash in. It's not likely we'll get to Blyn Court until tomorrow…All right. I'll meet you at Blyn Court tomorrow afternoon…All right, I promise to call you between now and then if *anything* happens. Cheers."

"So kind of him," Frederick said, "to step in during your father's absence."

She gave a mock groan. "He has been pretty much swaddling."

"Where were we before he called?"

"I had just informed you I was going to fascinate you with my brilliant conversation so you don't go to sleep at the wheel."

"I could use some brilliant conversation after what I've had to listen to the past five hours."

She started laughing. What he'd said wasn't funny. She was giggling so hard she was wiping away tears. "What is so bloody funny?"

It took a minute before she could stop giggling and reply. "It's sort of like the queen in her lovely pastel hat, clasping her handbag with white-gloved hands and sitting patiently in a tattoo parlor. Your being in that lobby this morning was just as incongruous."

"I'm glad you find it so funny. It was rather educational. A woman sitting across from me demonstrated a remarkable aptitude for finding cranial orifices on which to hang pierced earrings."

"Cranial orifices? Now you're talking like Simon."

"Shoot me if I start talking like *Doctor* Steele."

"Do you have a gun?"

He lifted a brow. "Do you mean rifle or pistol?"

"I forgot all British gentlemen *shoot* with rifles, as opposed to guys *hunting* in America. So I guess I'm asking about pistols."

"Then, no."

"I figured as much."

As they drove on, the skies turned a pale blue, and the traffic thickened with morning commuters. It took him nearly two hours to get through the London-area traffic. When he finally began traveling north, it was still slow going, but nothing like the snarl going south.

"Have you ever been to Blyn Court before?" she asked.

"Once. When I was a lad. The present duke's son was at Eton with me. A couple of years ahead of me, but he kindly invited me to one of their shooting parties up in Yorkshire. That sort of thing was quite thrilling to an eleven-year-old boy."

"Killing foxes? I think it's disgusting."

"Actually, it was grouse."

"Same thing. It's killing innocent creatures."

"But you eat meat and aren't opposed to wearing leather."

"That's different."

He would pick his battles with Antonia, and this wasn't one he cared to wage.

"So," he said, "what kinds of questions did Patel ask you?"

"The idiot asked the very same questions he'd asked the day of the murder. Like I would change my story. I'm pretty confident my answers were exactly the same as they were that first day."

"I suppose he was hoping to nail you on inconsistencies."

She nodded. "He also accused me of faking the theft at my flat and at the offices in Siddley's basement."

"How did you respond?"

"With the truth. I suppose I was pretty outraged."

"Did he offer you the chance to obtain legal counsel?"

"In an underhanded way. He said if I wanted counsel, he'd have to put me in a holding cell until that was accomplished— which sounded too much like an arrest. So I declined."

He wondered if he should let her know he would find her an attorney, if the need should arise, but was afraid it might upset her. "If he takes you in again, you need counsel."

"I have nothing to hide."

Her phone rang.

Instead of *hello*, she said, "I'm still alive."

Surely Simon wasn't pestering her again.

"You just go on to bed and don't worry about me. I've two men looking out for my well-being...Love you. Cheers."

For a split second, he thought she was telling Simon she loved him, then he realized if she were speaking of going to bed, she must be talking to someone in the States. Her sister? Had she really been talking with her sister the other night?

"My sister's been reading the articles in the *Guardian* online and is terrified that the murderer will target me next." She leaned back in the seat and sighed. "I'm really very grateful to Hard Ass for not arresting me. If he had, Simon would have been forced to revoke his letters of introduction for me to have access to the archives at the stately homes."

"That wouldn't do. No one except you can lead us to the monstrance."

"That's not true, but I may be able to. I can't understand why you're putting yourself out so much for a monstrance that probably won't belong to your family anymore."

"It's not about the monstrance. It's about catching the person who ruthlessly killed my valued employee. I believe the trail to the monstrance will lure the killer."

"Do you know what you're saying?" Her eyes widened. Her voice quivered.

"Yes." He drew in a deep breath, his grip on the steering wheel tightening. "In my quest for the monstrance, I'm not only exposing myself to possible death, but I'm also exposing you. That's why I'm so bloody concerned for your neck. I'm bloody responsible for endangering it."

"And I'd hoped you've been clinging to me because you had the hots for me. Of course, that was before I knew about Lady Caroline Hinckley."

His foot on the accelerator drew up. "What do you *think* you know about Caroline?"

"That you're either officially or semiofficially pledged to one another."

He frowned. "We are not pledged to one another." Even to his own ears his voice did not register protest. He spoke as if he were making a dull observation on the weather.

"There are apparently a lot of people out there—including Bessington—who believe you and Caroline are an item."

Including my own mother. "I can't help what others think. I have never said anything that would make Caro think I plan to marry her. At the present, there is no woman with whom I have a romantic interest." *Except you.* Even as he thought this, he caught a whiff of her lavender scent. How had she managed that?

He felt like one of Pavlov's dogs. The smell of lavender was beginning to have a physical effect upon him. If he never again set eyes on Antonia, every time he smelled lavender, he would think of the long-legged American beauty who'd once kissed him with such incredible passion.

"I get it. You're a confirmed bachelor."

He hoped he hadn't come off as sounding as if he thought of himself as a bloody George Clooney.

A few minutes later, she said, "I can't leave the country."

"I didn't know you wanted to."

"The point is, Hard Ass confiscated my passport."

"Nothing like innocent until proven guilty," he mumbled.

"So," she began after a moment of silence, "since you studied art history, you must tell me who's your favorite painter."

"What does that have to do with anything?"

"I told you I was appointing myself to keep you from sleeping while driving."

"Right-o. Why don't you try and guess who's my favorite painter? You seem to think we like the same things. Let's see you put your theory to the test."

She sighed. "Of course you could like impressionists or cubists or something modern, but I think not. Am I hot?"

"You're hot." *In every way.*

"It would be easier if I knew which period of history you were partial to, but I really don't. You seem pretty well rounded—about your historical periods. So, I'll just tell you who my favorite artist is, and since he's British, I'm hoping my shot in the dark hits the target."

"You believe we might share the same favorite artist?" he asked skeptically.

"More than once you've commented on how much we think alike."

"OK, who's your favorite artist?" he asked.

"Gainsborough."

How in the hell did she do that? He took his eyes from the road—something he never did—and glared at her. "How did you know?"

"I got it right? Really and truly?" She sounded like a teenager.

"How could you have known?"

"I didn't. And I'm not clairvoyant, either. I was merely remembering the Holbeins, van Dykes, and Gainsboroughs—all of which you've got at Siddley—and asking myself which I preferred."

"So you only picked Gainsborough because we've got one at Siddley?"

"I did not say that. In all the world, Gainsborough's my favorite artist. I've seen him at the Huntington in California, the Met in

New York, the National Portrait Gallery in London, and at various stately homes in England, including Siddley Hall."

"He really is your favorite?"

"Absolutely. And I can't even tell you why. You'd think I'd go for Holbein because his subjects are the ones I study the most, but give me one of Gainsborough's lovely full-length beauties with their big, powdered hair any day."

"Did you find my great-great-great, many more greats, great-grandmother beautiful?"

"Very much. I've often wondered if Gainsborough only painted beautiful women, or if he just painted all his subjects to embellish their beauty."

He had wondered the same thing, but he didn't want her to know that. He didn't want to be that close to any woman. Especially not now.

Would he ever?

By the time they got to the outskirts of Peterborough, he knew they had to stop to eat. "Fancy a brunch?"

"I thought you'd never ask."

That damned Rockford had broken up their attempt to grab the American. Damn, but he'd like to take out that arrogant aristocrat. He'd thought he could scare the earl away with taunts aimed at his blonde lady love. But apparently that hadn't worked.

Rockford had now attached himself to the American bird. When she led them to the monstrance, he would have to take out both of them. It couldn't look like another murder, though. It had to be staged to look like an accident.

He was clever about electronics, but how could he take out the pair of them and make it look like an accident?

He fished his state-of-the-art mobile from his pocket and called his associate. "I can't get away today. Rockford and the American are going up to Blyn Court Castle."

"Then I'm on my way there."

"You won't let them see you?"

"Let's put it this way, if they see me there today, it'll be the last thing either of them ever sees."

CHAPTER 22

When she first awakened, she wasn't sure where she was. The room was so dark she couldn't see a thing. As her consciousness returned, she remembered Frederick had checked them into a hotel in York. One room with two beds. Again.

An advantage to traveling with Frederick was the quality of the hotels he selected. They were luxurious. Not like some of the crappy ones where she'd stayed—the worst of which provided individual folded sheets of toilet paper scarcely big enough to cover her palm. She and Sophia had called them Barbie wipes.

Among the amenities in this fancy hotel was an alarm clock with nice, big digital numbers. She rolled over and squinted at it: 5:27 a.m. Which meant they had been asleep for…over eleven hours!

Frederick had been so exhausted from the long drive and the sleepless night before that when he'd lain on the bed to rest, he'd fallen straight to sleep even though the television was blaring and he was still wearing his clothes and shoes.

She'd been surprised to discover that he snored. Somehow, snoring seemed like something a Green Bay Packer might do, not the urbane Lord of Siddley Hall. He'd been a pretty quiet sleeper previously. Maybe there was a correlation between exhaustion and a man's snoring. She'd read of the correlation between liquor consumption and snoring.

Quietly removing herself from the bed, she grabbed her suitcase and went to the bathroom for a shower, shampoo, and blow dry.

When she emerged from the bathroom half an hour later, fully dressed in Monday's outfit with her hair dry, he was sitting at the desk, looking at the laptop.

"Hope you don't mind that I've booted up your computer," he said. "Thought I'd see the press's latest regarding the Stately Homes Murder."

She came to peek over his shoulder. "They really do call it the Stately Homes Murder?"

"I wouldn't have made up such a thing." He got to his feet. She had to tilt her head back to look up into his finely chiseled face. It was one of those clean-cut kinds of faces one would expect to see touting air force officers or something equally as gentlemanly.

He had on shoes and she didn't. It made her feel really short, even though she knew she wasn't. He drilled her with his smoky, simmering eyes. "I need to tidy up," he said, his voice husky.

Not what she'd wanted to hear.

She dropped into the chair he'd vacated and read the *Guardian*'s entire story. It quoted Hard Ass. *We're investigating all avenues and hope to have an arrest within the week.*

Was that a week from today? A week from when he was quoted yesterday? Or a week from the day the murder had taken place?

If he ever tried to arrest her, she'd get the best lawyer money could buy. Her daddy was no pauper. The Townleys were marginal millionaires. Especially when you counted the big-ass suburban McMansion her daddy had paid cash for with one of his patent bonuses.

She surfed the Internet link by link and was surprised when Frederick came out of the bathroom with fresh clothes and wet hair after what seemed like about ten seconds. She looked at the time on her monitor: 6:30.

"Fancy breakfast?" he asked.

"Sure."

There were so many men in suits taking breakfast in the hotel's dining room, Frederick and Antonia got one of the last tables. It was a half dozen steps from the busy kitchen. Swinging doors opened and slammed with regularity, and the clanking of heavy plates and cups accompanied their bits of conversation. Which was perfectly fine with her. She didn't want others listening to them.

Over their square, white-clothed breakfast table, he asked, "Will you be able to gain access at Blyn Court before it opens to tourists?"

"I think so. Tours usually start around ten, but the librarians typically start around nine." Her gaze traveled over the menu, but since she didn't have any special dietary needs, she decided to go for the buffet.

"I was hoping we could get in the building before nine o'clock."

"I can't help you there."

"I might ring the duke."

"That's a ballsy thing to do with a duke." She really needed to watch her tongue in front of this very proper earl. "How do you know he doesn't sleep until noon? The fifth Duke of Devonshire never rose before four p.m."

"That was in the eighteenth century!"

She shrugged. "What can I say? I live in the past."

He eyed her. "You don't look like a woman from the past."

"Darn it. Given away by a pair of blue jeans." She stood and told him she was opting for the buffet. He joined her.

"Hey, I've got an idea," she said.

He raised a brow.

"Have you told Hard Ass about the listening devices at Siddley?"

He put index finger to mouth, a clear warning for her to watch her language as they moved along the buffet line. "I had hoped to tell the inspector during last night's interrogation, but he obviously wasn't interested in anything I had to say."

"Because you're a peer," she said, as she scooped bran cereal from a clear canister into her bowl, "I'm sure you get preferential treatment in the UK."

"I assure you, he's no nicer to me than he is to you."

"Yeah, right. He treats me like I'm Lucrezia Borgia." Trays piled with food, they returned to their table. "The DCI needs to know about your bugs."

"Are you thinking what I'm thinking?" he asked.

Her smile unfurled. "Maybe we'll wake up the weasel."

"You are wicked." He took his cell phone from his jeans pocket and called the DCI, whose number was in the phone's memory.

She watched as he held the phone to his ear. Nothing. After a moment, he said, "I got voice mail. Should I leave a message?"

"Yes, do. Make it really, really long."

He grinned. "Wicked woman," he mumbled, then a few seconds later spoke distinctly. "Patel? Rockford here. I wanted to inform you that someone has placed sophisticated listening devices at Siddley Hall. I hired a consulting firm to run a scan for them. My secretary, Emerson Berwick, has all the details and can direct you to the firm whose services I procured. We don't know how long the devices have been at Siddley, but I feel safe in saying they were likely there before Ralph Ellerton's murder. If you call my Siddley number, you'll get Emerson. If you need me, ring my mobile. I'm up in York with Miss Townley. We are not giving up our quest to find the Percy Monstrance." He poked something on his phone as he met her gaze. "Long enough for you?"

"It'll do. It's a shame you couldn't have awakened him after what he did to our night's sleep."

"You must remember he's a public servant. He does appear to be going over and above what's expected."

"You sound like Simon."

"Shoot me."

"Even if I had a gun, I wouldn't. I don't like violence, present or past. I won't watch violent shows, nor will I watch shows like *CSI*, which depict the aftermath of violence."

He nodded knowingly. "Too dark for you."

"I do prefer comedies. Even in Shakespeare."

"Allow me to guess…"

"Which is my favorite of Shakespeare's comedies?"

"Yes." He pursed his lips for a moment, then said, *"Taming of the Shrew?"*

"How did you know?"

He did not answer for a moment. "I suppose in the same way you knew about my affinity for Gainsborough."

Now she knew why he hadn't answered her right away. He didn't like to admit that any woman could be that close to him.

Which was fine with her. Really. Until the murderer was apprehended, she could trust no one. Not even this man whose thoughts so closely mirrored her own.

Frederick looked at his watch and grimaced. "I suppose it is too bloody early to call the duke."

"Don't worry. You forget we've still got at least an hour's drive to reach Blyn Court, fighting the morning commuter traffic."

"That's true. I kept thinking about Blyn Court being in York, not Yorkshire. Which are two completely different things."

"Will we stay at this hotel again tonight, or do you want something closer to Blyn Court?"

"Bird in the hand," he said. "It's best not to take chances with the unknown when the known is so satisfactory."

"And returning by night, the roads should be much less congested."

He nodded. "So the return journey would likely be half an hour."

He dug into his full English breakfast while she ate from her fruit cup and cereal.

"I don't see how you could choose that over this," he said, slicing into his bacon.

"I can honestly say there's nothing on your plate that even remotely entices me."

He shoved a fork of bacon into his mouth and chewed. "Not even bacon?"

"That's not real bacon."

"It is, too."

"Real bacon's crispy. You can't find real bacon in the UK. That stuff you're eating looks more like a thick slab of elongated ham."

He shrugged and took another bite. "A rose by any other name smells as sweet…"

"Oh, please! How can you compare that heart-attack-on-a-fork to one of nature's prettiest creations?"

Fork in one hand, knife in the other, he held out his arms and shrugged. "I'm a guy."

She nodded. "You and Keith Hernandez."

"Ah, the fellow in that *Seinfeld* episode?"

"I can't help it. Every time someone says *he's a guy* or *I'm a guy*, I hear Elaine Benes in that episode. *He's a guy, Jerry,*" Antonia mimicked. "Now, if my daddy were here, he'd be highly offended that all you know of Keith Hernandez is that he was a guest on *Seinfeld.*"

"Why?"

"Because Daddy thinks the world should honor his favorite sport, which is baseball, which is the sport Keith Hernandez excelled in once upon a time. Six years, his batting average exceeded three hundred, and he won eleven Golden Gloves for his play at first."

"You can recite statistics like that off the top of your head? How do I know you're not making it up?"

She whipped out her phone, went to Wikipedia, and scanned the write-up, nodding. "See for yourself, I'm right."

"That's not necessary. I believe you." He waved her off. "Can you do that for all the baseball players?"

She shook her head. "I'm not a computer."

"So I noticed." His reality check flicked to that part of her upper torso that revealed her gender.

She liked that he appreciated her femininity. "There are hundreds, if not hundreds of thousands, of current and former baseball players. I probably do know the stats for most of the MVP players in my father's lifespan." She shrugged. "He had no sons, so I fell into the role."

Frederick's lazy gaze perused her. "No way could you pass for a son."

"You wouldn't say that if you'd ever seen me squat behind home plate in a catcher's mask and chest protector."

His gaze flicked to her chest once more. "I stand by what I just said."

She got a case of the warm fuzzies. "Thank you."

"I'd wager your father couldn't name a single cricket player."

"You'd be right." She took a sip of her coffee.

They grew quiet. Her thoughts strayed to Mr. Ellerton's murder. How totally terrifying it was to think the cold-blooded killer was still lurking somewhere, possibly watching her this very minute.

But he couldn't be Frederick.

Then who? She finished her breakfast, pushed her two bowls aside, settled back, and eyed Frederick. "So, do you care to enumerate suspects?"

"I've never felt so clueless."

"Come on, there must be someone you suspect."

"Simon."

"Just because he tried to beat you up."

He leveled a stern gaze at her. "Simon. Could. Not. Beat. Me. Up."

She gave an apologetic shrug.

"His attempt to beat me up is *not* why I suspect him. He just acts suspicious. He wants to follow you everywhere you go. He's obsessed with being present when you find that monstrance."

She didn't like to admit the truth in what Frederick said. "It's back to that paternal thing, I suppose. Because my daddy's not here to look after me, Simon feels he has to. That's all it is."

"Right-o. And I'm Mary Poppins."

"I think we need to change the subject."

"No," he said, his voice stern. "We need to get all of our suspicions out in the open. Tell me who you suspect."

Her stomach somersaulted. Simon had repeatedly tried to convince her that Frederick could be behind the evil deeds, but she had difficulty believing that. "I'm clueless. I know it's someone we know, but I can't believe anyone I know would kill somebody in cold blood."

"You have no suspicions?"

She shook her head. "The only people with access to Siddley—besides you and me—are Alistair and your Emerson. I have difficulty believing that dim-witted Alistair has the slightest clue what a monstrance even is, and I've never met Emerson."

"I trust her completely."

The way he said that brought out Antonia's rare jealous streak. Was Emerson young and pretty? Of course, she'd have to be. Antonia found herself wishing Emerson were the murderer.

While also wishing Emerson a persistent case of rosacea.

"Great, so that leaves Alistair," she said.

"He is someone who does have some access to Siddley. Not to the main house, though. And he doesn't have a key, as Ellerton did."

"That's right," she said. "I remember that morning with Simon he was waiting for someone to come open the door." She glared at

Frederick. "If you could suspect Alistair, you couldn't have spent five minutes with him."

"He does seem a bit of a slow top."

"And I think the person who put a device in Mr. Ellerton's phone and in your quarters must have some cranial activity going on—which Alistair has failed to demonstrate on numerous occasions."

Frederick nodded. "Poor Ellerton had commented on the lad's stupidity—in a good-natured way. Ellerton wasn't one to ever complain."

"All of this brings us back to this question: Do you agree the murderer is someone we know?"

"I do."

"What about maids or gardeners?"

"It's a possibility, but unlikely. The...mastermind, for lack of a better word, has to be someone with vast knowledge of the history of these old families." His brows hiked. "Agreed?"

"Agreed."

"And it's not me, no matter what that damned don has told you."

His comment caught her off guard. It was a moment before she could think of what to say. "Like I'd be sitting here with you if I thought you were a murderer."

"Or sleeping with me." He nailed her with a penetrating gaze.

She felt guilty for staying awake all night the night of the abduction. Of course, she'd been so distraught that night, if Hard Ass had come walking through the door, she would have thrown herself into his arms.

Even though it would never have felt as good as kissing Frederick. Just thinking about that did funny things to her chest.

Frederick's claims of innocence reminded her of Sophia's comment about the Marquis de Sade. No way, of course, that Frederick should ever be thought of along with that perv. Frederick was far too nice. Just a moment ago his voice had softened when he remembered Mr. Ellerton.

"Let's discuss other suspects," she suggested. She thought of the matronly woman who'd led her tour of Siddley months ago. She had been fairly knowledgeable not only about the Percy family but also about English history. "What about your tour guides? They're certainly well acquainted with the Percy family history."

He gave her one of those *Are you delusional?* looks. "We have two. Both have white hair. Need I say more?"

"You said yourself the mastermind needs to be knowledgeable. Why can't the mastermind hire thugs? We're talking five million pounds."

"Let's think about the money for a moment." He dipped his toast in the gooey yellow of his egg. "For the sake of this discussion, let's say my Mrs. MacIntosh decides to try to take possession of the monstrance. How would she go about trying to sell it without being accused of being an accessory to Ellerton's murder?"

"And Mrs. MacIntosh is?"

"My longest-serving tour guide. She turned seventy-five last fall."

"Oh," Antonia said, her voice wimpy. "Think of this. A lot of these genteel tour leaders may very well be the poor relation of a peer. One of them could be working in tandem with her aristocratic relation."

"To humor you, I'll have Emerson do background checks on the white-haired duo."

He poured tea into his cup. "The person who seeks the monstrance should be an aristocrat who could naturally come up with it, say he found it at his home, and no questions would be asked. Anyone else—like Mrs. MacIntosh—would arouse suspicion."

It made perfect sense. "Someone like Richard Bessington?"

"His name is Richard Craine, Earl of Bessington."

"Yes, Frederick Percy, Earl of Rockford." Her solemn gaze met his. "Should we suspect your cousin?"

"Distant cousin. I'm not close to him, but I can't see Bessington as a murderer."

"True. And how could he have found out about the monstrance? All his archives are at the University of Portsmouth." She poured coffee from her individual carafe.

"It's not like he's desperate for money," Frederick said. "That's a sizeable amount he's getting from the university."

"What about Lord Granworth? Maybe his dinginess is a ruse to mask maniacal tendencies."

He raised a brow. "I thought the same thing. He's far more shrewd than he lets on, and we can't discount the fact that he knew about the monstrance."

"No matter what Simon says, I don't trust his Mr. Bly at all." She told him about the missing letter.

"I need to tell Patel. Perhaps he can get a warrant to search for that letter, maybe even get statements. It would be useful to know if they knew of the monstrance *before* Ellerton's murder."

"Now I feel like we're getting somewhere."

He gave her another of those *Are you delusional?* looks.

She shrugged. "I'm just throwing out ideas."

"The problem is that we can't believe someone we know is a murderer."

His phone rang. He took it from his pocket, looked at the screen, then said, "Hello, Mother." He flicked his other wrist and looked at his watch. "You're up exceptionally early." He listened a moment, then cut in, "I'm sorry you're having difficulty sleeping, but I assure you I'm perfectly safe...No, I'm not getting a bodyguard...Actually I *have* beefed up security at Siddley...All right,

I give you my word, I shall apprise you the moment an arrest is made…Yes, it is a pity they've done away with hanging…Love and kisses to you, too."

As he ended the call, their gazes locked. "Your mom must be reading the same *Guardian* accounts my sister's reading."

He nodded.

"OK, where were we?" he asked.

"We were trying to discover which peer might be murdering to get the monstrance. What about peeresses?"

He glared at her. "My mother's in Italy."

"I wasn't talking about Lady Rockford. I refer to Lady Caroline Hinckley."

His glare had not diminished one iota. "I've known her my whole life. She's neither a murderer nor would she have a clue what a monstrance is."

"I never implied that she was working solo. Someone could be pulling her strings." She drew in a breath. "She was at your computer just before my flash drive was wiped."

He made no reply. From his total lack of response, she almost wondered if he'd suddenly been struck deaf. Then he finally spoke. "It appears I need to investigate the finances of both the Marquess of Granworth and Caroline's father to see if either is desperate for funds."

After he finished his breakfast, he said, "Shall we hope it's the Duke de Quincy? Or…who's got Castle Paxton now?"

"Viscount Swinnerton. You don't know him?"

He shook his head. "There's a reason we're called the Upper Ten Thousand."

She shrugged. "I thought half those ten thousand aristocratic families died out in the first world war."

"Sadly, that is the case."

"Well, finish your tea, and I'll finish my coffee, and we'll go see if the Duke de Quincy is our murderer."

CHAPTER 23

As soon as Frederick got off the motorway onto a rural road, Antonia realized this was the same road she'd traveled each day to research in the dungeons at Blyn Court Castle. She recognized the distinctive thatched cottage with wisteria trailing from the pediment over its curved front door. The half dozen hanging baskets plump with pink and white petunias hadn't hung there when she'd last passed by here in her bus during the winter. Each day then, her bus had driven past this cottage on the rural road Frederick had just turned onto. This country lane led directly to Blyn Court Castle.

She was disappointed the sun that had favored them all week had now disappeared. "Such a shame we had pretty blue skies yesterday when we were on the motorway, and now that we're in the lovely countryside, we've got gray skies."

He nodded. "I'm just hoping we don't get rain."

"I've brought an umbrella. I go nowhere in England without one. And a slicker, too. It folds up like a handkerchief."

"I'm surprised a California girl even owns an umbrella."

A smile sprang to her face. "Since it never rains in California?"

"Of course."

"That's a myth."

"If Antonia Townley says it's a myth, it must be. So what can Miss Townley tell me about Blyn Court Castle's history?"

"It's by far the oldest of all the five Catholic families' homes. The first de Quincy came over with the Conqueror, and shortly after the Battle of Hastings he started heading north to claim his reward, which was many thousand hectares. Then he started construction of the castle."

Frederick's brows lowered. "So what we'll see today is original?"

She hesitated a moment before answering. "A few sections of the original castle wall remain, and Blyn Court still has the old motte and bailey, but they're mostly a little conversational nod to the past. Today's castle with turrets and crenelated battlements came a couple of centuries later—I believe in the fourteenth century."

"If I remember correctly from my single visit there many years ago, the castle was expanded and remodeled in the late Victorian period."

She nodded. "I expect you saw much more of it than I. Besides the dungeons where the archives are located, I've only seen the public rooms the current duke allows on tour. Those are the great hall, the old kitchens and larders, and, of course, the thrilling armory. As one paying my eight pounds to see the castle, I wasn't privy to the family's chambers, which I understand are exquisite. I saw a spread on them in *Architectural Digest*."

"Opulent would be the correct description, if my memory serves me correctly."

"So an eleven-year-old boy noticed that?"

"I just remember being amazed because it was much grander than Siddley Hall." He turned toward her while still looking at the road. "At the time, Siddley was being run by my grandfather while we lived at a much smaller residence. Up to that point, I'd been rather in awe of Siddley Hall."

"I like Siddley best because it doesn't look like a cold palace. It looks like a home where one could raise a family."

"Just a homey residence that happens to have three hundred and sixteen rooms."

"The armory homey? Not so much."

"I take it you don't like armories."

"I'll take an armory any day over a dungeon with torture devices."

"I'm betting you've never set foot inside of a torture chamber, even though you're mad for medieval history."

"That's one bet you'd win. Torture is one facet of medieval history I detest reading about, although I've had to."

"Richard III and all that, I expect?"

He'd nailed the trail of her thoughts. She nodded. "I'm so glad I live in a civilized society."

"When you did your research at Blyn Court earlier, you came by rail?"

"In a roundabout way. From the York rail station I took a train to Ridlington, and from there hopped on the bus in front of the Bombay restaurant. That bus came along this road. It was a thirteen-minute ride to Blyn Court from the Indian restaurant." She looked ahead. "Any minute now we should see the castle's turrets."

No sooner had she spoken than Frederick's car rose over the crest of a small hill and Blyn Court came into view. The proud gray stone castle looked every bit as formidable as it must have looked centuries earlier. Even the unspoiled setting of hilly terrain had probably not changed in the past millennium. Too rocky and uneven for farming, the land proved good for raising sheep, and it looked as if the duke owned many hundreds.

"Wow!" Frederick said. "Looks like the duke still owns a sizeable chunk of Yorkshire."

"Yes. I believe all that sheep-grazing land surrounding the castle does belong to the de Quincys."

"Or their family trust."

"You'd know more about that than I."

"That I do. I feel like a bloody caretaker."

"But, because of your love of Siddley, you don't mind."

"That's true. The days of primogeniture are really over. I'm not the trust's chief officer because I succeeded as earl, but because of my four siblings, I'm the one who wanted it most, the one who loves Siddley most."

"It surprised me when I first started touring stately homes to realize that some are run by female descendants."

As they drew near Blyn Court, he turned off the road they'd been traveling and started up the rocky road to the castle. The skies were turning even darker, and she thought the castle's gray stone nearly matched the graphite skies.

She was seized by a menacing feeling. She'd been there maybe a dozen times before and never experienced any sense of foreboding like this.

He boldly drove right up to a timbered entrance to the castle, swerved to a complete stop, spraying gravel, then got out of the car and came around to open her door.

She looked at her watch. It was 8:36. "We're too early for the tour."

"Thank you, Sybil, for pointing out the bloody obvious."

"So that makes four! Ken Burns, *Vicar of Dibbley*, *Seinfeld*, and now *Fawlty Towers*."

"I didn't know they even showed *Fawlty Towers* in the States."

"Once upon a time, it was on our public television network. My parents were huge fans, and I grew up watching that same handful of episodes over and over."

She followed him to the massive door. She seriously didn't like being here in remote Yorkshire with no one else around.

As they stood there with Frederick pounding on the door's thick wood, the winds howled eerily through the endless fields behind them and mist clung to her. She felt like she was in the eightieth remake of *Jane Eyre*.

The sound of a car coming up the drive caused her to turn around. A blue Ford Taurus slowed down next to them, and a middle-aged man with a full head of dark hair rolled down his window. "Tours don't start until ten." He was well spoken. Not aristocratic, she decided, but possibly public school—which was the opposite in England of what it was in America.

"I've come to see the duke," Frederick said.

The man's gaze shot to Frederick's expensive sports car. He was obviously pegging Frederick—and likely deducing that he was one of the duke's fellow peers. "Is His Grace expecting you?"

"Not exactly."

The man didn't respond for a moment, then he spoke in a respectful tone. "Give me a few minutes, then I shall come let you in. May I have your name so I can announce you to His Grace?"

"Lord Rockford of Siddley Hall."

The man's eyes widened at the mention of Siddley Hall. If the Siddley Hall murder was so prominently featured in the newspapers, she knew it must be on television, too, even though she hadn't managed to see any of the reports. Poor Frederick. This was not the kind of notoriety he wanted for Siddley.

The man in the Ford drove off, and ten minutes later, dressed in formal tails, he let them in the castle's front door. "I've announced you to the duke. If you will just follow me, I shall show you to the drawing room."

They followed him upstairs, and when she reached the second floor it was all she could do to hold her tongue. What kind of lunatic wanted the inside of a medieval castle to look like Versailles? Everywhere she looked was marble and gilt and sparkling crystal chandeliers. Where were the iron lanterns and chunky wood furnishings? Every stick of furniture here was gilded in the straight lines of Louis XVI.

The drawing room was so large it had four sofas and many more chairs. She and Frederick sat side by side on one of two velvet sofas that faced each other before the large fireplace. Over its marble mantelpiece hung a painting of what she assumed to be one of the early Dukes de Quincy. Because of his long, curly dark locks, the man in the portrait appeared to be a contemporary of Charles II.

She and Frederick sat there in silence, solemnly listening to the whistle of the winds outside. Soon rain began to pelt the tall casements, and the skies darkened even more.

A chill penetrated her shivering limbs.

A few moments later, the duke entered the room, and she and Frederick stood. Dressed in tweeds and woolen sweater, he walked erectly and spoke stridently, though he must have been well into his seventies. "Pray tell, Rockford, what brings you here so damned early?" Despite the tone, he offered Frederick a handshake, and before allowing Frederick to respond, he turned to Antonia and said, "Forgive the duchess's absence, but she's not yet dressed."

Antonia flashed a smile. She'd been told that one didn't address a duke until one was formally introduced to a duke.

"First, Your Grace," Frederick said, "allow me to present Antonia Townley. She's an Oxford doctoral student studying our families in the days of Henry VIII. In fact, she's worked in your archives before, but she's got to replicate that research because hers was stolen."

She kept thinking the duke was going to ask them to sit, but he neither asked, nor took a seat himself.

"Let me ask you this, Rockford. Was the theft of her research connected to that nasty murder at your place?"

"Yes, Your Grace, it is connected."

"I'm afraid until the murderer is apprehended, I can't allow you or your friend at Blyn Court." The haughty duke rudely turned his back on them and began to leave the room, saying, "I trust you can find your way out."

The rains came down with such relentless force, Frederick's wind-shield wipers were incapable of clearing the windows for more than a split second. He'd had to turn on his headlights in an attempt to see the country road beneath the night-like skies, and his hands tightly gripped the steering wheel as he battled against the howling winds that threatened to topple the small sports car.

"How long do you calculate it will take to get to Castle Paxton?" she asked, hugging her own arms to ward off the chill. She was ter-rified they would end up in a deadly collision.

"Under normal driving conditions, a little over three hours."

She unconsciously eyed the clock on his dashboard. Nine.

"But," he continued, "these are *not* normal conditions."

"Thank you, Basil. My guess is you couldn't make it in six hours—under these conditions."

His face was grim. "I know."

A fierce gust of wind caught the car, pulling it toward a hedge-row, but Frederick managed to keep the car stable.

How different this drive was from their first together. To think that she'd been frightened that night just because of his speed. Now, she would happily exchange this drive for that.

For so many reasons.

"I don't think it's such a good idea to try to drive to Staffordshire in this monsoon," she said. "We probably wouldn't get there until closing time, anyway. If we don't get killed on the road first."

"You don't have to twist my arm. I'm not terribly keen about driving in this."

"I wonder if we even need to continue to Castle Paxton. I think we've found our man."

"The duke?"

"Yep."

"I'll admit he's most suspicious, but dukes are a different breed."

"I think you've got one more peer whose finances bear scrutiny."

He rolled his eyes. "All right."

"Why don't we just return to our hotel? To tell you the truth, I could use a breather. I might be interested in spending the rest of the day in the hotel room going over the research we've accumulated." The very idea of their warm, dry hotel room sounded wonderful.

"That'll work."

"What will you do while I'm going over the notes and letters? Read your Scandinavian thriller?"

"Any way I can help you?"

"I don't need help at this point, but you're free to read over some of your ancestors' letters to see if anything sets off any bells for you."

"I don't know the original five families as well as you."

"But you're knowledgeable enough to look for clues that might point us to the monstrance."

"I should like to try."

"We could probably find a printer at the hotel if you'd like me to print out some of the pages for you to read, or I can just send files to your smart phone. How are your eyes?"

"Good enough to read from a phone. I've read entire books that way before."

Once they returned to the hotel room—which the maids had already tidied—she sent pages of her notes to his phone. She remained at the long, built-in desk in their room. She really liked the high-quality wheeled chair. If she had to spend hours reading at the computer, this was much more comfortable than propped against the bed's headboard.

He sat in the room's big upholstered chair, crossing his legs ankle to knee, and settled back to read.

She was utterly grateful to him for allowing them to stay in the warm, cozy hotel room as the winds outside whistled and howled like forlorn creatures of the night. She still hadn't shaken the foreboding feeling that had washed over her as they'd stood in the mist when Frederick had pounded at the tall, weathered door of Blyn Court Castle.

She wanted to feel safe. And she did. But she remembered her vow to herself that she would trust no one until the murderer was apprehended—or the monstrance found. She would not put her trust in Simon, nor would she trust Frederick completely.

This chick was on her own.

And the murderer was someone she knew. The very notion sent prickly goose bumps racing down her arms.

She spent the next hour perusing her copied correspondence, concentrating on the sisters' letters to one another. Even though these Percy sisters were intimate, there remained a formality in the letters they wrote to one another. It was so different from the way she and Sophia wrote to each another.

For a moment's comic relief, she turned to the shit document. First, she read the *shitty* passages written about Martin Luther. Then she suddenly thought of something. *Something that might be significant.* Hadn't Simon said he and Mr. Ellerton had discussed the shit document? And wasn't Mr. Ellerton's dying word *shit*? *Which he'd said twice.*

Her heartbeat began to roar.

There must be something in this letter that pointed to the location of the monstrance!

Hands shaking, she started at the beginning.

My Dear Son, It grieveth me to tell you that yesterday I handeth up my much-loved daughter, your wife's sister Katherine Farr, to the Infinite Care of Our Blessed Lord and Savior. Because she hath been failing since the birth of her son, My Wife and I came hither to Castle Paxton to be with our beloved Firstborn during her last days in This Kingdom. We hath buried the most precious Jewel amongst Heavenly

Gold and Jewels in her tomb at the Farrs' chapel. I doth trust the Jewel will stay entombed until The One True Faith triumphs over the tyranny of Sinners and Adulterers.

Castle Paxton! It could not have been more clear! How could no one during these past five hundred years have realized this letter blatantly pointed to the hiding place of the Percy Monstrance?

She remembered the tiny little stone chapel in the parkland surrounding Castle Paxton. She'd even gone inside, genuflected, and quietly strolled among the stone tombs with effigies carved upon their lids. In her mind's eyes, she could still picture the effigy of Katherine Farr lying still for eternity. In spite of the hundreds of years that had passed since the young mother's death, Antonia had teared up as she looked at the young beauty whose life had been cut so short. How painful it must have been for the father who wrote this letter.

Antonia must go there. To the tomb of Katherine Farr.

She could trust no one.

Men had already killed to possess the monstrance. And the five million pounds it was worth.

Even though this letter made the location of the monstrance look obvious, Antonia did not want to look like a fool. She would go to Castle Paxton and investigate for herself. Then she would tell Hard Ass.

She'd thought about telling him first, but what if she were wrong? If he came all the way to Staffordshire for nothing he'd be seriously pissed. He would be bound to think she was merely attempting to deflect suspicion.

Another problem with telling Patel was that Frederick would then have to be included in the information loop, and she didn't have 100 percent confidence in Frederick's innocence. She kept remembering how suspicious Range Rover Girl was. What if Frederick was the one Range Rover Girl was helping?

Antonia must go today. Alone. Even though the weather was abominable.

Now to divert Frederick.

She tried to stretch casually. "I'm so glad we're staying at a large hotel that caters to the business traveler."

He looked up from his phone, which he was charging as he read. "Why?"

"Because they always have business centers where you can use their faxes, copiers, and such."

"Something tells me you're going to send me on an errand."

"You are brilliant. Do be an angel and go print out these letters on my flash drive. I'll need the ones written by Elizabeth Montague printed out. Reading on the computer is really straining my eyes." Her gaze flicked to his phone. "You ought to print out your stuff while you're at it. It can't be good for your eyes to do that much reading from your phone." She hoped he did. Anything that would keep him away longer.

"I just might." He rose. "Anything else?"

"No. When you come back, we can order lunch from room service—unless you want to try to rustle up some sandwiches while you're down there?"

He grinned sheepishly. "Rustle up? Certainly." He grabbed his key card, then came to her and held out his palm. She placed her flash drive in it.

By the time he'd left the hotel room, she was trembling all over. She donned a hoodie, covered it with her hooded slicker, and checked her purse to make sure the umbrella was there. Now she was as ready as she could be to brave the unmerciful elements.

Global positioning chips were one of the greatest inventions ever. The one in Antonia Townley's handbag had been most useful in tracking her to the York rail station. As she stood in line to purchase a ticket, he stood watching her in a far corner of the busy terminal.

That the hood of his jacket covered his head would not draw attention in this chilly, rainy weather, and it helped to keep him from being recognized.

Once her ticket was purchased, he watched to see which train she would board. He was able to keep an eye on her while staying inside the terminal. She crossed on a catwalk to get to the far side where she waited for her train.

She made it easy for him. He saw where she stood, then looked up at the electronic messaging. Staffordshire. He knew very well what was in Staffordshire: Castle Paxton. There was only one reason she'd be venturing out alone on a day like this: she had to have learned the monstrance was at Castle Paxton. Did the bitch hope to keep it for herself?

How convenient that she'd dumped the lord. It was so much easier to make one death look natural. How easy it would be to strangle the life from her, then stage a suicide by hanging.

Once he had the monstrance, that is.

EPISODE 9

CHAPTER 24

The rail journey from York to Stoke-on-Trent took three and a quarter hours. Trains had a distinct advantage over cars in bad weather. Rain, sleet, hail, or snow, rail timetables never varied.

When Antonia got to Stoke-on-Trent, she knew exactly which bus to board to take her through the countryside to the gates of Castle Paxton. She had traveled that route every day for more than three weeks earlier in the year when she was researching at the castle.

Unfortunately, the bus stop she needed was not in one of the rail station's covered areas but some hundred yards from the main door to the terminal, where she now stood.

She had stood at that bus stop many a time, awaiting the 2579 to Paxley. She'd been there in a mist so thick it soaked into her bones. She'd been there once during a light snow. She'd been there, too, on the odd sunny day in midwinter.

But she had never been there on a day like today, when the midday skies were charcoal and the rains slanted sideways. She had hoped by the time she reached this western amalgam of cities famed for their potteries that the worst of the rains would have dissipated.

If anything, the rain had strengthened.

Up until now, she had managed to stay dry. Taxi from the hotel's portico to the rail station. Covered terminal at the rail station. Nice warm rail car—though the ride wasn't so great. The windows were fogged up, and there wasn't a view of anything but dark skies and pounding rain outside.

More of the same faced her now as she stood in a covered area of the train station, eyeing with apprehension the bus stop that was at a hundred yards' distance. Wasn't it just this morning she'd bragged to Frederick that she never went anywhere in England without her slicker and umbrella? She had sounded invincibly cocky then. Now, though, the prospect of standing there in a slicker feebly grasping an umbrella was even less inviting than jumping in the ocean fully clothed.

She must focus on the triumph of announcing to Hard Ass Patel that she had single-handedly found the monstrance. Proving her innocence to him would be worth all this discomfort. She tied her fleece hood under her chin. She hated it when wind like today's drilled into her ears. Then she put up the slicker's hood and secured it. Last, she opened her umbrella and pushed through the driving rains to stand at the bus stop, awaiting the 2579. She couldn't remember its exact schedule, but she knew one came every half hour, and she'd already stood at the entrance to the rail terminal a good ten minutes, gathering courage to take the plunge.

Her face was the only thing dry on her whole body as she stood with the umbrella smooshed onto the crown of her head. At least the slicker kept her shoulders and arms from becoming soaked, and she was really glad she'd worn boots. They kept her feet relatively dry. For now.

Her gloves, unfortunately, were with the rest of her belongings that had been taken from her flat in Oxford to Siddley Hall. It had been weeks since she'd had to don gloves, but today they would have been worth ten times their initial purchase price.

At least she was outfitted better than many a wet straggler she watched run through puddles up to the rail station as she stood waiting not-so-patiently for the darned bus. Where in the heck was it? It would be just be her luck if this was the day the normally punctual 2579 got swept up in floodwater while she stood there freezing off her tush.

She'd been confident her three-hundred-dollar leather boots would keep her inner foot dry, but she soon found out that even three-hundred-dollar leather boots were incapable of offering non-permeable protection against this kind of saturation. What she needed was her polka-dot wellies, but they, too, were awaiting her at Siddley Manor.

She momentarily wished she were back in Bagsy's warm, dry room at Siddley—even though the rooms had been bugged by a dagger-wielding killer.

Her cell phone was vibrating. Again. Frederick and Simon both had tried to call her. She took it from her pocket. This time it was Simon. She wasn't going to talk to either of them before she gave Patel the monstrance.

Finally, after an almost forty-minute wait, the bus came, spraying more water onto her jeans as it rolled to a stop in front of her. She couldn't get on it fast enough. She dropped four one-pound coins into the meter and began to move as far away from the doors as possible. Since there were only three other passengers in this miserable weather, she had her pick of seats. She wanted to be as warm as she could for the ride to Castle Paxton. Under normal driving conditions, the drive from Stoke-on-Trent's rail station to the castle had taken forty minutes. Today might be quite a bit longer.

After he'd boarded her train back in York—at the opposite end from where she'd boarded—he had nervously watched his railcar's glass doors for her, fearing that she might wander into his compartment. It wouldn't have done for her to see him.

When he reached Stoke-on-Trent, he was able to hire a car and take possession of it before her bus ever came. He supposed bus schedules were running behind because of these treacherous driving conditions.

There was no need to follow her bus. He knew Castle Paxton was her destination. He would arrive first and find a place to hide his vehicle, a place where he'd be sure to see her arrival. Then he would have to play it by ear.

One thing was sure. Tonight the monstrance would be in his possession, and the bitch would be dead.

If it hadn't been for that damned abduction attempt, Frederick might not have been alarmed that she wasn't in their hotel room when he returned. When he'd come through the door and not seen her at the desk, he'd thought maybe she was in the lavatory, but that door gaped open. Surely she hadn't left the door open while she did her business? That wasn't like Antonia. She might toss out a careless piece of slang, but deep down, she was a lady.

As he neared the dead-still loo, his stomach dropped; his pulse accelerated. She wasn't there, either.

They had her!

His first panicked instinct was to grab the phone and report her abduction to 9-9-9, but as he crossed the room to the phone on the nightstand, he slowed.

He scanned the room for signs of a struggle, but there was nothing that indicated she'd been carried away under duress. Her laptop was still here. Wouldn't they want that? And the laptop was neatly shut. Just as if she had closed it herself.

If a murdering madman were striding toward her, the last thing on her mind would have been logging off her laptop. It was almost as if she had logged off to prevent someone from seeing something. Something important.

Something she had discovered.

Suddenly, he had a good idea what it felt like when a husband discovered his wife had been cheating on him—at the same time he grasped an electrified fence.

Antonia had deliberately withheld vital information from him. She'd discovered the hiding place of the monstrance, and she didn't trust him enough to tell him.

He collapsed onto her desk chair. How could one woman have such a devastating effect upon him? He was shaking all over. Did she think he was a bloody murderer? He was so mad, he could wring her lovely neck.

But as he sat there, it wasn't anger that exploded within him. It was fear. Fear for Antonia. On her own. Without his protection. His spine stiffened; his fists balled. What in the hell was she thinking?

Simon must have screwed with her thinking, convinced her that Frederick was not trustworthy. Lest he judge Simon too hastily, Frederick had to admit he'd done the same damn thing, trying to show her that Simon was guilty of Ellerton's murder.

He couldn't blame the poor girl for running away from both of them.

It also crossed his mind that Antonia wanted the monstrance for herself. Antonia could have murdered Ellerton.

No matter how many things pointed in that direction, Frederick could not, would not believe that of Antonia. He'd gotten to know her pretty well this past week, and God may strike him down, but he believed in her innocence. He had come to the conclusion she was incapable of murder or even of theft.

He bolted from the chair and tried calling her cell phone. It rang and rang; she did not answer. Damn it!

As he was shoving the phone back into his pocket, it rang. Antonia? He yanked it out. It didn't register as her number. Perhaps she'd had to find another phone. He answered promptly.

And was deflated. It wasn't Antonia, but Simon. "Say, Rockford," he started, "I'm not getting an answer on Antonia's phone, so I got your mobile number from your secretary. Told her it was a bloody emergency."

"What's the emergency, Steele?"

"I just left Blyn Court, where I discovered you and Antonia had been shown the door, so to speak. I told Antonia I'd meet her this afternoon. Where are you two?"

"I'm in York. At our hotel room."

"And Antonia?"

"Apparently, she's bolted."

"What do you mean, *she's bolted*?"

"I think she's discovered the location of the monstrance and didn't trust me—so she's gone off."

"She didn't leave you a note or anything?"

"Nothing."

"Listen, Rockford, this could be serious. Are you sure those thugs didn't abduct her again?"

The way Simon sounded made Frederick think that maybe, just maybe, he hadn't had a thing to do with that previous abduction attempt. But one couldn't be too careful when dealing with... actually, when dealing with murderers.

"There's no sign of a struggle or quick exit. She apparently methodically shut down her computer and closed it up, almost like she didn't want anyone to trace what she was doing."

"I need to see that computer. Maybe I can figure out what she saw."

Frederick hesitated. He didn't like the sound of that word *need*. Why in the hell did Simon *need* to see the damn notes? At this point, though, Frederick would welcome any help he could get to find Antonia. Also, he had full confidence he could defend himself. "I'm at the Stanson Arms. It's relatively close to the York rail station."

Even as he said it, he wondered if Antonia had gone to the rail station. If only he could clone himself and go ask around about Antonia. He could count on the fact that men would not forget her once they set eyes on her.

"I know where it is," Simon said. "As it happens, I've stayed there before. For a conference. I'll be there in ten minutes. "

"Cheers."

While waiting for Simon, Frederick booted up the laptop and began to read the passages, avoiding the ones she had sent to his phone earlier. What she'd seen had to have been in the passages she was reading.

Before she'd sent him to the hotel's business center—and lunch counter. She'd deliberately gotten rid of him. Fury pounded into him.

He eyed the two sandwiches, but he had no appetite.

As he scrolled through her files and pages, he knew he needed to concentrate on the sisters' correspondence. Isn't that where she had concentrated her efforts?

Ellerton had admitted that something he'd learned from the pages she'd discovered had given him the location of the monstrance. Frederick knew the correspondence would not have actually used the word *monstrance* because Antonia—with her damn-near-infallible memory—would have immediately remembered an uncommon word like that when Ellerton initially revealed his discovery.

When a knock sounded at his hotel room's door, Frederick's gaze whipped to the bedside clock with the big digital numbers. Ten minutes since he'd talked with Simon. As he moved to the door, he wished to God he had a pistol.

He had a strong feeling he was going to need one today.

His only defense was to suspect everyone. He would not let Simon—or anyone—come up behind him. He needed to be ready to defend himself, if the need should arise. He did possess a Swiss Army knife. His hand coiled around it in his trousers pocket as he went and opened the door.

There Simon stood in his mackintosh.

"Come in," Frederick grudgingly said. The coat would have to go. Frederick needed to look for concealed weapons. "Why don't shed your coat and sit here?" He indicated the chair where he'd been reading earlier, before Antonia drummed up her excuse to get him out of the room.

He watched as Simon removed his coat and tossed it on the bed. The man looked incredibly professorial in his rumpled tweeds and sweater that really didn't match anything. And, of course, there were the thick glasses.

Frederick paid particular attention to his pockets or anywhere a gun could be hidden. Simon appeared to be unarmed.

"You really have no idea what she was reading just before she left?" Simon asked, lowering himself into the chair.

"None whatsoever."

"Pity."

Frederick returned to Antonia's laptop and started reading where he'd left off before Simon came. He was careful to turn his desk chair in the direction of Simon. No way would he turn his back on him.

"I wouldn't be here," Simon said, "if I weren't so bloody worried about her." He glared at Frederick. "I know you've poisoned her against me, told her not to trust me. That's why she's not answering my calls."

"Can you deny that you did the same thing? Told her I was a murderer?"

Simon shrugged. "I never said you were a murderer. I merely suggested that you were wealthy enough to have hired thugs to kidnap her." He looked into his lap and began to speak in a lower voice. "And I might have said that only two men knew Antonia was working in the basement that night: you and Harold Bly, and I've known Harold for more than twenty years. He's an honorable fellow."

"And I'm not?"

"I haven't known you a week!"

"Add yourself to those two persons, and that makes three."

Simon's eyes narrowed. "What in the hell are you implying?"

"You could have hired slimeballs as easily as I—not that I would ever do that!"

"My pockets aren't as deep as yours, old boy."

"Maybe we should make it four or five or six or seven who knew she was there that night."

Simon's brows lowered. "What are you implying?"

"If Bly knew, there's a good chance his employer did, and Lord Granworth's pockets appear to be deeper than mine. Then there are the two abductors—"

"That goes without saying."

Frederick froze. "I've just thought of something chilling."

"What?"

"I wonder if the electronics expert who bugged Siddley Hall may have found a way to place a global positioning chip in…" He thought of that big purse she carried everywhere. "In her purse, for instance."

"In that gargantuan bag? She could go for months and never discover it in there!"

"Exactly."

A look of sheer terror flashed across Simon's face. "Bollocks! Do you know what you're saying?"

"That he could be following her right now," Frederick answered, his voice grim.

"We've got to find her. Damn it! How much time's passed since she left?"

Frederick shrugged. "I was gone about twenty minutes." His gaze shot to the bedside clock. "A little over thirty minutes, I should say."

"If only we knew where she was going."

"That's what you and I have got to discover." Because it now could be a matter of life or death, Frederick returned to the document he was reading, and Simon came to stand beside him.

"If only Ralph Ellerton could have given us a dying clue," Simon said.

Dying clue? Good lord, the man had! "Doctor Steele, you are brilliant!"

Simon gave him a puzzled look.

"You never heard about Ellerton's dying word?"

"No. What was it?"

"*Shit.*"

Frederick watched as recognition slammed into Simon. "The shit document!"

"Exactly." Frederick fleetingly thought that maybe he should have kept his assumption to himself, but just as he knew Antonia was innocent, he believed now that Simon was, too. The man's concern for her could not be feigned.

And besides, Frederick might need Simon's help.

"Let's have a go at those letters."

In less than five minutes, they hit pay dirt. "It's at Castle Paxton!" Frederick said.

Simon peered at the laptop screen and nodded. "Are you driving, or should I?"

"In this weather, we'll make better time by train."

"Time is of the essence." Simon snagged his mackintosh and headed for the door.

"I don't suppose you've a gun?" Frederick asked.

"Heavens no!"

CHAPTER 25

From here, he had a view of Castle Paxton that was obstructed only by the violent rain. In his hired car, he'd gone down a dirt lane into a wood with a lot of low-lying shrubbery. He managed to hide his vehicle behind some of the brush. It was just a few hundred feet from here to the private road up to Castle Paxton.

There was no way he could miss seeing Antonia Townley when she arrived. He settled back and watched through the windshield that was being swiped by wipers every fraction of a second. The rains hadn't abated. His handkerchief came in handy for wiping the fog away from inside the car's windows.

His driving conditions would have been the same as the bus's, but he wasn't sure how long she'd had to wait for her bus. His guessing game was cut short as he saw the bright-red bus come creeping along the watery street. It stopped directly in front of Castle Paxton. She was the only person to exit. Who in the hell else would be out on a day like this?

To his shock, she didn't walk up the gravel drive to Castle Paxton. Instead, she began walking west. What the hell? He wiped the fog from his window, shoved his face up against the glass, and eyed her as she pushed against the heavy winds and rains. Where was she going? There was only one other building in sight: the little church located a short distance from the castle walls.

She was going there! That's where the monstrance had been hidden.

This was much worse than the bus stop had been. There, she'd had the protection of buildings that blocked some of the heavy winds. But here she was in the middle of nowhere, surrounded by vacant fields. And a wind strong enough to topple a small person.

The second she'd departed the comfort of the bus, she had known this was going to be tough. The wind whipped her umbrella inside out and darn near yanked it from her hands. She fumbled with it for a moment, but it was useless in these fierce winds. She ended up tossing it and taking off at a jog toward the chapel.

All she needed now was to go too fast, catch the sole of her boot on a wet rock, and fall into the mire. And probably break a bone while she was at it. Therefore, she went in a slow, sure-footed jog, heel first for stability.

She didn't remember the distance from the castle road being this long. It looked like she could walk for a minute and be at the little church. Looks could be deceptive. She grew winded as her legs powered her through the mud. And still she wasn't there.

To think, she could have been in Frederick's *dry* car, having him drive her right up to the church door. Why had she ever listened to Simon when he planted doubts about Frederick's innocence? She'd thought long and hard about Frederick throughout that three-plus-hour train ride.

And she'd come to regret striking out on her own—not trusting Frederick when every cell in her body told her he was a good man. She wished she were with him right now.

Finally, she made it to the church. It would be just her luck for the doors to be bolted.

But they weren't.

She opened one of a pair of old, timbered doors, and the wind caught it, slapping it against the wall of the stone church. Closing it was no easy task because she had to fight against the winds, but she managed to close it and enter the church.

The socks inside her boots were so wet, she could have wrung them out. Just like the legs of her pants. A slicker could only cover so much.

The little church wasn't the sanctuary she'd hoped for. It was much darker than she remembered. There was no sun to shine through the stained glass windows today. And with its slick stone floors, it was cold. How she longed for warmth!

She stood there a moment, her gaze fanning over the ancient chapel. It had one central nave, and the pews on either side could accommodate no more than eight adults each side. The marble altar was set off from the rest of the church by an altar rail, and the pulpit was of carved oak that had aged to a dark brown, much like the crucifix that hung front and center. Christ's flesh had yellowed with age.

Off to the side on the right was an attached, windowless room that held tombs of early members of Sir John Farr's family.

Antonia's destination.

There was no wall or door separating the vault from the rest of the church, but there were iron bars in the mode of a Gothic fence, and a gate. *I hope it's not locked.*

It hadn't been locked when she was last here. She moved toward it, and the gate creaked open. She went straight to the sarcophagus bearing the remains of Katherine Farr, the beloved daughter of the Percys.

Antonia stared at Katherine's effigy, which had been carved on top. She appeared about the same age as Antonia. The young mother's hands were folded as if she were in prayer, and a veil covered her head in much the same way veils covered women's heads in biblical times. She looked so serene. And achingly pretty. Antonia wondered if the sculptor had ever seen her. How could he carve a likeness from someone who was dead?

Five centuries had not obliterated the lettering on her tomb. Antonia could clearly read: *Katherine Farr, 1545-1566.*

As Antonia stood there, she realized what an idiot she'd been to think she could just waltz in there and grab the monstrance she knew was in Katherine Farr's sarcophagus. First off, she had not calculated how heavy the effigy was. It was of carved marble, for God's sake! Life-size. Heavy.

Secondly, Antonia had completely forgotten the remains of the beautiful Katherine Farr lay there. How sickening it would be to see the evidence that the lovely woman had turned into a horrifying skeleton. Would her burial dress have disintegrated? Would there still be a foul odor?

Out of the blue—well, not really out of the blue, since this was on a related topic—she remembered the story of King Tut's curse, that those who had opened up the tomb in 1922 had mysteriously died soon thereafter. Decades later a scientist suggested the deaths could have occurred from toxins that were a byproduct from the decay of foods buried with the pharaoh, as well as toxins from the embalming, all because the tomb was sealed so tightly.

She glanced at Katherine's sarcophagus. Was it airtight? Had it trapped deadly toxins nearly five hundred years ago?

Her stomach turned queasy.

The more she thought about it, though, she didn't think Katherine would have been embalmed, nor did she think any foodstuffs would have been buried with her. Just a bejeweled monstrance made of almost solid gold.

She moved closer, eyeing the marble on top of the sarcophagus. She took a deep breath and gripped the lid on either side and attempted to give it the shove upward. It didn't budge.

Next, she squatted at the tomb's end and gave it an upward heave. It actually moved that time. Not enough, but it did move. She drew a deep breath in preparation for her next shove. She thought she heard a sound like the closing of a car door right outside the chapel. Who on earth would be coming here on a day like this?

Then the door of the chapel opened.

Alarmed, she stood statue-still, watching the chapel's shallow vestibule. At first all she could see was the silhouette of a man. A man of medium height and build. Because he was in shadow, it was impossible to determine the color of his hair.

Then he stepped into the chapel. Even in the dim light, the man was unmistakable. She knew him. It was the Earl of Bessington.

In that instant, she realized why he was here, realized that he was the killer. Her heartbeat thundered. In spite of the chill in the air, perspiration slickened her.

He would kill her, too.

She was already squatting. He hadn't seen her, so she moved behind the tomb, completely out of his view.

She knew as soon as she'd done it, hiding had been an idiotic thing to do. If he was here, he'd obviously followed her. All the way from York. And if he knew she was here, he knew she hadn't left the church. If she'd been capable of intelligent thought, she should have taken off running to the side door the moment she'd seen him.

The queasiness in her stomach turned to roiling, and she trembled uncontrollably. Was it too late to dash away? She heard his footsteps. Not coming down the nave but coming straight to the vault. She inched around to the front of the sarcophagus, then lunged toward the gate.

Bessington blocked her exit, a menacing smile on his face. "How kind of you to lead me to the monstrance, Antonia." His gaze flicked to the tombs. "It was fortuitous that you came alone. So much easier to deal with a lone female."

Deal with? He meant to kill her. Why oh why hadn't she trusted Frederick? "I understand everything now," she said, her voice shaking. "Alistair's not the moron he appears to be. Is he even your cousin?" The moment she spoke, that fuzzy memory from the day of the murder sharpened. When Alistair came into Mr. Ellerton's office as she stood over the body, she noted—although it didn't register properly at the time—that Alistair's shoes had fresh mud on them.

Now she understood. When she'd come to Ellerton's door, Alistair had been forced to retreat from the other door and go up the stairs to the gravel drive, which was wet from the previous night's rain.

If only she'd put two and two together before now. Everything should have been so clear. That's why Alistair hadn't heard her original scream. He'd been outside.

"Of course he's not my cousin." He moved toward her like a tiger on soft paws. "I made his acquaintance when he did the security installations at Chumley—and I caught him trying to nick some of our silver. I could hold that over his head in order to get him to do my bidding."

Her eyes narrowed. "You mean he'd kill an innocent man just to keep from being charged with a minor theft?"

"There were other...considerations. I promised him half of what the monstrance would bring." His voice was amplified in the stony little church.

"How did you even learn of the monstrance's existence?"

"Before shipping off the family archives to Portsmouth, I came across a letter from my ancestor to Sir Percy that rather bluntly referred to the fact the monstrance had not been destroyed, as everyone thought. That's when I remembered the Cardinal Wolsey painting. A Holbein, wasn't it?"

She nodded. She remembered Frederick telling her he'd just had the painting moved to the chapel. Its previous location must have been in the family rooms that Bessington was likely to have seen.

"With that kind of provenance, it should be worth a fortune," he said.

"Five million pounds—or eight million dollars."

His green eyes flickered with satisfaction. "That will go a long way toward the restoration of Chumley to the grand home it once was."

"You place a house above a human life?"

"Chumley is not just a house. It's a unique stately home that's more than five centuries old. I'd put up a dozen lives to preserve it."

She swallowed. And she would be one of those lives sacrificed for the sake of Chumley. What could she do to fight for her life? She couldn't get past the gate because he stood there. Her gaze darted to her drenched purse, which she'd dropped to the floor when she'd decided to do the heave-ho. If only she could call 9-9-9. But by the time she got the phone from her purse, he'd be on her.

And Antonia knew her strength—even if she had gotten the huge marble effigy to budge—would be no match against a man's.

She couldn't think of one darn thing she could do to preserve her life. For some odd reason, she thought if she could just keep him talking, that would buy her time. Time for what? No one knew she was here, and no one was likely to be stopping by for a quick prayer in this weather. Maybe something would come to her if she could just keep him talking.

She forced herself to try and speak with stridency, but it was a poor effort. Her voice cracked. "So Alistair an electronics expert?"

"Yes, he bugged Rockford's rooms, and no one ever suspected he had, or that youthful, clean-cut, dim-witted Alistair could have done it."

"And was Alistair the prowler at Chumley the other night?"

He began to laugh. "There was no prowler. I was rather convincing, though, wasn't I? Even to the point of suggesting—several times—that we ring the constable."

She wouldn't give him the satisfaction of knowing how cleverly that ploy had managed to deflect suspicion. "So how did you trace me here?"

"GPS chip in your purse, courtesy of Alistair."

"And Alistair's the one who ransacked the offices and stole my laptop?"

"Yes. He made a good show of not having his own key to Siddley when, in fact, he'd managed to "borrow", Ellerton's—before his death—and copy it. As for your flat in Oxford, that was my handiwork."

"How did you even know where I lived?"

He gave her a wicked smile. "Alistair's very good at locating where people live. He passed it along to me since he thought he'd stay at Siddley until the police left the night of the murder."

"And today? You were in York, of course."

"Of course."

"Did you also board my train?"

"I did, but that's enough questions." His gaze swung around the vault. Parallel to Katherine's sarcophagus lay her husband's. His effigy showed a much older, shriveled-up old man. There were compensations to dying young. "Since Katherine was Percy's daughter," Bessington said, "I'm betting the monstrance was placed in her tomb by her father, probably just before they closed it."

"Why don't you take a look?" she asked.

He chuckled. "And let you escape? I think not. I'll just take care of you first, then come back here for my reward."

Her heartbeat soared. More sweat trickled down her back. She lunged for her purse. And the phone within it.

He lunged for her, grabbing her wrist as she pulled him with her to the hard stone floor. She tried to break free, but she wasn't strong enough. They were both breathing heavily. "One good thing about this vile weather," he said, his voice harsh, "is that no matter how loud you scream, no one's going to hear you." He had not let go of his viselike grip on her sore wrist.

As they sat on the cold floor in a tangled mess, it occurred to her to use her feminine charms on him. She remembered the way he had practically drooled over her when they met. Could she use his attraction to her advantage?

The idea of his filthy hands on her made her nauseous. This man was so far removed from Frederick it was hard to believe they were the same species.

She ended up spitting in his face.

Fury flashed in his eyes. He let go of her wrist so he could raise back that same hand and slap her in the face. The force knocked her against the floor as if she were a rag doll. *Ouch!* There was going to be one big, fat knot on the back of her head. If she lived to feel or see it.

Which didn't look like a probability right now.

Never mind the pain throbbing in her head, she told herself. She had to stay alive. What was it her father had always told her to do to disable an attacker? Kick him in the groin. That's what she had to do. It could immobilize him long enough for her to make a dash for the castle.

Had he left the keys in the rental car? That would be so sweet.

But first, she had to give him the old kick in the nuts. Slowly, she raised herself to a seated position. "Won't you help me up?" she asked in a pleading tone, tears filling her eyes, and one hand caressing her reddened face where she was pretty sure his hand had left an impression.

He got to his feet, sneering down at her, his brows lowered. Then he offered her a hand. As she was getting to her feet, she drove her knee into his groin with every ounce of force she could muster.

He yelled out like a man ripped with a bayonet.

And she took off running for the front door.

It opened just as she got there, and she collapsed into Frederick's arms.

CHAPTER 26

"Antonia! Thank God!"

Frederick gave her a humungous bear hug. Even though he—who wore no rain gear whatsoever—was wetter than she.

He didn't even sound mad at her, as he had every right to be. She started weeping. She'd wept more this past week than any time since prekindergarten. And at each of her crying sessions, Frederick had offered her comfort. Like he was doing now.

"Where's that Bessington?"

It was Simon's voice. She raised up on her tiptoes and peeked over Frederick's shoulder. Simon was right behind him, but he was so much shorter than Frederick, she hadn't seen him.

How did they know it was Bessington? She whirled toward the vault, but now Bessington had raced through the gate and was heading for the side door of the church.

Simon went to give chase. Then Frederick dashed off, calling over his shoulder, "Don't leave, love."

He called me love! Even though she'd practically accused him of being a murderer. She couldn't have felt more guilty had she published her accusations against him on the front page of the *Guardian*.

"Please take care!" she called out. "Both of you." Big sniff. Twice.

Frederick sped past Simon, and as she saw the last of their backs disappear through the side door, she got really scared.

A horrifying, paralyzing, terrifying thought rammed into her. What if Bessington had a gun? If he shot Frederick dead, she'd just...die. She raced back to her purse, whipped out her phone, and called 9-9-9. "Please help! There's a murderer right here in front of Castle Paxton. Please hurry."

Before she terminated the call, she added, "It's the Stately Home Murderer." That ought to get their attention! A high-profile case like that.

This once she was going to attempt to do what Frederick asked of her. He'd told her not to leave, so she was going to stand there in the drafty chapel as if her boots were glued to the stone floors.

What if Bessington went for the car? Maybe she could prevent him from leaving. If he'd left the keys in the ignition, she could yank them out.

Then she remembered Frederick's request. She couldn't afford to do one more thing to make him mad at her. She was still amazed that her welfare had weighed heavier with him than his bruised pride.

Besides, now they knew who the murderer was. If Bessington wanted to get away from this little section of Staffordshire, let him. She had full confidence that Hard Ass would make sure Richard Craine, the Earl of Bessington and mastermind behind the Stately Home Murder, was arrested. And Alistair, too.

So why in the heck didn't she encourage Simon and Frederick to back off for the exact same reasons? She darted toward the side door with the intention of seeing if she could request that they allow Bessington to leave.

Before she got to the door, she heard sirens. No way could the police have gotten here that quickly!

When she reached the door, she saw Bessington lying belly down on the saturated ground fifteen feet from the church. Simon, his rumpled mackintosh dripping, stood on Bessington's back, and Frederick—who was covered in mud and sitting in the quagmire next to Bessington—was sopping bright red-blood from his face.

She charged at him. "Oh, my poor Frederick! What has he done to you?" Never mind that he was sitting smack in a muddy puddle, she plopped down right next to him and placed a gentle hand to his muddied brow.

Before he could answer, a police constable's car door slammed, and he came running up, his rain slicker flapping behind him. "Which of you is Lord Rockford?"

"That would be me," Frederick said. "This man we've more or less apprehended," he said, nodding toward a sobbing Bessington, "is responsible for the Stately Home Murders."

At least her poor Lord Wonderful could talk! It was a huge relief to know he hadn't been seriously injured, because if he had been, it would have been completely her fault. If she hadn't gone off like a lunatic, he wouldn't have had to come chasing after her and go face-to-face with a madman.

As Frederick spoke, two more police cars started bearing down on the site. Now she understood why the first policeman had gotten there so quickly after her phone call. Frederick had called 9-9-9 *before* she had.

He'd obviously been worried about her. But how had he learned about Bessington?

The constable handcuffed Bessington as two more constables came to offer assistance, even though Bessington wasn't putting up any resistance.

Her eyes narrow with disgust, she watched as Bessington quietly got to his feet. The whimpering, sniveling dirtbag hadn't uttered a single word. Nor did he face Frederick. He had to be smart enough to realize how loathsome he was to them.

She and her two dear friends watched as Bessington hobbled away. It appeared as if he was incapable of straightening up all the way, and his gait had a pronounced limp. "I want a lawyer," he finally said just before he was locked into the backseat of the police car.

Knowing that the police had the situation well in hand, she spun back to face Frederick. "What happened to you, my dearest?" *Oops.* What right did she have to call him that?

Now, he stiffened. "That's an odd thing to be saying to someone you suspected of murder."

Simon stepped forward. "It's my fault, old fellow. I take complete blame for telling her not to trust you."

Frederick flashed a smile at him. "No offense since that's exactly what I told her about you."

All three of them started laughing.

"I am so sorry, Frederick." She looked into those honeyed eyes of his.

"I understand."

"Now please tell me what's happened to you." There was so much mud and blood on his face she couldn't tell the source of the bleeding. "Do you need stitches?"

"No!"

"How can you be sure?" she asked.

"Because the bounder punched me in the nose."

"You gave worse than you got, old chap," Simon said. "Did you see how Bessington could barely stand, barely move without wincing in pain?"

Antonia cleared her throat. "I may have, er, had something to do with the slowing of his movements."

Frederick smiled at her. "What did you do to him?"

She wished she hadn't opened her big mouth. She shrugged. "If you had a daughter, what would you advise her to do to disable an attacker?"

Both nodding, Simon and Frederick responded at the same exact time with the same exact response: "O-o-o-o-h."

"If you knew the police were coming," she said, thrusting hands to her hips, "why would you and Simon jeopardize your lives trying to catch that awful man? You could have been killed!"

A somber look passed over Frederick's face. "If it weren't for Steele, I might have killed him."

"You're not a murderer," she said, her voice soft. "As soon as I boarded the train, I knew that, knew what a terrible mistake I'd made, knew you were innocent."

"I should be mad at you." He continued to hold the muddy, bloody handkerchief beneath his nose.

"How did you know it was Bessington?" she asked. "You already knew it when you arrived at the chapel."

Simon moved closer. "The man is an incredibly stupid criminal. He used his own name, his own credit card, when hiring the car in Stoke-on-Trent."

"How clever of you to think to check the car rentals." She eyed Simon.

"Actually, it was Rockford's idea."

Frederick gave a shrug. "On occasion, I'm useful."

"But how did you know to come to Staffordshire?" she asked.

"Lord Useful figured it out." Simon did not look happy.

She turned to Frederick. "The shit document?"

He nodded, a slight trace of satisfaction on his face. "I could not have done it without Steele. It was he who said what a pity it was that Ellerton hadn't said any dying words."

"Oh, and because I had so recently shown you the…ah, shit document, you put two and two together?" Antonia asked.

Frederick nodded, his gaze linking with hers. "It had always bothered both of us that a nice man like Ralph Ellerton, a man who never resorted to slang or expletives of any kind, would have used that word in his final breath on earth."

"He was a loyal employee until the very end," she said, her voice choked with emotion. "He used his dying breath to help you find the monstrance instead of identifying his killer."

"How much simpler it would have been for all of us if he'd just fingered Alistair," Frederick said.

"So you've pieced together Alistair's part in all this, too?" she asked.

Frederick nodded. "Once we knew it was Bessington, it wasn't hard."

"I'm exceedingly proud of you, Antonia, for using your research to figure it out where the monstrance was being hidden," Simon said.

"Thank you, Simon. I guess it was smart of me, but I negated one smart thing with one really, really stupid decision." She sent Frederick an apologetic gaze.

Frederick cocked a brow. "Might I suggest we get out of this bloody rain?"

She leaped to her feet and offered Frederick a hand.

He shook her off. "I can bloody well get up without any help from a female."

Men and their pride! "Might I suggest," she said, "we go see if we can get the monstrance?"

Frederick was eyeing one of the policemen, who was coming back. "Will you be so good as to step in the church and give statements?" asked the constable, who didn't look as old as Antonia.

Once inside the church and at the constable's request, the two men produced identification. When he finally asked Antonia for hers, she said, "You'll have to get mine from the Metropolitan Police's Detective Chief Inspector Patel, who confiscated my passport because he was so clueless he suspected me of being the Stately Home Murderer."

"I'm terribly sorry," the young constable said. "I'll make a note to ask Scotland Yard for verification."

They spent the next twenty minutes answering his questions. The subject of the monstrance did not come up. After he drove away, Antonia said, "Can we get the monstrance now?"

Frederick met Simon's gaze, and both men nodded.

Antonia led them to Katherine Farr's tomb. Frederick stood on one side, Simon on the other, and each of them began to lift. Antonia moved away. If there was a foul smell, she didn't want to catch a whiff. And she most certainly did not want to see the remains of the lovely Katherine Farr. "Please, hold your breaths," she cautioned. "You don't want to inhale any toxins."

"Give her a little encouragement," Simon mumbled, "and now she thinks she's a bloody scientist."

Both men grunted as they lifted the lid of the sarcophagus high enough over the rim that they could turn it at enough of an angle to allow for an opening when they set it back down on the sides. When they eased it down, she was half afraid it was going to crack in two.

One corner of the sarcophagus's base was open, but neither man was looking inside. "Why don't you have a go at it, old chap?" Simon said.

She couldn't blame Simon for not wanting to see the grim sight.

Frederick nodded. Then he poked his head into the dark corner. "Not on this end."

They grunted all over again, hoisted, and twisted the heavy lid to expose a corner at the foot of the sarcophagus.

"Be my guest," Simon said, bowing toward the sarcophagus.

Frederick came closer and looked in. "I see it!"

A couple of seconds later he was showing them the monstrance. It was difficult to believe anything so beautiful—and so religiously symbolic—could have led men to commit murder. Its gold and jewels were still every bit as brilliant as they had been in the Holbein painting.

"So," Simon said, "what are you going to do with it?"

"What do you think I should do with it?"

"If I were in your shoes, old fellow, I'd take the damned thing home. You're the one who risked your neck to find it."

Frederick turned to her. "And you? What do you think I should do?"

A few hours ago, she may have doubted Frederick, but not anymore. She knew without a doubt that Frederick was too intrinsically honest to claim something he didn't think he had a legal right to. God knew, he had a right to the monstrance. But a legal right? Not bloody likely. "It wouldn't be right to just give it to Lord Swinnerton at Castle Paxton. If it hadn't been for *your* archivist, the monstrance would never have been found."

"So, are you suggesting I should keep it?"

She shook her head. "I don't think you'll do anything you perceive as being unlawful. What I would suggest is that you propose some kind of plan where you and Lord Swinnerton share ownership."

"Thank you." His eyes shimmered. "Fancy a meeting with Lord Swinnerton?"

Three days later…

Frederick had thought he would never again have to come to this police station where he'd spent that unfortunate night waiting for Antonia. "Last time I was here," he told her as they entered the building, "I had to explain that my lady friend was *not* a prostitute."

She giggled. Thank God the tears were behind her now. They had done a lot of laughing these past couple of days.

When they entered DCI Patel's office, he stood and came to shake Frederick's hand. Then he faced Antonia. "I'm returning your passport." She stood there stiffly as he placed it in her hand. "I'd also like to offer you my apologies for being so harsh with you."

She waited a moment before responding. "I understand. You told us that first day it was your job to suspect everyone."

The man cracked a smile.

So Hard Ass had finally fallen under Antonia's spell.

They tied up all the loose ends of Patel's case against Alistair and Bessington and left. As they walked to the car park, she asked, "Who's Brat?"

He stopped. "What do you know about Brat?"

"Just that Brat put out a hit on me."

He gave her a puzzled look.

"When you were in the shower at the hotel."

"Oh, the text."

"Yes, *Get rid of the American.* I was terrified to go to sleep that night."

"I'm sorry. It wasn't what you thought."

"I think I figured that one out, Sherlock."

He started walking again.

"You haven't answered my question."

He really didn't want to tell her. But he also didn't want mistrust to ever again put a wall between him and this woman he was coming to care so much for. "Caroline Hinckley is Brat."

"So, she hates me?" Antonia was actually smiling with considerable glee.

"I wouldn't say she hates you. She thought that perhaps you might…disparage her to me."

"You don't know how happy this makes me."

His brows lowered. "Why?"

"Because now I will have no compunction whatsoever about running that peroxided, rancorous, pretentious, haughty, mean-spirited Range Rover Girl into the dirt where she belongs."

He didn't know what was coming over him. He was on a busy street in broad daylight, yet he found himself hauling her into his arms and giving her one hell of a scorching kiss.

ACKNOWLEDGMENTS

Once again, I must thank my ultra supportive husband, Dr. John Bolen, who brainstorms, beta reads, built and maintains my website (and a lot more techie stuff), and is a skilled writer himself.

AUTHOR BIOGRAPHY

A former journalist who, in her own words, has "a fascination with dead Englishwomen," Cheryl Bolen is the award-winning author of more than a dozen historical romance novels set in Regency England, including *Marriage of Inconvenience*, *My Lord Wicked*, and *A Duke Deceived*. Her books have received numerous awards, such as the 2011 International Digital Award for Best Historical Novel and the 2006 Holt Medallion for Best Historical. She was also a 2006 finalist in the Daphne du Maurier for Best Historical Mystery. Her works have been translated into eleven languages and have been Amazon.com bestsellers. Bolen has contributed to *Writer's Digest* and *Romance Writers Report* as well as to the Regency era–themed newsletters *The Regency Plume*, *The Regency Reader*, and *The Quizzing Glass*. The mother of two grown sons, she lives with her professor husband in Texas.

Kindle *Serials*

This book was originally released in episodes as a Kindle Serial. Kindle Serials launched in 2012 as a new way to experience serialized books. Kindle Serials allow readers to enjoy the story as the author creates it, purchasing once and receiving all existing episodes immediately, followed by future episodes as they are published. To find out more about Kindle Serials and to see the current selection of Serials titles, visit www.amazon.com/kindleserials.

Made in the USA
Charleston, SC
14 September 2013